BLOOD
&
BOND

BLOOD
&
BOND

BLOOD & BOND

THE BOUCHERS
BOOK TWO

Nicole Jacquelyn

Blood & Bond
Paperback Edition
Copyright © 2025 by Nicole Jacquelyn

Love N. Books Press
An Imprint of Wolfpack Publishing
1707 E. Diana Street
Tampa, FL 33610

www.lovenbookspress.com

Cover design by Jennilynn Wyer Designs
Edited by My Brother's Editor

Paperback ISBN 979-8-89567-167-2
Ebook ISBN 979-8-89567-166-5
LCCN 2025942745

For my children.
Never forget that family is everything, and your mother
loves you.

BLOOD
&
BOND

AMBROSE

The room smelled like death. Even the chemicals they used to clean and the little air freshener in the corner couldn't hide it. A morgue smelled like dead bodies. It was impossible to make it smell like anything else.

I stared blankly at the body draped in a clean white sheet.

Logically, I knew that they hadn't made a mistake. They knew what my baby brother looked like. They had records of his DNA and fingerprints. Vampire Command didn't make those kinds of errors. They wouldn't have brought us all the way there if they hadn't been sure.

I still couldn't make myself believe it.

There were pieces of him on that table, lined up like they were about to sew him back together again. It was revolting, abhorrent, and there was no need. They weren't hiding anything by placing him that way. They weren't helping anything. Every single one of us could see that our youngest brother—my father's youngest son—had been chopped up like meat about to be sent to a butcher.

"You know who did this?" my father asked, his voice hoarse.

"Strike Team Three eliminated all of them," the commandant replied. He sounded nervous. Good. "It took them less than a day to get back into the compound."

"Why weren't we informed?" I ground out. We should've known the moment he'd been taken.

The commandant's face paled. "It was a fluid situation."

"Bullshit," I replied flatly.

"How much less than a day?" my brother, Chance, asked angrily. "A fucking hour? You can't tell me this didn't take a while."

I forced myself to unclench my fists. Killing the commandant of the United States Vampire Command wouldn't bring my brother back, even if it would feel really fucking good for a few moments.

"It took them twelve hours," the commandant replied.

I couldn't believe that we'd always considered him like an uncle. Arthur had been friends with my father for longer than any of us had been alive. They'd fought together before my father met my mother, and they'd stayed close through our childhoods. Now, I could barely stand to look at the fucking coward.

"We should've been there," my brother, Danny, said. "We should've known."

"We did know," my other brother, Beau, replied. "All of us knew."

He was right. We had known that something was wrong, but we hadn't known what. There had always been a connection between the five of us, a little niggling feeling in the back of our minds when one of the others was hurt. But it wasn't as simple as knowing immediately which one of us it was or what the problem was. The four of us had reached out immediately, checking on the others, and Zeke had been the only one we hadn't been able to find.

"You're sure this was some small group and not part of a larger—"

The commandant cut our father off. It was either very brave or very stupid. "They were locals who noticed that the team didn't get injured like they should've," he said. "They knew what we were, and when given the opportunity—"

"How the hell did they even have the opportunity?" I barked. That theory didn't make any sense. "How the fuck did they keep him down?"

"That we don't know," Arthur replied.

"And no one thought to ask?" Chance scoffed.

"I give you my word—"

"Fuck your word," Beau said darkly, glaring at the commandant.

"Bjorn," my father chided.

"It's all right, Erik," Arthur murmured. "This is unprecedented aggression."

"What the hell did you all expect when you went public?" Danny asked incredulously.

"We went public sixty-four years ago, Daniel," Arthur replied. "And since that time, targeted assaults have been minimal. The benefits of no longer having to hide our species from the rest of the world far outweigh the consequences of living openly."

He was wrong. The assaults hadn't been minimal. Vampires just chose to deal with them when they happened instead of running to daddy every time someone spat in their cereal. The only time anyone notified command was when they needed help cleaning up a mess.

"Tell that to our brother." Danny spat.

"We're doing everything in our power to make sure that this is an isolated event and not part of a larger plot," Arthur said placatingly.

He was so full of shit. I couldn't believe he was actually spouting that nonsense to our faces. No one in that room believed that some random group of humans had been able to take down a Vampire in his prime without serious planning and resources.

"You have all that you need from him?" my father asked after a moment of all of us staring at Arthur like he'd lost his mind.

"We do," Arthur replied.

"I'll expect him by dusk tonight," my father informed him.

"I don't know if it'll be possible to..." Arthur sputtered.

"Tonight, Arthur. No later." He reached out and touched my youngest brother's head softly before cutting a small lock of hair.

I looked away.

It was all my mother would have left of her baby.

I couldn't leave that room fast enough. That body on the table was no longer Ezekiel Boucher. It was a shell, nothing more. My baby brother was gone.

TWO MONTHS LATER

My stomach churned as I stood in the center of the room, spinning in a slow circle. We'd followed every lead and chased every piece of information and come up with nothing. Someone had paid for this facility—there was no doubt in my mind—but I still had no idea who it was.

The huts in the middle of the jungle looked like nothing from the outside. An abandoned village that hadn't been occupied in a long time. It wasn't until you looked closer that you saw the little things that didn't fit. A door with a dead bolt. A lone antenna on one of the roofs. Clear paths that hadn't become overgrown with the passage of time.

We'd come here when we realized that our investigation was getting nowhere, hoping to find anything that the other team had missed.

I hadn't realized how viscerally it would affect me.

My brother had been held in this room with the moldy blanket and the bucket in the corner. How long had he looked at these walls, waiting for his team to rescue him? Had he thought that his brothers knew and hadn't come for him? I couldn't believe that.

He must've been waiting for us, sure in the assumption that we'd reach him in time.

I swallowed against the bile rising in my throat and moved to the wall, running my fingers over the rough cement. There had to be something in that room. *Anything* that could point us in the right direction. We'd hit wall after wall, and if I hadn't known better, I would've thought that command was actively trying to keep us running in circles.

That didn't make any sense, though. They had as much stake in finding out how the hell these people had captured Zeke as we did. Their soldiers were all over the world, entering into conflicts that command agreed to support. If there was a group out there targeting Vampires, all of us needed to know about it.

Crouching down, I moved along the walls, staring at the lower section as I went. My fingers caught on something that I hadn't immediately seen, and I pulled them away, reaching for my flashlight.

It was bright enough in the room to see easily, but the symbol wouldn't have been noticeable if I hadn't felt it.

It felt like the wind had been knocked out of me when it came into focus.

When Zeke was young, he'd been obsessed with becoming a rancher. It was all he talked about for a solid year. At one point, he'd even packed up his belongings, fully expecting my parents not to notice that he'd run away to play cowboy. He'd begged them for a pair of spurs.

He'd also designed his own crude brand for all the cattle he was going to buy someday. An intertwined Z and B.

I traced my finger over the letters.

"Boucher," someone called from outside. "You about done? It's going to take us a couple of hours to get back."

"I'll be out in a minute," I called back.

None of them had wanted to spend more time in the room than they had to. I didn't blame them. It stunk of blood and fear.

Leaning closer, I fanned out my fingers and lightly scraped them along the concrete. There had to be a reason Zeke had left his brand there. It wasn't anywhere near where the blanket had been discarded—*there*.

There was a little lip. Taking out my knife, I carefully slid it alongside the piece I'd caught my finger on. Almost immediately, a small crude rectangle of cement fell to the dirt floor, leaving a small hollowed-out space in the wall.

My heart pounded as I reached inside. It stopped when I felt the little objects beneath my fingertips.

Slowly, I pulled the first one out. It was a St. Christopher medal, tarnished with age and dirty with blood and who knew what else. I didn't recognize it, but I knew someone would. I reached into my vest and pulled out the plastic bag that came with my travel blood. It was double wrapped to protect from spillage, and I'd never found a use for the extra bag before, but I always saved them. Gently, I dropped the medal inside and reached for the next item.

It was a piece of light pink ribbon about three inches long that had once been silky but had been worn down over time, probably by someone smoothing it between their fingers.

Next was a silver ring with some kind of crest on it that I couldn't read. Very old. Someone's family heirloom.

I gritted my teeth and pulled out a small lock of hair next, the memory of my dad cutting Zeke's weighing on my chest like a boulder. It was very dark, almost black, and tied together with thin string.

A broken tooth, next. The root was still half-attached. Closing my eyes, I told myself it wasn't Zeke's. I'd read his autopsy report. It hadn't said anything about missing teeth.

Then another ring. This one smaller than the last. Plain gold. A wedding band.

My fingers reached the bottom of the hole, and I slid them side to side. There was something—paper—in there about halfway back. Pinching it between my fingers, I pulled it out.

My world tilted as I saw the faces staring up at me.

Oh Gods. My hands began to shake.

The photo was tiny, square, and printed in black and white, but it was impossible not to recognize my baby brother's beaming face. He was wearing a shirt that my mother had bought him for his birthday, and his arms were around a man who was laughing at the camera.

Zeke's hand rested lovingly on the side of the man's throat. They both looked deliriously happy.

I fell to my ass.

I couldn't look away from him. I'd never seen my brother look like that, his face so fucking relaxed and happy.

I would've known without the note on the back, but I was still floored when I turned the photo over and found *my mate* written in Zeke's handwriting.

My baby brother had been mated, and I'd known nothing about it. How was that even possible? I'd known the moment our brother, Beau, had found his mate. I'd felt it, like someone setting their hand on my shoulder.

I wiped at my wet face with the back of my arm. I could hear my unit moving around restlessly outside. I needed to finish what I was doing so we could head back to camp.

Carefully, I slid Zeke's photo into my front shirt pocket so the dirt and gore from the other items didn't soil it further.

When I reached into the hole again, I found another ring and a toothpick. I wasn't sure what the significance of the toothpick could be, but I put it away with the rest of the items. If nothing else, command may be able to get some DNA off of it.

Before rising to my feet, I gently placed the cement block back into the hole, covering it nearly seamlessly. How many Vampires had been held in that room without knowing that there was somewhere to hide a sign that they'd been there? How many had stared at those walls, hoping someone would come to rescue them? Even worse, how many had stared at those walls, knowing that no one was coming?

Arthur's assurances that it was an isolated incident

were utter garbage. Whoever had killed my brother had killed countless others, and we still had no idea why.

Brushing off my trousers, I strode to the doorway and stepped out into the sunlight.

I'd go back to camp with the others, but I wasn't going to stay there. I'd done everything I could, and now it was time to go back home.

My family needed to know that the other half of Zeke's soul was somewhere out in the world, suffering without his mate.

Everything else could wait until we'd found him and brought him home.

CHAPTER 1
LUCY

We shouldn't have split up.

The thought played on a loop, even though it wasn't like my brother would've been any real help. Charlie was a lover, not a fighter. I'd been defending him since I was seven years old, and a boy made him cry on the playground. To be fair, he *would* defend me to his last breath...and at least I wouldn't have been alone as I watched the doorknob to my motel room turn.

I knew I'd locked it. I'd double-checked before I took a shower.

I wasn't sure who was on the other side, but if I had to guess, I'd say that the baseball bat in my hands wasn't going to do much but piss them off. I tightened my fists around the handle, making sure I didn't choke up too far so I could really swing. I'd have seconds to do whatever I could to get away.

Light shone in from the streetlamps as the door swung open slowly. So slowly.

As soon as a shadow stepped inside, I swung as hard

as I could. Aluminum connected with flesh with a sickening *thunk*. Gasping, I pulled back and swung again as the man closest to me went down. The one behind him was smarter or had better instincts, because I watched in horror as he caught the bat in mid-swing and ripped it out of my hands.

I didn't wait to see if he'd use it. With a grunt, I rushed him. My shoulder hit his sternum, and he let out a whoof of air as I knocked the wind out of him. He stumbled backward, and I shoved past.

Straight into the arms of the third man.

"Stop," he ordered quietly, carrying me back into the room as I bit and scratched, shoving at any part of his body I could reach.

Nothing I did seemed to have any effect. He wasn't even breathing heavily as I kicked my legs and twisted back and forth. His arms were like frigging rocks, tight enough to keep me contained, but not tight enough to hurt. *He also smelled really good.*

I scoffed and dug my chin into his collarbone.

"We're not going to hurt you," the man holding me said softly, gently closing the door with his foot.

"Pretty sure I blacked out for a second," the man on the floor groaned. "Fuck."

"You're such a dumbass," the one with the bat said, prodding him with it.

"Lucille, stop," the man holding me ordered, grunting as I twisted enough to elbow him in the gut. My hair had fallen in my face, and I could barely see in the dark, but I didn't stop trying to shove him off.

He knew my name.

"Get off of me," I wheezed, my breath seesawing in and out of my lungs.

He dropped me to my feet instantly.

I stepped backward toward the window as he flipped on the light, making the man on the floor curse.

"We're here to help you."

"Get the hell out of my room," I growled. It sounded very impressive, considering the fact that I was two seconds away from shitting my pants.

"Sorry, no can do," the man with the bat said, his words cutting off as his head snapped to the side to look at the man who'd been holding me. "No shit, Ulf?" he asked.

The man nodded.

"Awesome," the man on the floor said with a sigh, lying back flat.

Something about these men felt familiar, which ratcheted up my panic. Where had I seen them before, and how the hell did they know who *I* was?

"We're looking for Charles," the man who'd held me said carefully.

"You'll never find him," I replied without thinking.

Then I actually looked at him, and it felt like the floor had dropped out from under me. He was *gorgeous*. His light brown hair was long enough to brush his collar, but it was smoothed away from his face and looked like it hadn't moved in our tussle. A little demoralizing that I couldn't even mess up his hair, but whatever. His light blue eyes were framed with dark lashes, making them pop, and his chin and cheeks were covered in five o'clock shadow a few shades darker than his hair.

He looked like a model or something. It was a little disconcerting.

"We found *you*," bat man said with a shrug.

I clenched my teeth together and lifted my chin. I wouldn't tell them *anything*. Charlie might've been my older brother by thirteen months, but I'd been looking out for him since we were kids. If they thought I was the weak link that would lead them to him, they were dead wrong.

I looked back at the handsome one, almost reflexively. God, he was...

"We're Zeke's brothers," he said, running his hand down the back of his neck.

He was fidgeting. What did that mean? Was he lying?

"I don't know anyone named Zeke," I lied. "Sorry, you must've gotten the wrong room."

The man on the floor laughed, then groaned.

"I'm Ambrose Boucher," the handsome one said, pointing to himself. "The asshole with the bat is Chance. The one you knocked out is Danny."

I stared at him blankly.

"Do any of those names sound familiar?" he asked, his eyes searching my face.

Of course they sounded familiar. They were my brother-in-law Zeke's brothers' names. There was one missing, though. Barry? Brandon? No, Beau. It was Beau. But just because he knew the names didn't mean those were *their* names.

I tried and failed to look away from him. It felt compulsive. I had to fight the urge to speak.

What the hell was going on? Had I hit my head or something?

"You're Lucille Franklin," Ambrose said. "Your brother is Charles. He was my brother Zeke's mate, right?"

I stared at him blankly for a moment. His sentence sounded wrong, but it took me a moment to realize why.

Was. He said *was.*

I took an involuntary step backward, that small word hitting me like a blow to the solar plexus. We'd known that Zeke was missing. When he hadn't come back for me and Charlie in Belgium, we'd followed his directions to the letter, quietly making our way across Europe and taking a merchant ship home. I'd stashed Charlie and come back to Baltimore, even though Zeke had warned me not to. I'd figured that I could be in and out quickly enough that no one would notice.

I'd hoped that by the time I got back to my brother, Zeke would've already caught back up with him, ready and willing to rip me a new one for taking the risk.

"She didn't know," Chance—no, Danny—said quietly from the floor.

Ambrose winced.

I tried to control my breathing, but it felt like I couldn't draw in enough air.

Zeke was *gone*? That couldn't be true. They had to be lying. Zeke had explained it to us. Vampires had long lives and were harder to kill than humans, but once a Vampire was mated both the Vampire and the mate became *immortal*.

I took another step backward, a lump in my throat. I wasn't sure how I was going to get away, but I had to. I needed to get back to Charlie. I wasn't sure what these men had done to Zeke, but we needed to find him. Maybe his real brothers would help. From what Zeke had told us, they were the best of the best. If they hadn't realized yet that their brother was in trouble, I had my doubts, but Zeke had told us a hundred times that if we were ever in trouble to find the Bouchers.

"She's panicking," the one with the bat—fake Chance—mumbled.

"Our brother Zeke has the night sky tattooed across his chest," the handsome one said quickly. "He's missing the end of his third toe on his right foot. He lost it by dropping an axe on his foot when we were children. He maintains to this day—" His voice grew rough, and he cleared his throat. "He maintains that Chance startled him, and that's why he dropped it. *Not* because it was too heavy. His favorite food is marshmallows. Can't get enough of them. When he smiles, the left side of his mouth rises a little bit higher than the right. He's not a drinker. He takes his coffee with cream but no sugar."

"Stop," I snapped, the weight on my chest growing heavier and heavier.

"He was closer to our mother than our father because he was the baby," Ambrose finished quietly. "And she coddled him."

Chance and Danny were silent.

Shit. I believed them.

"Who did we meet in Europe?" I asked, watching Ambrose's face closely for any kind of tell.

"Matthias," Ambrose replied easily. "Zeke probably called him our cousin, even though there's no blood relation. You also met his mate."

"What did Zeke want to be when he grew up?"

"A cattle rancher. He even designed his own brand."

My shoulders slumped.

"We *are* Zeke's brothers," Chance said, helping Danny up from the floor.

"Is he dead?" I asked, glancing between them.

My eyes moved back to Ambrose almost instinctively.

He gave a tight nod.

"That's impossible," I whispered.

"How much did Zeke explain to you?" Danny asked gently.

"Everything," I hedged. I believed these males were his brothers. I could see the resemblance now that I no longer felt like the panic was going to suffocate me, but that didn't mean that I was going to blindly trust them.

Zeke may have promised that we could trust his

family if anything went wrong, but he'd also promised that he and Charlie would live forever, and look how that turned out.

Chance moved behind Ambrose and used the baseball bat to slowly pull back the curtain. "Sun's coming up, Ulf."

"We need to leave," Ambrose told me. He hadn't looked away from my face since the moment we met, and it was beginning to make me a little self-conscious. Did I have dried spit on my cheek or something?

"Feel free," I said, waving at the door. "Don't let the door hit you."

"We can't leave you here."

"You absolutely can," I argued.

"Do you have any idea the kind of danger you're in?" Danny asked dubiously.

"Oh, I think I have a better idea than you do," I shot back. "Where have you been the past few months?"

The *audacity* of these Vampires.

"Ambrose," Chance called, his voice low.

"Problems?" Ambrose asked, his eyes still on me.

"Don't touch that," I ordered as Danny reached for my bag.

"Same human male has crossed the parking lot twice," Chance told Ambrose.

"That happens at a hotel," I snapped, stomping over to tear my bag out of the Vampire's hands.

"You can't stay here," Ambrose told me, stepping into my path. "If we can find you, so can anyone else."

"No one is looking for me."

"If they think they can use you to get to Charles, they are."

"They're not looking for Charles either," I lied. We actually weren't sure if they were looking for Charles or not, but we'd erred on the side of caution. Zeke had been adamant that we needed to be vigilant if he didn't come back.

"Then why did you stash him somewhere?" Chance asked drily.

"Who says I stashed him?" I shot back.

"Can we stop talking in circles?" Danny asked tiredly. "You know, and *we* know, that you're on the run. We need to get the hell out of here. Are you carrying the bag, or am I?"

"You carry it," Ambrose ordered his brother. He looked at me. "Is there anything else to pack?"

"I'm not going anywhere with you."

"I'll take that as a no," Ambrose replied. He glanced over at Chance. "All set."

"Now's the time," Chance agreed.

"Then we're moving."

Ambrose reached for my arm, and I don't know what it said about me, but I allowed him to usher me out of the room and across the parking lot to a nondescript sedan. I didn't think anyone had followed me to the hotel, but their little chat about some guy walking back and forth through the parking lot creeped me out. I climbed into the back seat without a word, the feeling of someone watching me crawling up the back of my neck. When Ambrose let go of my arm, I shuddered and scooted down in my seat so only the top of my head was visible from outside.

"We can't stay in Baltimore," Danny said as Chance drove the car into the morning traffic.

"It's a big city—" I began, peering out the window.

"Not big enough," Ambrose said quietly from beside me. "You shouldn't have come back here."

"I had to," I replied.

"Where are we going?" Chance asked, glancing at me in the mirror.

"You tell me," I replied emotionlessly. "I would've stayed in the motel room I paid for."

"Where's Charles, Lucille?" Ambrose asked quietly.

I just stared at him. I'd had chemistry with plenty of men. Sometimes it was a fleeting thing, and sometimes it led to longer relationships, but it always ended eventually. Whatever was happening with Ambrose wasn't that. Instead of butterflies filling my belly, it felt like a tether had pulled tight between us. I looked away and took a deep breath, which was a mistake considering I got a huge whiff of him, and he still smelled distractingly good.

"I'm not taking you to my brother."

"Are we really still doing this?" Chance asked in irritation.

"Leave my brother alone."

"We're here to help him," Ambrose said kindly. "He's Zeke's mate. He's part of our family."

"He's *my* family," I argued. How dare they try to claim Charles. He was *my* brother. The only family I had left after our parents had died within a year of each other when we were teenagers. *Zeke* was family. *They* weren't anything. Charlie didn't even know them.

"I don't envy you," Chance said from the front seat. I wasn't sure who he was talking to or what the hell he was talking about.

"Listen," Ambrose said as Chance suddenly took a side street and smoothly pulled out at the next intersection, driving in the opposite direction. "Zeke was murdered. Our brother, Beau, and his mate were ambushed and barely made it home. We're not sure what's going on, but we need to get you and Charles somewhere safe, and Baltimore isn't safe."

"Charlie isn't in Baltimore," I replied smugly.

"But you are," Ambrose countered flatly. "And I've seen what these people do. You may think that you'd be able to hold out against them. You'd be wrong. If they get their hands on you, it'll be a matter of hours before they know where your brother is."

I opened my mouth to argue, but snapped it shut again when he shook his head angrily.

"You will not withstand torture," he said slowly. "Tell me where Charles is so we can get you both somewhere safe."

I bit the inside of my cheek. On one hand, I couldn't ignore the sense of relief that filled me when I imagined the Boucher brothers taking over the job that I'd been doing since we'd realized that Zeke wasn't coming back for us. I was exhausted from being on constant alert. On the other hand, I didn't know these brothers of Zeke's, and neither did Charlie. If I showed up with them, there was a good chance that we'd scare the hell out of my brother.

Charlie had been through enough, and he wasn't in any condition to deal with more.

Plus, for all I knew, the brothers were the ones being followed. If someone had found me, maybe it was because they'd led those mysterious people right to me. I wasn't about to let them lead any assholes to Charlie.

"Take us to the house," Ambrose ordered after a few minutes of silence.

Chance sighed in irritation and nodded.

The car was quiet as we drove in circles. Back and forth through the city, never taking the same streets or crossing previous paths. It took us two hours. Finally, we drove down a quiet suburban street, passing someone walking a dog, a couple of toddlers and their mother drawing on their driveway with chalk, and an old man sitting on the porch in a lawn chair.

Chance reached above his head, and as we pulled into a driveway, the garage in front of us began to open. The minute the door was high enough, we pulled inside. No one moved until the door had closed behind us again.

"I'll do a quick sweep," Danny announced as he left the car.

"Whose house is this?" I looked around the garage. A few tennis rackets hung from pegs on the wall. Beside them, a tool bench sat deserted, an array of tools scattered across the surface like someone had only set them down for a moment and planned on coming right back. Two bicycles were parked in the corner, helmets dangling from the handlebars.

"Clear," Danny called from the doorway to the house.

Ambrose and Chance thrust their doors open and climbed out of the car. I sat for a moment, wondering if I should just stay where I was. I didn't want to go into some strange house with them. I didn't want to be dealing with any of the shit we'd been slogging through since the day Zeke approached Charlie at an outdoor café and our lives were upended.

We'd been saving for years to take the year-long trip through Europe. We'd never had enough money when we were kids to take any kind of vacation, and we'd promised each other in middle school that someday we'd leave it all behind and see everything that we wanted to. Architecture and artwork and parks and gardens and restaurants and shopping centers and canals and beaches—the world was our oyster, and we'd finally had to opportunity to reach for it all. Then everything had imploded.

"Come on," Ambrose ordered, throwing open my door.

"Where are we?" I demanded as I followed him into

the house, clutching my bag. What the hell had they done with my baseball bat?

"A friend's place," he replied easily.

"A friend. *Right*," I shot back sarcastically. "A friend who just gives you the remote to his garage door"—I looked around the house—"and isn't even here."

"Where is Charlie?" Chance barked, glaring at me.

"Fuck you," I enunciated slowly.

Chance looked at Ambrose like he would help. When Ambrose said nothing, Chance's glare moved back to me.

"We're not fucking around here," he snapped. "We need to get your brother somewhere safe *yesterday*."

"Forgive me for not putting a lot of stock in your promises of protection," I scoffed, waving him off like an annoying fly. "Considering your brother is the entire reason I'm not sunbathing topless in France right now."

"Don't you—" Chance began to round the kitchen island separating us, but stopped instantly when Ambrose lifted his hand.

"Enough," he said quietly. He looked at me. "How about you go pick a bedroom. The primary at the end of the hall has a connected bathroom."

"Fine," I replied, moving in that direction.

"We don't have time for this," Danny said as I left the kitchen. "We need to get back—"

I reached the bedroom and slammed the door behind me.

Taking a deep breath, I dropped onto the end of the bed and set my bag between my feet. The sun shone through the blinds of the simple room. There was no dresser, just a bed and two nightstands with small lamps. The door to what I imagined was the bathroom was closed, but the one to the walk-in closet was open and empty. There wasn't even a random pair of shoes left inside.

Where the fuck were we? No one lived here. The place was clean and tidy, but there was no sign that anyone had been here in a long time, despite the lack of dust.

Jesus, Charlie had really fucked us when he fell in love with Zeke. My poor, heartsick brother.

Carrying my bag with me, I walked into the massive bathroom and closed the door behind me. A little window above the shower filtered in enough light that I didn't even have to turn on the vanity lights, but I did anyway. Might as well waste a little electricity since I'd basically been kidnapped. I grimaced at my reflection in the large mirror behind the sinks. My hair was a mess, falling out of my ponytail and hanging around my face. My eyes had dark circles beneath them, with good reason. I couldn't remember the last time I'd had a full night of sleep. My clothes were wrinkled past the point of worn and strad-dling the line of slept in. I looked like shit.

I told myself it didn't matter as I tidied my hair and changed my shirt into a slightly less wrinkled one from my bag, but somewhere inside, it did. These were Zeke's brothers, and even though my resentment was so strong I could practically taste it, I'd still loved my brother-in-law. It was impossible not to after I'd seen the way he treated Charlie. The way he'd looked at him. The way he'd spoken to him.

Clearing my throat, I pulled out my toothbrush and toothpaste and got to work. There was no reason to think about Zeke. Not yet. Not until I had a little more time to really sit in it and mourn the life my brother could've had, and now never would.

When I finally came out of the bathroom, Ambrose was sitting on the bed, waiting.

"I thought you said I could pick my room," I greeted as I set down my bag. "I didn't hear you knock."

Dear God, he was incredible to look at. I couldn't really accept how attractive he was. I'd been around other Vampires—Zeke and his cousin—and I'd noticed that they were both good-looking, but they weren't even in the same league as Zeke's eldest brother.

"Tell me what I can do to make you feel more comfortable about trusting us."

"Drop me off at the nearest bus station," I replied instantly.

"You know I can't do that."

"Won't," I corrected.

"Can't," he reiterated. I stared as he slid his fingers through his hair in frustration. The strands fell neatly back into place, and as I dropped my gaze, I met his. My stomach somersaulted.

I was fucking trapped in this house in some random neighborhood with Vampires I didn't know. By tonight, Charlie would be losing his mind with worry if I hadn't shown up yet. I was on the run, *maybe*, from some shadow organization that was searching for my brother, and I couldn't stop staring at this guy. Why should I give a single fuck that he was good-looking? How had I even noticed with all the craziness swirling around me? I couldn't think of a less appropriate time to lust after someone, especially this guy. What the hell was—

I stumbled back a step as a thought raced through my mind. Familiar. *He seemed familiar.* That was what Charlie had said to me on the day we'd met Zeke.

No. No fucking way.

Ambrose rose to his feet.

"Stop," I snapped.

"It's all right," he said gently.

The only reason I didn't start screaming is that he held still. He didn't make a single move toward me.

That's when I noticed the expression on his face. The look in his eyes. The tone of his voice.

Every time I'd found myself staring at him, he'd already been staring at me.

He hadn't said that he needed to get Charlie somewhere safe. He'd said he needed to get *me* and Charlie safe.

After the moment I'd run into him at the hotel, neither of the other brothers had touched me. Not in passing, not to help me, nothing. They'd kept their distance.

Chance had looked at him in the kitchen, expecting Ambrose to do something about me.

They already fucking knew.

CHAPTER 2
AMBROSE

"**W**hen were you going to tell me?" she choked out, her eyes wide with a mixture of panic and disbelief.

"Tell you what?" I hedged.

This was not how I'd wanted things to go down. In a perfect world, we'd already be picking up Zeke's mate and on our way home. We would've gotten them settled at the house, and things could've progressed naturally from there.

"Don't give me that," she hissed, crossing her arms over her chest. "Did you know before you came looking for me?"

"We've been searching for Charles."

"Charlie," she corrected angrily.

"Charlie," I conceded.

"Were you going to tell me we're mates?" she asked, glaring as the last word came out stuttered and breathy.

My gaze swept down her body. When I'd first realized who she was—what she was—I'd been shocked. I hadn't really ever had a type. I just liked women, all kinds of women. Almost every woman I'd ever met had something —her smile, her eyes, the way she carried herself, her laugh, her intelligence, her ass or tits—that made her attractive. Lucille was no different. She was beautiful, with her cupid's bow mouth and her wide brown eyes and heart-shaped face.

I also couldn't wait to get my hands on her ass.

But I'd been stunned anyway that she was my counterpoint. After all those years of waiting, all those years of wondering who my mate would be, I'd been completely shocked when I realized I'd found her. What about her made her my ideal mate? Why was her soul specifically the perfect match to mine?

"Oh my god," she said, still staring at me. "I'm not, am I?" she choked out, her eyes widening in horror. "I'm sorry. I'm such a frigging idiot."

"You are," I replied quietly.

"Are you sure?" she wheezed.

"Yes."

"But how can you be sure?" she asked.

"Because I can feel it."

"That doesn't clear anything up for me," she replied, throwing her arms in the air.

I took a step toward her and then paused as she shook her head.

"It's like..." I tried to think of a clear way to explain it. "If you saw photos of a hundred hands, could you pick out yours? Your brother's? You mother's?"

"Yes."

"I could pick you out," I said, watching as understanding filled her eyes. "I could pick you out of thousands. Millions. With my eyes closed. I would know you *anywhere*."

"Oh," she breathed.

"I thought Zeke explained—"

"Other stuff," she said, cutting me off as her gaze dropped somewhere to my left. "He, uh, didn't explain that kind of thing. It wasn't for me, you know? That was Charlie's."

"I understand." Gods, did I understand that. The constant ache in my chest intensified as I thought of my baby brother finding this *thing*. This sense of belonging and exhilaration and wonder and surety that we'd all been waiting for, only to die.

"I don't think this is the same," she said, shaking her head. "I don't think this is what Charlie had. Charlie was *glowing* when he found Zeke. They were both..." She flung her hands into the air again, at a loss for words.

"It happens differently for everyone."

"This is not happening," she said to herself.

"Look, we can figure all of this out," I said, taking a step forward. The few feet that separated us felt like too much. Now that I'd found her, any space between us felt wrong. "We need to go get your brother and get home. We can protect you there."

She let out a humorless laugh. "Protect us?" she said scornfully. "You're the ones who put us in this position in the first place."

"Lucille—"

"It's Lucy," she burst out, beginning to pace. "The only person who called me Lucille was my mother."

"Lucy," I repeated. It fit her. She looked like a Lucy.

"I'm not going to let you descend on Charlie like fucking vultures," she stated, shaking her head. "No. No, he's been through enough."

"We need to get him somewhere safe."

"Tell me where to go," she said stubbornly. "I'll go get him and bring him to you."

"That's not happening."

"You can't just keep me here." She glared. "I'm leaving."

"You're not."

"What are you going to do about it?" she sneered, shouldering her bag. "It's not like you're going to *hurt* me, right? You can't. And you wouldn't let your brothers, either."

"So you do know a little something about mates," I replied dryly.

"I know enough," she snapped. "Tell me where to meet you."

"Listen—"

"No, you listen," Lucy cut me off. "*I* will get my brother and bring him to you, if that's what he wants."

"I can't let you go by yourself."

"You can't stop me."

"I can."

"Bullshit."

"I won't ever hurt you," I told her seriously as I stepped to the side, blocking her path to the door. "I also won't ever stand by when you're in danger. If that means keeping you here, I'll do it."

"I need to get back to Charlie," she argued, trying and failing to hide the desperation in her tone. She glanced at the window.

"I understand," I soothed. "But you're not going anywhere without me."

"That's ridiculous!" Her voice rose. "You can't just make decisions for me. That's not how this mating thing works. I haven't even accepted you, and let me tell you something, buddy. Your odds aren't looking good!"

It was impossible to hide my wince at the sharp pain that flared in my chest. She wasn't wrong. There was a chance that she could walk away at any time before we'd cemented our bond. It would be uncomfortable, but with time and distance, she could live her life like any other human.

It would be agony for me.

I'd survive it. My brother Beau had walked away from his mate eighty years ago and survived it, but he'd never been the same afterward.

Now that I'd found her, the idea of never seeing her again made my skin crawl.

"What if just you and I go get Charlie?" I asked, hoping the concession would be enough to calm her down. "Would that be better?"

My brothers were going to kill me.

Lucy stared at the floor and crossed her arms. The room was silent for a long moment.

"Just you?" she said tentatively.

"Just me and you," I agreed.

"Tweedle Dee and Tweedle Dumb will never go for that." She jerked her head toward the doorway.

My lips twitched as I tried to hold back a relieved smile. "I'll deal with it."

"I don't know," she hedged. "I think it would be better if I went alone."

"It isn't safe."

"I've kept us safe this long."

"You've gotten lucky, sweetheart."

"Let's keep the pet names to a minimum," she grumbled, glancing at me and then away again.

"All right."

"I don't think that it's a good idea for Charlie to know about you and me," she said with a grimace, looking me over. "Oh, for fuck's sake. Couldn't you chip a tooth or something? Get a zit? Why do you look like that?"

"Like what?" I glanced down at my jeans and thermal.

"Forget it."

"I'll go talk to my brothers," I said, not bothering to hide my smile anymore.

"Stop it," she snapped.

My smile grew.

"The window doesn't open," I warned her, pointing to the bedroom window that looked over the backyard as I headed for the door. "And we'll hear if you try to break it."

"Haven't you ever heard of fire safety?" she called as I left the room. "Shit."

I found Chance and Danny still standing in the kitchen where I'd left them. Chance raised his eyebrows and glanced behind me as I joined them.

"Lucy and I are going to go get Charlie ourselves," I announced firmly. "You two fly home and let the family know what's happening."

"Fuck that," Chance snapped.

"That's a really bad idea," Danny agreed, his hands clenching the edge of the counter. "You have no idea if Charles is even still where she left him. You guys could get there to find him missing, and we'll be across the fucking country."

"Or you'll get there and it's a fucking trap," Chance said, looking toward the bedroom. "How much do we know about her?"

"I know enough," I replied flatly.

"So...nothing," Chance said derisively. "Cool, cool."

"She won't bring all of us," I said with a sigh, leaning against the counter. "So our options are to try and wait her out, try to figure out where Charles is without her help, which I'm guessing will be an impossible task, or go along with the plan that she actually agreed to. I'll go with her to get Charlie, and we'll head straight home."

NICOLE JACQUELYN

"Why the hell wouldn't we just wait for you here?" Danny asked. "You find Charles and bring him back here, and we'll take the fucking plane home."

"We've got no idea where he is," I reminded him. "And bringing him back to Baltimore isn't an option."

"This is going to end badly," Chance said, staring out the kitchen window.

"You don't know that. She knows we're mates. I think if we give her a little space, we'll find that she—"

Chance started laughing, cutting me off. Leaning away from the window, he pointed. "You were saying?"

My mate was sneaking, badly, across the backyard toward the gate.

"Fuck." I strode toward the front door.

By the time Lucy opened the gate that led to the side of the house, I was standing right outside, waiting.

"Dammit," she said with a sigh. "You forgot to paint the bathroom window closed."

"How far did you think you'd get?"

"Well, I figured you'd be arguing with them for at least another ten minutes," she said, letting me lead her back through the yard.

I stopped her by the back door. "Is it really so bad that we want to protect you?"

"Zeke wanted to protect us too," she said as she pushed the door open. "You've seen how that turned out."

"Nice stealth work," Danny said drolly as we entered the kitchen.

"Shut up," Lucy grumbled.

"Seriously?" Chance asked me, staring at me like I'd lost my mind. "You still think it's a good idea for the two of you to go off on your own?"

"I don't like you very much," Lucy said conversationally to Chance. "You're kind of an asshole."

I smiled.

"It's part of my charm," Chance shot back.

"Huh." Lucy crossed her arms over her chest. "I missed the charm. Where is it exactly?"

"You're pretty mouthy for someone we just saved."

"Saved from what? Bedbugs?" Lucy scoffed. "If I remember correctly, you broke into my perfectly safe hotel room—"

"Which obviously wasn't as safe as you were pretending since it took about fifteen seconds with a lock pick to get in," Chance interrupted flatly.

"Considering that I'm not even sure anyone was looking for me to begin with—"

"You can't be that fucking naïve," Chance barked.

I took a step forward, but Lucy didn't need me. Her eyes widened as she sneered at Chance.

"You don't know anything," she spat. "You're just a bunch of bumbling idiots. Oh, I'm supposed to *trust* you? *Thank* you? I met you like five minutes ago. Vampires are the ones looking for us, you frigging asshole! They're the ones selling out other Vampires to humans for their sick experiments. Why do you think Zeke left my brother, even though it was excruciating for both of them? Huh? He *loved* Charlie."

I stared at Lucy in horror.

"What do you mean Vampires are the ones searching for you?" Danny asked softly.

"I mean..." Lucy snapped, oblivious to the undercurrent drifting through the room. "That Zeke was sure that Vampires were the ones selling out the mates to the humans. Apparently, you guys have some kind of reporting system or something, and that's how they were finding the new mates. That's why he didn't report Charlie."

I didn't want to believe it. The idea that our own kind was setting up others to go through what Zeke had gone through before he died. It was abhorrent. *Mates were sacred.*

"That's why Zeke went back to his unit," Chance said quietly, his hands braced on the kitchen counter.

"He thought if he poked around, he could get more information," Lucy said, crossing her arms over her chest. "He wasn't sure who was behind it, but he was working with Americans and the guys from Europe, and he thought he could narrow it down or something."

"Fuck," Danny whispered. "Fuck. Fuck. Fuck."

"He had names. Dates. He was trying to piece it all together." She went quiet, and her gaze dropped to the floor. "He was due back, so he said he was going to do one more job, see what he could figure out, and then he'd be back for Charlie, and they could take everything he'd gathered to you guys."

"Someone's leaking classified information to the humans," I said out loud. The words sounded just as strange out loud as they had in my head.

"Money can do horrible things to people," Lucy replied, almost sympathetically.

"Most Vampires have money," Chance said tiredly. "Benefit of a long life."

"Not this kind of money," Lucy replied. "Zeke said he thought the whole thing was funded by that billionaire. You know, the tech guy. The one who invented those electric boats that can go underwater."

Danny's gaze shot to me.

"I can never remember his name," Lucy continued quietly to herself. "Dammit, what is that guy's name?"

"François Baudelaire," I answered as Chance's head snapped up. "Am I right?"

"How the hell did you do that?" Lucy asked suspiciously. "You can't read my mind, right?"

"Of course not."

"Good. Just checking."

"He's well known in some circles," I explained. "High in the United States government."

"Oh, goody," she said tiredly, leaning back against the wall. "Because this shit wasn't crazy enough."

"Why did Zeke think that Baudelaire was involved?" Chance asked.

"How the hell should I know?" Lucy snapped. "That's just what he said. That he thought Baudelaire was funding the research or something. I don't even understand what the hell they could be researching."

I knew. I'd suspected since I'd walked into the hut they'd tortured my baby brother in, but I hadn't wanted to believe it.

"If they've got that kind of funding, they could be tracking us by fucking satellite," Danny said, straightening. "We need to get rid of our phones."

When we'd begun searching for Charlie, it was for the sole purpose of finding our brother's mate and bringing him into the fold. Ignoring his existence would've been impossible. He was Zeke's soul match. The other half of the baby brother we'd lost.

We'd realized early on that Charles and his sister were in hiding. The fact that they'd suddenly dropped off the grid was proof of that. It hadn't been until our brother, Beau, and his mate, Reese, were attacked that we'd begun to understand exactly how much danger Charles might be in.

Lucy would've been collateral damage if the group that was hunting mates had caught up with them. Their only interest in her would've been as an avenue to

Charles. Now that we'd met and the mating heat had begun, she was in as much danger as her brother.

I tossed my phone onto the counter.

"I don't have one," Lucy said with a shrug. "Those were the first to go. Amateurs."

"We need to leave," Chance said, glancing toward the front door. "We've been here too long."

"You two go straight to the airport," I ordered. "Take my phone with you. Toss them all when you get there."

"This is fucking stupid," Chance said, stuffing my phone into his pocket.

"Probably better that we're splitting up," I replied, actually believing it. With any luck, whoever was watching would assume that I was flying home with my brothers. Maybe they'd think that we hadn't found anything because Baltimore was a dead end. "Hopefully, it'll give us a little time to get to Charles before anyone notices."

"You take the car," Danny ordered. "We can make it back to the airport—"

"We're biking, aren't we?" Chance bitched. "Excellent."

"Stop whining," Danny replied.

I caught the keys that Chance tossed my way.

"Go," he ordered. "We'll clean up here. Make sure no one knows we stopped by."

"I'll call as soon as I can," I said, gesturing for Lucy to follow me. "Give me a few days before you call out a search party."

"No promises," Danny said, moving in for a hug. "This is fucked," he murmured in my ear.

I nodded as I let him go. It *was* fucked. We had more questions than answers, and I didn't see that changing for a while, at least until I could get Charlie and Lucy back to my parents' place, where I knew they'd be safe.

"No details when you call," Chance ordered.

"No, really?" I said sarcastically as I hugged him with a hard thump on his back.

"You sure about this?"

"If I need you, I'll call."

"With what phone?"

"I'll fucking buy one," I said in exasperation. "It's going to be fine. If no one has shown up yet, we've still got some time."

"Clock's ticking," he warned as I led Lucy toward the garage door.

"I'm aware."

"Love you," I called out as we entered the garage.

Both of my brothers replied, repeating my words as I opened the passenger side door for Lucy.

"They'll be okay on those bikes?" she asked dubiously, looking at the bicycles in the corner.

"Don't worry about them. They're resourceful," I assured her.

A few minutes later, I was driving two miles above the speed limit as we left the little neighborhood behind.

Lucy was quiet beside me, her arms wrapped around the bag on her lap. She'd pulled her baseball bat up from the back floorboard and set it next to her feet. Easily accessible.

I wanted to assure her I wouldn't let anything happen to her, but since I'd seen what she could do with that bat, I kept my mouth shut. If she felt more comfortable with it in reach, she could sleep with the thing.

"Where am I going?" I asked as we made our way closer to the freeway.

"North," she replied, resting her chin on the bag.

"Still not going to tell me where he is?"

I thought she'd ignored me. She didn't reply for a long time. We'd been on the freeway for half an hour before she finally spoke again.

"Lancaster," she said quietly, staring out the windshield. "Charlie's outside Lancaster."

I understood instantly and almost laughed at the brilliance of their plan. Zeke must have told them where to go if things went sideways. My brother had been a pain in the ass since the moment he was born, but he'd also been the kindest of us, and arguably the smartest. If Lucy hadn't gone back to Baltimore, there was a good chance we wouldn't have ever found the Franklin siblings.

"Are you hungry?" I asked after another half hour of silence.

She was killing me. Our proximity inside the car had ratcheted up the heat that was currently racing through my veins, and I knew that she wasn't immune to it. Every few minutes, she shifted uncomfortably in her seat. She'd already dropped the bag between her feet and had spent most of the last fifteen minutes pulling on the chest of her shirt like she was fanning the skin beneath it. Even her hairline was becoming a little damp.

"I'm not hungry," she said. "Could we turn up the air conditioning? Why is it so hot in here? It's starting to make me feel sick."

"It's not hot in here," I replied as she messed with the controls. "I turned it up as far as it will go."

"Maybe it's broken."

"It's the heat."

"That's what I said," she snapped. "It's frigging hot in here."

"The mating heat," I clarified.

Her head snapped to the side. "The *what?*"

"Didn't Zeke explain anything?"

"He explained plenty," she said slowly, staring at me. "What are you talking about?"

"It's a biological process—"

"Cut the shit."

"It's basically nature's way of making sure that mates complete the bond. Can I try something?"

"No."

I ignored her and set my hand carefully on her knee.

Lucy's breath left her in a whoosh of air. I understood the feeling. The pulsing in my veins slowed. Not completely, but enough that my skin stopped crawling. If that small point of contact could settle it that much, I wondered how it would feel to have her pressed against me.

Naked.

Lucy jerked my hand up a few inches so that it was partially wrapped around her thigh and sighed in relief.

"Good?" I asked, glancing at her.

"A little better, yeah," she said quietly. "This is how Charlie felt?"

"I think it's a little different for everyone," I replied. "But yes."

"No wonder they were always touching," she said to herself as she relaxed into the seat.

"Even after the bond has been completed," I explained. "The urge to be close to your mate doesn't go away. It gets easier to manage, but it's never fully gone."

"I can see the draw," she said. "Who wouldn't want someone literally unable to leave you?"

"It's more than that," I countered. "You're my other half. The reason humans ever heard the word soulmate."

"I don't even know you."

"You will."

"You seem pretty sure of that."

"Anything else is unacceptable," I replied before I could think it through.

Lucy just huffed.

The rest of the drive was mostly quiet. With my hand on Lucy's thigh, my mind had quieted enough that I felt able to think through exactly what we were dealing with. The men we'd encountered when Beau and Reese were attacked in her apartment were all human, so the conspiracy didn't spread far enough that they'd had enough Vampires to do their bidding. My gut told me that the group of Vampires who knew what was going on was small, probably only a few.

There had always been plenty of infighting between Vampire factions. There'd even been wars hundreds of years ago, but even then, mates had been off limits. For the most part, Vampires with mates hadn't even been participants in those wars. It went against everything we lived for to squander that gift.

The Vampires responsible for the death of my brother didn't have mates. The sudden belief was unsubstantiated, but it felt right. No one who'd gone through that jolt of recognition, of knowing, would've been comfortable taking it from another.

It was still pretty early when we pulled up to the old farmhouse and climbed out of the car. Chickens pecked in the grass under an old oak tree, and the sound of children playing out back made a hundred memories drift through my mind. It was like stepping into a different time.

I rested my hand on the base of Lucy's spine, both for the connection and what the move represented, as the front door opened and a familiar face came into view.

"Renn," I greeted.

"Ambrose Boucher," Isaac Renno replied, taking measured steps toward us. "It's very good to see you."

"You too, old friend," I said, reaching out to shake his hand. "I hear you have a houseguest."

"He's still in bed," Renn told Lucy, jerking his head toward the door.

Without a word, Lucy raced past us and disappeared into the house.

"Ezekiel?" Renn asked quietly.

"Gone."

He was silent for a moment. "I'm very sorry to hear that."

"How's Charles?"

"To be expected," Renn replied, leading me around the back of the house. "Every day he grows worse."

"I'm going to bring them back to my parents."

"Yes. That would be best."

"Thank you for taking them in," I said softly as we came to a stop behind the house. Two children were completely oblivious to our presence as they exited the small chicken coup and headed toward the barn.

"It was a privilege," Renn replied, sitting down on a bench. "You know that."

"How are things?" I asked, sitting down beside him.

"Quiet, mostly."

"Not a lot of people to hide anymore?"

"There will always be those who have nowhere else to turn," he responded. "The monsters are just more easily hidden now. It is mostly mothers and children these days."

"Do you need anything—"

"The Lord provides."

"You're a stubborn old goat."

Renn scoffed.

"How are your wife and the children?"

"Well. Your parents?"

"Grieving," I replied with a sigh. "Angry. Scared."

"Trying times."

"Has Charlie said anything to you about what's going on?"

"No," Renn answered. "And I do not ask. Better for everyone that I do not know."

"If there was any way I could've kept you out of this mess, I would've. Zeke trusted that you'd keep them safe. That's why he sent them here."

"Put on the whole armor of God, that ye may be able to stand against the wiles of the devil," Renn replied calmly. "I have no regrets."

"Ephesians," I mumbled.

"You remember."

"I could recite the entire thing from memory," I said dryly, leaning forward to rest my elbows on my knees.

It was peaceful here. Quiet, except for the wind blowing through the trees and the occasional farm animal. It was the perfect place for Renn to do what he'd been doing for longer than I'd been alive, sheltering and protecting those who needed it for as long as they needed it. If there was anyone in the world who deserved recognition for the good they'd done, it was Renn, but he'd never accept it. He believed that he'd been called upon to be a shepherd in a world of wolves, and he'd never wavered in his dedication to the cause.

"Ambrose," Lucy called as she stepped out of the back door.

I rose to my feet as a slender man followed her outside. He was thin to the point of being delicate, with a sharp chin and dark brown eyes that matched his sister's. It looked like he'd attempted to tame his hair and only been half successful, but he was fully dressed, complete with shoes, as he strode toward me and reached out his hand.

"Hello," he said, his voice low and raspy.

"Charlie," I greeted. I couldn't stop the smile that pulled at my cheeks or the ache in my chest. "I'm Ambrose."

"I would've recognized you anywhere," he replied with a nod.

He was perfect. It was easy to imagine him sitting with my baby brother, scolding him for dropping his shoes near the door or warning him that marshmallows would rot his teeth out of his head.

"It's good to finally meet you."

"I wish it were under better circumstances," Charlie said, his voice cracking as he let go of my hand. He cleared his throat. "Sorry."

"I told Charlie that we're going with you," Lucy announced. "To your parents' house, right?"

"That's right." I nodded. "It's the safest place for you right now while we get to the bottom of all this."

"That is a wise choice," Renn told Charlie as he stood. "There is no safer place for you than beside Erik Boucher."

"I'm standing right here," I joked, glancing at him.

"A babe in swaddling cloth," Renn replied, smiling gently at Charlie. "But he'll do."

"Thank you so much for everything," Charlie told Renn, his eyes welling with tears.

"Say nothing of it," Renn replied. He gathered Charlie to him, one arm wrapped around his back and one hand resting on the crown of his head as he prayed over the younger man.

"Erik is your dad?" Lucy asked me softly as we took a few steps away to give them some privacy.

"Yes."

"And he knows about Charlie?"

"He knows. He'd be here too, if he could leave my mother for longer than a few days."

Lucy nodded. "I'm going to go get Charlie's bag. Tell him I'll meet you guys out front."

She went back inside just before Charlie turned back to me.

Someone screeched inside the barn, and Renn twisted to look over his shoulder.

"It was good to see you again, Renn," I said as wailing commenced inside the barn.

"You know where to go next?" he asked.

I nodded.

"God go with you, Ambrose," Renn replied as he strode away.

"Lead the way," Charlie said, waving me ahead of him as we rounded the house.

"Lucy said she'd grab your bag and meet us out front."

"She doesn't like goodbyes," Charlie replied. "Never has."

I couldn't stop looking at him. This man held the other half of my brother's soul. He was Zeke's perfect match in ways that I would never understand. He was responsible for the happiest moments in my baby brother's life. The immediate sense of protectiveness I felt shouldn't have surprised me, but it did.

"You look a lot like Zeke," Charlie said softly.

"We both got my father's eyes."

"Around the jaw and mouth too," he said with a small smile. "Strong genes."

I tried to put myself in his place, but I couldn't imagine it. I'd only met Lucy hours before, and I still couldn't fathom losing her and then coming face-to-face with her lookalike brother. It must've been a complete mind fuck for Charlie and painful as hell.

"I got your shit," Lucy announced, bounding down the front steps. "You ready?"

"You didn't have to do that, Luce," Charlie said as she tossed him his bag.

"I didn't mind. You take the front seat."

"Back," Charlie countered as we reached the car.

"Your legs are longer," Lucy argued.

"I want to lie down. Take the front."

I watched the two of them in fascination. Lucy seemed bigger when she was near Charlie. She hadn't been some wilting flower when we'd found her in that motel, but it still seemed like she'd grown a couple of inches just by the way she was holding herself now that her brother was present. She was more sure of herself and more assertive than she'd been before.

Her gaze softened as she reached out and squeezed her brother's bicep. "All right, but we're waking you up for lunch. No sleeping through it."

"Deal," he said, throwing open the back door.

I rounded the hood as Lucy climbed into the passenger seat. By the time I sat down beside her, Charlie was sprawled out across the back seat with his head resting on the bag his sister had thrown him.

"Where are we going?" Lucy asked, her body twisted in the seat so she could watch the farmhouse disappear behind us a few minutes later.

"West," I said dryly. I knew she'd gotten my reference to her earlier reticence when she shot me a look before settling back into her seat.

"Ha. Ha."

"Oregon," I clarified.

"Or bust," she said with a sigh. Reaching back without looking, she rested her hand on Charlie's knee.

Twenty minutes later, Charlie was snoring softly in the back seat when Lucy finally brought her hand forward. I didn't react when she silently reached for my hand and pulled it to her thigh, but I felt it in every millimeter of my body.

CHAPTER 3
LUCY

I was in a rundown hotel room somewhere in Indiana, and I was pretty sure I was dying.

Staring at the bathroom door, I both wished that Charlie would finish his shower to come say his final goodbyes and that he'd take long enough that, by some miracle, the heat racing through my body in agonizing waves would be gone by the time he came out of the bathroom. The air conditioner was running full blast, complete with a loud clanking noise that didn't happen with any kind of regularity, but it didn't put a dent in the heat. I couldn't even open a window to let in a breeze. Ambrose thought that we hadn't been followed out of Pennsylvania, but of course nothing was sure.

Charlie had slept for hours while we'd made our way west, and I hadn't had the heart to wake him for lunch even though I'd said I was going to. It seemed like the only time that his face lost the pinched, haggard look was when he was asleep. I wasn't sure if being unconscious was the escape or if he saw Zeke in his dreams. Either way, sleep had been his reprieve since we left Europe. We'd gone through a drive-thru at dinnertime and only stopped for gas and bathroom breaks once. Ambrose was clearly on a mission to get us to Oregon as soon as possible.

After the day cooped up with him in the car, I couldn't say I was mad about the rush. Once Charlie was with us, and I'd lost the panic I'd felt while we were separated, my attraction toward Ambrose had amped up so much that more than once I'd found myself fantasizing about making him pull the car over so I could strip him bare on the side of the road. I obsessed over the flex of his forearms while he drove. The grip of his fingers around the steering wheel. The tendons in his neck as he looked over his shoulder while switching lanes. To say it was inconvenient was an understatement.

It didn't make any sense that I was his mate. Beyond the fact that the odds of that happening, which were very low, he was ridiculously gorgeous. And me? I was average at best. I'd never had a problem finding men to date or sleep with, but I was under no illusion that I was some kind of beauty. My face was round, my body wasn't slender or voluptuous, but somewhere in between. My hair was plain brown and slightly wavy. Nothing about me stood out. We didn't *fit*.

I probably would've been in shock about the whole thing, but after the last few months, I felt numb. I'd already done the whole holy-shit-you're-a-Vampire's-mate thing with Charlie. *That* had been a shock. Then we'd done the whole someone-is-out-to-get-Vampires-and-their-mates thing. That was both shocking and terrifying. Then we'd gone through Zeke leaving and the aftermath—more terror. Realizing that he wasn't coming back —terror and numbness. Sneaking our way through Europe and back into the United States—numbness and determination. And finally meeting Zeke's brothers.

The sustained trauma and strain had made me feel like I'd lost my ability to feel almost anything.

Ambrose had rented us adjoining rooms for the night, and I was glad that I could put some distance between us, but almost immediately after I'd closed and locked the door between the rooms, I started to feel like garbage. It was almost the same sensation as I'd had in the car when we weren't touching, but so much worse.

I didn't remember Charlie having this kind of reaction to Zeke. Though, the more I thought about it, the clearer it became that once Charlie and Zeke had met, they'd been inseparable. They'd gotten their own room the first night and every night after until Zeke had gone back to his unit.

I groaned as nausea rolled through my belly.

Maybe it wasn't the mating heat or whatever. Maybe I'd gotten food poisoning or something. That seemed more logical. Why would nature make someone feel like they were going to vomit their guts out or poop themselves when they found their mate? It seemed like that would put a serious damper on any romance.

Kneeling on the bed, I tucked my arms tight against my chest and curled over my thighs until my forehead pressed against the comforter. I would've given anything to be able to fall asleep. Miserable, I took deliberate deep breaths and blew them out through pursed lips. It didn't help, but it at least gave me something to focus on while I sweated through my shirt.

By the time Charlie came out of the bathroom in a fresh set of clothes and his hair neatly combed, I was a groaning mess.

"What the hell is wrong?" he asked urgently as he hurried toward the bed. "Luce?"

"I feel like crap," I complained.

My skin felt too tight to hold everything in, like at any

moment it was going to burst and splatter my insides all over the walls.

I closed my eyes and leaned into the pressure of his cool palm as he checked my head for a fever.

"Shit," he muttered. He turned toward the adjoining door, then back toward the bathroom, then toward the adjoining door again, before spinning toward the bathroom and running inside. He came back seconds later with a cold washcloth. "This should help a little."

"Feels good," I mumbled as he laid it over the back of my neck. "Just leave me. Save yourself."

"So dramatic," he joked, brushing my hair out of my face.

"I'm never eating at a drive-thru again."

"You're spoiled after all that good food we had in Europe," he said softly, still smoothing his hand over my hair.

"Or someone shit and didn't wash their hands before assembling my taco," I panted.

"Gross."

"Very," I agreed.

I closed my eyes and groaned as a new wave of heat ran from my scalp to my toes, leaving me lightheaded. I was so busy trying to breathe my way through it that I didn't notice that Charlie had stopped rubbing my head and had crossed over to the door between our room and Ambrose's room.

"Lucy's sick as a dog," Charlie said.

My eyes shot open, and I lifted my heavy head to see him standing in the open doorway.

"We need some kind of fever reducer and probably anti-nausea medicine."

"Fuck," Ambrose said from the other room.

Then he was there in the doorway and striding toward

me. I wanted to glare at him or swipe my hand over my neck or something to stop him, but I was too weary to do anything as he came over and sat on the side of the bed. The moment he set his hand on my back, my entire body shuddered, and my stomach stopped cramping entirely.

"Give it a moment," he told me quietly, running his hand lightly up and down my spine.

His hair was a mess.

"What happened to you?" I rasped, feeling my body relax more and more with each sweep of his palm.

"Same thing that happened to you, I'd imagine," he replied softly.

I grimaced. I could feel the hand on my back everywhere as my muscles started loosening, one by one.

"Oh," Charlie said from behind Ambrose, his voice trembling. *"Oh."*

Remorse filled Ambrose's eyes as a lump formed in the base of my throat. I could barely swallow, much less say something that would make the whole situation less terrible for my brother.

How the hell was I supposed to explain that for some ungodly reason, I was also the mate of a Boucher brother? It didn't make any logical sense. Vampires went hundreds of years without finding their mates. The chance of two siblings being the mates of two Vampires of the same family must've been astronomical. It would've been more believable to win the lottery *twice*.

The universe had a sick sense of humor. The only reason I'd even met Ambrose Boucher was because my brother's mate had died. The whole situation was horrific.

"Charlie," I wheezed, pushing myself up. "I'm sorry."

"What the hell are you sorry for?" he warbled back with a hiccup.

My brother was bawling, and my heart was breaking.

"This isn't fair," I cried, tears filling my own eyes. "I didn't—" I shoved Ambrose's arm away. "Stop touching me."

"Don't stop touching her," Charlie countered, glaring at Ambrose.

"Shut up, Charlie."

"If he stops, you're going to feel awful again," Charlie sniffled.

"Then I'll be in good company," I replied softly, my breath hitching.

"I don't want that for you," he said, his words so garbled I could barely understand him. "I'd *never* want you to feel like this."

"It's different," I tried to explain as I climbed awkwardly off the bed. Ambrose's hands gripped my hips as I stumbled. I shoved them away. "You were...you were in love with Zeke."

Charlie let out a sob.

"That's not what this is." I gestured between Ambrose and me. "This is some weird biological joke. I'm fine. I promise. It'll pass."

"No, it won't," Charlie countered, slapping away the tears on his cheeks. "No, it won't. You think it will if you ignore it, but it won't. He's *it* for you."

"Maybe not," I argued. "Maybe he's awful."

Ambrose made a noise, but I ignored him, keeping my eyes on my brother.

"Don't do that," Charlie ordered, crossing his arms over his chest.

"Do what?"

"Don't downplay it."

"I'm not downplaying anything."

"Yes, you are."

"No, I'm not."

"Yes, you are, and it's insulting!"

My mouth dropped open as I stared at my brother in surprise.

"Do you have any idea what you have?" he asked, his voice cracking. "I would give anything to have that back. *Anything*."

"Bub," I whispered. I had no idea what to say to him. I'd always been able to shield him. I'd always been able to cheer him up. Until Zeke, we'd never encountered a situation that we couldn't handle together.

I couldn't help him. I couldn't even understand what he was going through. The loss of a partner was hard for me to grasp because I'd never really been in love with anyone. The loss of a mate? It was inconceivable.

"I'm fine," Charlie said, using the shoulder of his shirt to wipe off his cheeks. "Really. I'm so happy for you."

"That feels a little premature," I replied with a scoff. "But thanks, I guess."

"I'm not usually like this," Charlie told Ambrose, lifting his chin a little like it would hide the fact that his eyes were bloodshot and his face was swollen from crying.

"He is," I countered, looking over my shoulder at Ambrose.

"I am not," Charlie shot back.

"You're a little bitch baby, and you know it," I joked, my laugh watery as I dodged the arm he swung at me.

"She can say it," Charlie told Ambrose seriously. "But just saying, you better not."

"Oh no," I agreed with a sniffle. "I'd kill you. Dead."

"Noted," Ambrose replied.

Charlie dropped onto the other bed with a sigh. "So... mates. I didn't see that coming."

"Join the club," I said as I sat down next to Ambrose.

I wouldn't have asked him to start rubbing my back

again, but I couldn't hide the relieved slump of my shoulders when I felt his fingers sliding down my spine.

"It surprised me too," Ambrose said with a smile. "My brothers and I have been waiting a very long time, and now suddenly three out of five of us have found our mates in the last few months."

"Who else?" Charlie asked curiously.

"Beau," Ambrose replied with a grin. "His mate's name is Reese."

"That's great," Charlie said. He smiled sadly.

"Zeke was first, though." Ambrose nodded.

"Well, not really," Charlie said softly. "Didn't one of your brothers find his mate during the war?"

"Wait," I interrupted. I hadn't heard this story. "What war?"

"The Second World War," Ambrose replied. "Yes, that was Beau."

"But I thought you said—" I frowned. Something wasn't adding up.

"When Beau met his mate, she was already married and had a baby on the way."

Charlie visibly flinched.

"But I thought Vampires only have one mate," I argued. "So how did he find another one?"

Ambrose smiled gently. "Only one soulmate," he said slowly. "Same soul."

"Oh, ew." I grimaced. "You guys think that we're reincarnated or something?"

"Yes."

"So you could've met an earlier version of me and mated *her* up?"

Ambrose choked out a laugh. "Basically."

"Huh." I wondered what that version of me was like. Maybe I'd been a bombshell, gorgeous with long, flowing blond hair, huge boobs, and a tight ass. That version would've fit with Ambrose. Too bad he didn't find *her*.

"I didn't know that," Charlie said quietly. "Zeke didn't explain the reincarnation thing."

My stomach twisted. God, if old Charlie and Zeke had met a hundred years before, what would their life have been like? Nothing like it had been when they'd met outside that café. They wouldn't have had those nights out dancing like no one was watching, or the time at the theater when they'd held hands and whispered to each other the entire time, irritating the hell out of me since I actually *wanted* to see the movie we'd paid for. I had a hundred memories of Zeke pulling Charlie in for a kiss, no matter where we were. At the time, I'd been almost as happy as Charlie, watching my best friend get everything he'd ever wanted. It hadn't even occurred to me to be afraid. But if they'd met a hundred years before, I didn't know if I'd have felt anything but fear. The world had changed so much in the last century.

"We believe that we find our mate when we're meant to," Ambrose said. "I don't know why Beau met his twice, but there must've been some cosmic reason."

"It must've been awful for him," Charlie whispered.

"It was," Ambrose confirmed. "But he's happy now. More than happy."

"What a mind fuck," I announced, falling over until my head hit the pillow.

My body was twisted, with my feet still resting on the floor, until Ambrose reached down and pulled them onto his lap.

"Zeke was with Beau when he met his first mate," Ambrose said, rubbing his palms over my feet. "Did he tell you about that?"

"He mentioned it," Charlie replied with a nod. "During the Blitz, right?"

"From the stories I've heard, they found her in a collapsed building," Ambrose confirmed. "About thirty seconds after they realized who she was, her husband came running."

"Ouch." I grimaced.

"Yes," Ambrose agreed.

"You didn't fight in that war, right?" Charlie asked, lying down on the other bed until he looked like a mirror image of me.

"Not at first," Ambrose explained. "The United States hadn't joined the war yet. We could see where things were headed, but politics tied our hands. We fought near the end, though."

"That had to be frustrating."

"You have no idea." His hands tightened on my feet for a moment before they resumed the massage. "The truce between humans and Vampires has always been held by a very fragile thread. If one side pulls too tightly, even for a moment, the entire thing could snap."

"Like, say, if humans were targeting Vampires and their mates?" Charlie asked knowingly.

"That would be more like cutting the thread with a pair of scissors," Ambrose replied flatly. "Which is why I think that whoever is responsible for what's going on has kept the information very contained."

"Zeke was sure that if he had more time with the unit's computers, he could follow the threads until he found out who was leaking information," Charlie said with a yawn. "But he said it was impossible to get into the systems from the outside. That's why he went back."

"That must've been painful for you," Ambrose replied sympathetically.

"It hurt like a bitch," Charlie confirmed. "Luce was convinced I had some kind of deadly virus."

My head snapped up in understanding. Charlie had been sick when Zeke left, but I'd never imagined that it was *because* Zeke left. He'd spent days in bed with a raging fever, but that had felt almost secondary to the constant weeping. I'd been desperate to keep him hydrated and terrified when he wouldn't let me take him to the doctor.

"Separating mates, especially after the bond is complete, has physical repercussions," Ambrose explained to me.

"Why the hell would *anyone* want this?" I griped, glaring at him.

"It's worth it," he replied simply.

"I remain unconvinced," I grumbled, closing my eyes.

"It eventually tapered off," Charlie told Ambrose, his voice faint. "It was manageable for a while. Until..." He let out a long breath. "Well, now it's more like a hollow spot. Empty."

"I'm sorry," Ambrose said quietly. "I wish I could've seen the two of you together."

"They were disgustingly adorable," I announced, opening my eyes again. I wiggled my toes so Ambrose would keep rubbing them. "So lovey-dovey all the time. You've never heard two men giggle so much."

"Zeke giggled?" he asked, his lips twitching.

"Oh, yeah. He giggled. Like a schoolgirl."

"He did not," Charlie protested with a small laugh.

"He did," I countered. "And he looked at you like you were the most beautiful and fascinating person on the entire planet."

Charlie smiled.

"And, I mean, you're handsome, brother," I continued. "But let's be honest, you're a little boring."

"Do you see how mean she is to me?" Charlie asked Ambrose.

"I keep you grounded."

"Is that what we're calling it?" Charlie asked.

"My brother was lucky," Ambrose said, ending our argument.

"I think so too," I added, blowing a kiss to Charlie.

"I was the lucky one," Charlie replied. "For a while there."

"Even the toe didn't gross him out," I told Ambrose with a little laugh. "And you've seen it. That thing was weird looking."

"It was not." Charlie rolled his eyes.

"You should've seen it when it happened," Ambrose replied with a grimace. "Blood everywhere. I thought our mother was going to faint."

"He dropped an axe, right?" Charlie said, curling his hands together under his cheek.

He looked so young. My older brother, who had always felt younger than me. Always sweet. Always helpful. Always kind. The world hadn't been able to change him yet, and I swore it never would, not if I still had breath in my body. There was something unmistakably pure in Charlie. He could curse like a sailor and got angry as much as the next person, but I'd never seen him take it out on someone else. I'd never seen him make anyone feel less.

He didn't deserve what had happened to him.

No one deserved it, but Charlie deserved it even less.

"Right on his foot," Ambrose confirmed with a nod. "He was always trying to keep up with us, even though he was the youngest. I think it was Chance's turn to chop wood. Back then, we kept the house warm with a wood-stove, so if we didn't have split wood, we'd go cold."

"Back in the olden days," I drawled.

Ambrose pinched one of my toes and continued with his story.

"So Zeke went out to do it himself, even though my parents didn't expect him to help with that chore yet. I think he was trying to get on Chance's good side, but it also probably had a lot to do with pride. Zeke hated being the baby."

"And that's how we all know that Zeke was insane," I joked, grinning at Charlie. "Being the baby is the *best*."

"So he's out there for a while," Ambrose said. "And nobody realized what he was trying to do, but eventually, my mother ordered Chance to go finish his chores. He stomps outside, grumbling and pissed, and half a minute later he comes running back in, and he's white as a sheet. We all go running outside, and Zeke's sitting on a log, swaying, staring at his mangled foot." Ambrose paused, staring at the floor. "He wasn't making a sound."

The room was quiet for a long moment before Ambrose spoke again. "He always said that Chance startled him."

"That's what he told me," Charlie added.

"But Chance says that he found Zeke already sitting on that log with a bloody foot." Ambrose shook his head. "Who knows what the truth is."

"Well," I mused. "Chance wouldn't have wanted to get in trouble for startling his baby brother and getting him hurt."

"Good point." Ambrose grinned at me. "But Zeke was always getting hurt, so I don't know that Chance would've gotten into trouble. One time, we were down at the river..."

Ambrose told stories for hours while Charlie lay across from us, soaking it all up. He smiled and laughed and cried a little, but it felt like I was watching in real time as a little of my brother's spark came back, if only for a little while. I would never be able to pay Ambrose back for what he gave Charlie that night—a glimpse into the life of his mate that he'd never see. More memories that he would've never had otherwise, even if those memories were second hand. It was such a gift.

I knew then that bringing Charlie to the Bouchers was the right choice. If Ambrose could give Charlie that, and he was just one person, maybe being surrounded by Zeke's family could give him even more.

I stayed awake as long as I could, but the hum of their voices eventually lulled me to sleep. When I woke up a few hours later, the only light in the room filtered out of the bathroom doorway, and there was an arm draped over my waist. Across from me, Charlie's bed was empty.

I shot up so fast that I made myself dizzy.

"He's in the other room," Ambrose told me softly. "He's fine."

"Why did he go in there?" I asked, glancing at the darkened doorway.

"I think he wanted some privacy."

"Then you should've left," I replied, turning to look at him. "That's your room."

"We wanted to let you sleep."

"I was already asleep."

"You wouldn't have stayed that way if I left you," he reminded me gently.

I let out a frustrated breath and looked at the doorway again. If I listened carefully, I could hear my brother's familiar snoring. It wasn't obnoxious or anything, at least I didn't think so, but it had always been noticeable thanks to a deviated septum he'd had since we were kids when a bully broke his nose.

"Thanks for what you did earlier," I said, keeping my voice low. "You know, the stories."

"You don't have to thank me for that."

"They didn't have enough time." I sighed. "They didn't get to make enough memories."

"They didn't," Ambrose agreed, laying his hand on my back. "But I think that would've always been the case. It's never enough."

"You're probably right."

"I wish I could've seen them together," he said with a sigh. "Just once."

I glanced at my backpack.

"We all waited so long. It's hard to explain. Humans fall in and out of love so easily—"

"Hey," I protested.

He let out a huff of laughter. "I just mean that there is one person for Vampires. One soul that is our perfect match. There is no *good enough* or *okay for now*. It's that one or nothing."

"Are you telling me you're a virgin?" I gasped mockingly.

"Fuck no." He poked me in the side. "I've had plenty of sex. I was having sex before your parents were born."

"That is *not* the flex you think it is."

He poked me in the side again.

"Don't worry," he said dryly. "I'll know what I'm doing."

"You seem pretty sure of that."

"Positive."

"For all you know, I'm into weird shit," I countered, turning to face him. "I could want you to meow like a cat while you go down on me. I could ask you to lie perfectly still and play dead while I ride you." I leaned down so I could see him clearly. "I could ask to paint your dick with hot sauce."

Ambrose's smile was so big it transformed his entire face. "Meow."

The word was so surprising that I let out a loud bark of laughter. Slapping my hand over my mouth, I looked at the bedroom door and waited, but Charlie was still snoring.

"You're a freak," I whispered.

"You're the one who wants to paint my dick with hot sauce," he whispered back.

"That was an example."

"It sounded like a fantasy."

"Bullshit."

"Baby, I'll do whatever you want."

I rolled my eyes and leaned back up. Carefully, I swung my feet over the side of the bed and padded over to my bag. It only took me a moment to find what I was looking for, and I carried it back over to Ambrose, crawling in beside him. It was so dark in the room that I had to power up the camera by memory as I lay back until we were sharing his pillow.

"I'm going to leave the sound off," I said softly as I scrolled backward through the photos until I got to the beginning. "I don't want to wake Charlie up."

"Oh." Ambrose breathed as I stopped on the first photo I'd ever taken of Zeke and Charlie.

Zeke was standing behind my brother, his arms wrapped around Charlie's chest, his chin resting on Charlie's shoulder. Their heads were tilted toward each other so that their temples rested together. Both were grinning. Huge.

The next photo was the two of them walking down the street. Zeke's hand rested on Charlie's lower back, and

Charlie's head was turned, only half of his smile visible as he looked up at his mate.

The next photo was of the three of us. We were sitting on a grassy hill, lined up. Charlie behind me with his arms around my shoulders. Zeke behind him, with his arms the same on Charlie's shoulders. Our heads formed little steps from the left, first mine, then Charlie's, then Zeke's. I was caught mid-word, and the other two were laughing. I was pretty sure I remembered setting the timer, and I'd been telling them to smile or else, but I'd misjudged how long I had before the picture was taken.

Then another photo of Zeke and Charlie. Sitting on the same side of the table. Charlie is telling a story, and his hands are out in front of him, mid-movement. Zeke is looking intently over at Charlie, his gaze soft. No smile that time, but more intimate.

Ambrose let out a choked noise, but shook his head when I looked at him, so I kept going. There were probably a hundred photos of the guys in my phone. I'd been so determined to get a picture of everything we saw that I'd bought the camera the week before our trip. I'd had no idea then that it would provide the only proof of my brother's love story.

None of us had known then how short-lived our trio would be.

Eventually, we got to a short video I'd filmed of Charlie and Zeke. We couldn't hear their voices, but my breath caught as we watched them move across the screen. They were roughhousing in a swimming pool. Zeke lifted Charlie in the air and tossed him to the side. My brother went under with a huge splash, and Zeke grinned proudly at me. Seconds later, he disappeared under the water because Charlie had yanked his legs out from under him. They came back up with a spray of water, both of them laughing hysterically. Zeke reached out and cupped Charlie's cheek affectionately. Charlie turned and kissed Zeke's palm. That's when the video stopped.

Ambrose let out a shuddery breath beside me. I turned my head to look at him as he cleared his throat.

"Thank you," he rasped. "If you—my parents would really love to see those, if you'd be willing to show them."

"That's up to Charlie," I replied. "But I'm sure he'd be glad to. I have more, you know. That wasn't the last one."

"I think, uh, maybe later."

"Okay," I whispered, hitting the power button. I set the camera next to me on the bed.

The room was silent for a long time. Eventually, Ambrose's hand found mine in the dark. When he threaded his fingers through mine, it didn't even occur to me to pull away.

"I'm glad he had that," he said softly. "Fuck, I'm really glad he had that."

Eventually, his breathing grew slow and steady as he fell asleep, but I was wide awake for a long time. I'd been very aware from the beginning how the loss of Zeke had affected Charlie, and even though I couldn't understand it fully, I'd tried my best to be sensitive to the fact that his life had been devastated.

But it was almost embarrassing to admit, even silently to myself, that I hadn't really considered how Zeke's death had affected his brothers. The same brothers who'd put their asses on the line to search for and protect a man they'd never met just because their brother had loved him. I'd been suspicious and catty and sarcastic, and they must've hated me.

Maybe not Ambrose. I was Ambrose's winning lottery ticket. But the other brothers, Danny and that asshole, Chance. They'd probably wanted to throttle me. They'd still been dealing with the loss of their baby brother when they'd decided to search for us, somehow found us when we were deliberately playing needle-in-a-haystack, and I'd refused to tell them where Charlie was and then tried to escape by climbing out a bathroom window.

I winced.

"Sleep, baby," Ambrose ordered, rolling to his side. His arm wrapped around my middle, and his breath feathered across my neck. "Whatever you're thinking about can wait until morning."

I bristled at the order, but closed my eyes anyway. He was right. I could continue berating myself for being a colossal pain in the ass once the sun was up.

CHAPTER 4
AMBROSE

"I'm fucking exhausted, Lucy," Charlie snapped from the back seat.

"You're not exhausted. You need to sit up and open your eyes and eat something. You've slept all day. You're *depressed*."

"So what if I am?" Charlie exploded, rising from the seat. "You have no idea what this is like. *None*. Leave me the fuck alone."

"Sorry, can't," Lucy shot back. She was twisted in the seat, glaring at her brother. "Since, you know, *I love you*."

When I glanced in the rearview mirror, Charlie was staring at his sister, expressionless.

"You think you're the only one who lost Zeke?" Lucy continued.

I reached out to put my hand on her leg in warning.

"I lost him too. Ambrose is his *brother*. Look at us, we're awake. We're talking. We're paying attention to our surroundings."

"It's not the same, baby," I told her quietly as Charlie continued to stare at her silently. "Not nearly the same."

"I'm not saying it's the same," she snapped. "And what's with *baby*? We're not at that point. You can call me Lucy."

"I'm not the one you're mad at," I reminded her.

"Well, I am *now*, since you're so interested in adding your opinion."

I opened my mouth and closed it again as she twisted back around and crossed her arms over her chest. I wanted to tell her that there was no way to fully describe the loss of a mate. It went so far beyond normal grief. There wasn't even a word for it. I'd heard it referred to as soul crushing in the most literal terms. It was why, in Vampire culture, suicide after the loss of a mate was commonplace and even widely accepted.

Her brother was immortal and alone. No matter how much she loved him, he was *alone*. Neither of us could comprehend the weight of that truth. Only Charlie could.

So, if he preferred to sleep twenty hours a day, who were we to judge?

"At least eat something," Lucy ordered. "You're skin and bones."

The car was quiet as we drove toward the setting sun, but Charlie didn't lie back down. He sat there silently until we found a drive-thru for dinner, didn't bother to give his order because Lucy already knew what it was, and ate his food without a word. I wasn't sure about Lucy, but I would've preferred him asleep. The grief that filled the car when he was awake was damn near stifling.

Gone was the man who'd smiled and laughed as I told him stories the night before, and in his place was a shell of a human. If I'd stopped the car and let him out on the side of the road, I was pretty sure he would've just laid down beside it and never gotten up again.

I didn't know how to help him. I didn't think I could

help him. If Lucy hadn't been there, pushing her way into his consciousness and making him see her and hear her, I didn't think we would've ever found him at all. He would've already been lost to us, along with Zeke.

Hours later, long after the sun had set, we finally stopped at a hotel right off the freeway. I wasn't sure how we'd made it so far without any issues, but it was beginning to make me twitchy. We still had two days on the road before we made it home, but the closer we got, the more careful I became. The group that had killed Zeke and was probably searching for Charlie at that moment would've been fucking ecstatic to know that they'd get two mates for the price of one.

I was just thankful that the heat seemed to be staying at a manageable level as long as Lucy and I were touching. At any moment, that could change, and then my attention would be split much worse than it already was, and we'd be fucked. I needed to stay focused for just a couple more days.

"I'm getting my own room," Charlie announced as we got out of the car.

"Oh, that's real nice," Lucy replied, throwing her arms up.

"Share with your *mate*," he snapped.

"It's not like I chose this," she sputtered, her eyes wide with hurt.

Charlie sighed tiredly. "I didn't say you chose it, Luce. Just share with Ambrose, all right?"

He led the way into the office. Lucy fell in beside me, practically vibrating with suppressed emotion. It had been a tough day for her, and I wasn't sure why. She'd been off since she woke up that morning. More quiet than usual. Thoughtful. She'd also been more demanding of

Charlie, and I wasn't sure why. It was almost as if she was embarrassed by how he was behaving.

When we got to our rooms, Charlie closed himself inside his without a word, and Lucy was near tears.

"What's going on?" I asked as I locked us in for the night.

"He's—" Her mouth snapped shut, and she shook her head angrily.

"He's in pain," I finished for her.

"That doesn't mean he gets to treat other people like shit," she blurted, throwing up her hands. "That doesn't mean he gets to treat me like shit or *you* like shit. Charlie doesn't *do* that."

"He hasn't treated me like shit," I argued carefully.

"You followed us to Europe," she spit out. "You found us, and you're driving us across the country because I refused to tell you where Charlie is, and your brothers had to fly home without you...and he's so ungrateful. He doesn't even care."

"I don't want him to be grateful."

"Well, he should be anyway." Her voice rose. "You lost Zeke too! Charlie doesn't get to act like—"

"Let me stop you right there," I interrupted carefully. "I don't know what's going on in your head, but I don't expect Charlie to do anything or act any certain way."

She just stared at me.

"Did you know that it's legal for Vampires to end their own lives?" I asked, moving toward her slowly. "Not only legal—accepted. There's no shame in it."

"That's fucked up."

"No, it's not. It's compassion." Cupping her face in my hands, I leaned forward so all she saw was me. "Because the grief of losing a mate is so all-encompassing that it

69

would be tortuous to force an immortal to live forever without them."

Tears welled up in her eyes and dripped unhindered down her cheeks.

"He can't *kill* himself," she whimpered, her chest heaving.

"I don't think he will," I assured her. Charlie may be lost in a sea of grief, but I had no doubt that Lucy was his tether to the world. He'd never leave her on purpose, no matter how much pain he was in. "But I do think that you should allow Charlie to live his life however he needs to in order to survive. If that means he sleeps most of the day, then so be it."

"I don't understand it," she rasped, shaking her head a little. "I just...I know that he loved Zeke, but—"

"You will," I promised her, wiping her tears away with my thumbs. "At some point in the future, you'll look at your brother and be amazed that he woke up at all, because just the thought of losing your mate will be that horrific."

"Losing you," she clarified dryly. She sniffled.

"Losing me," I agreed.

"You're pretty and all," she replied. "But I doubt it."

It may have been the most serious conversation we'd ever had, and none of it was funny, but I couldn't help the chuckle that fell from my mouth. "We'll see."

"I'm not going to lie," she said, her eyes crinkling a little at the corners. "I could go for a good kiss, though. With tongue. It's been a shit day and—"

I didn't even let her finish the sentence. I'd been dying to get my mouth on her, I didn't even care where, and I'd never in a million years deny her a kiss. The moment our mouths met, a surge of fire ran from the base of my spine, over my shoulders, and down my arms, and for the first time, it didn't hurt.

Lucy's arms wrapped around my neck as our tongues tangled, and my chest burned as I pulled her close. Gods, she was *everything*. I'd never wanted anything as much as I wanted her. Visions of her naked on the bed, her brunette waves just barely covering her nipples and her legs spread wide in welcome made my hands shake as I slid them down to grip her ass.

Fuck.

She tore her mouth from mine and took a step back as she dropped her arms.

"Okay, so you can kiss," she gasped. "I'll give you that."

"Where are you going?" I asked, following her.

"First, a shower." She held up one hand, ticking things off on her fingers. "Then to check on Charlie. Then bed."

I nodded. I was afraid that if I opened my mouth, I'd beg her to kiss me again. As she moved around the room, I walked carefully over to the side of the bed and took a seat.

I'd been in control my entire life. When you grew up as the oldest brother of five, you learned how to lead from an early age. I was in charge. I made most of the decisions. I kept the rest of them from getting into too much trouble or into situations where they could be hurt.

Of course, as we'd become adults, things had shifted. We'd stopped spending every second of the day together and started our own lives. My little brothers had started making their own decisions and stopped looking to me for advice. But still, that part of my personality had lingered.

Who would've guessed that a woman would be my downfall. I wasn't in charge of this situation. I had no control. Lucy held all the cards. She already knew that I was all in.

Flexing my hands, I stared at them as she carried her bag into the bathroom and shut the door behind her.

After two days in the car with Lucy and Charlie, it was easy to see that while she may have been younger, she'd also had the same role in their family. If I hadn't known better, I would've guessed that Charlie was the youngest and Lucy was the oldest. She spoke for both of them, made decisions unilaterally, and Charlie didn't seem to mind it in the slightest. It didn't seem like it was a new thing, either. Their roles hadn't reversed when Charlie lost Zeke. They'd always been that way.

Lucy was protective and opinionated and stubborn and tightly wound.

I was fucking dying for the day when she'd give up that control to me.

Rising from the bed, I walked over to the window and pulled the curtains aside just far enough that I could scan the parking lot. No new cars had pulled in since we'd arrived. How had we made it so far without being followed? Had they decided that our family wasn't worth going after? It would make sense. They'd already failed to kidnap Beau and Reese, losing four of their soldiers in the process.

Letting the curtain fall back into place, I stretched my arms above my head. I needed to stay focused. Lucy and I had nothing but time ahead of us. Once we were back on my family's property, we could spend time figuring each other out. Hopefully, naked.

Looking around the room, I spied a phone on the table. I needed to get in touch with my brothers soon. It didn't feel right being completely cut off from them, and they were probably climbing the walls waiting for me to make contact. I would've been if the roles were reversed. Losing Zeke had been a wake-up call for all of us.

We'd gotten complacent and assumed that all of us would inevitably be okay because we always had been. There had been no way to see it coming, and the blow had been so much worse because of it.

"All done," Lucy announced as she came out of the bathroom, running her fingers through her damp hair. Reaching up, she combed out the fringe across her forehead and shook her head a little to settle it into place.

"Feel better?" I asked, my voice raspy as I glanced down her body. The night before, she'd slept in her clothes, and I hadn't had to contend with the skimpy tank top and shorts that she wore as pajamas. My mouth was fucking watering at the sight of her peaked nipples.

"It's amazing what a cold shower can do," she said wryly. "You should try it."

"Funny." I rose to my feet.

Every molecule of my body was attuned to her. I wouldn't have been able to look away if I tried. The heat burned beneath my skin.

"I need to check on Charlie," she said breathily as I moved toward her.

"All right," I agreed. As I reached her, I lifted my hand and ran one finger gently across her nipple.

"Holy shit," she hissed, catching my hand as I dropped it. "Do it again."

I smiled.

That's when the door to our room swung open, and Charlie hurried into the room.

"Someone's at my door," he breathed, his eyes wide and frightened. "Two men. Not the manager."

"Stay here," I ordered, striding toward the door that

connected our rooms. When I got to his room, I paused next to the door.

It would've been easier to hear the two men if Charlie and Lucy hadn't been whispering to each other, but after a few moments, I'd heard enough of the men's conversation.

They'd been told to go in quietly, so they'd been hoping that Charlie would just open the door. While I stood there listening to the idiots, they decided to wait him out. They figured he'd have to leave the room at some point, and they'd take him then. No need for a fuss. He'd probably come quietly.

I waited for another minute after they'd walked away from the door before I headed back into the other room. Charlie and Lucy stood side by side just outside the bathroom door.

"Get dressed, baby," I ordered quietly, nodding to her bag.

"Who are those guys?" Lucy asked as she kneeled down to pull her clothes out.

"Not friends," I replied simply. "Charlie, go get your bag."

"They won't try to get in?"

"No."

"You're sure?"

"You think I'd send you back if I thought they would?"

He nodded and hurried away.

"The bogeymen found us, didn't they?" Lucy asked as she tugged a T-shirt over her pajama top.

"Looks like it."

"Fuck."

"They're idiots."

"That doesn't make me feel any better," she snapped as she shoved her sleep shorts down her hips. They fell to her ankles, and I nearly cursed at the sight of the tiny pair of panties that barely covered anything.

"You know I need to fucking focus, right?" I asked as she twisted and bent to grab a pair of jeans.

Her ass was bare. Fucking hell.

"Oh, please," she said, stepping into her jeans. "People wear these on public beaches."

"Someday," I said, turning to make my way over to the phone. "I'm going to pay you back for this."

"Oh, I'm scared." She shivered dramatically as she buttoned her jeans. "Are you going to strip while I'm trying to do my taxes?"

"No, I'm going to spank your ass."

Lucy's mouth dropped open in surprise.

"Don't worry," I said as I turned back toward the phone. "You'll like it."

Beau answered immediately. "Where are you?"

"I'm good," I said sarcastically as Charlie carried his bag into the room. "And you?"

Beau laughed.

"We're in Montana."

"You're making good time."

"Time's up," I replied flatly.

"Shit."

"How soon can you get here?"

"Couple of hours," Beau said. I could hear him moving through the house as his breathing changed.

"That'll work."

"Can you meet us at the closest airport?"

I looked over at Charlie and Lucy, who were watching me intently, both of them pale.

"No."

"Got it. We'll come to you. How many?"

"Two that I know of."

"So...double that."

"At least. I heard them talking about waiting Charlie out so they could keep things quiet, so I don't think they'll try to make entry. With luck, we'll have until morning."

"When have you had any luck?" he asked dryly. "Are you armed?"

Striding over to the backpack I'd carried all over Europe and back, I stuffed my hand inside and pulled out my always reliable Glock 19.

"One full magazine."

"Fuck."

"Probably all I'd need."

Beau chuckled, then quieted when I described exactly where the motel was and which room we were in. I fucking hated sitting on my ass and waiting for them to come bail me out, but I wasn't stupid enough to try to get Lucy and Charlie out on my own. It wasn't worth the risk. I just hoped that whoever was with those idiots at the door didn't convince them to come for Charlie while he was sleeping.

"Sit tight. We'll be in the air in half an hour, tops," Beau said quietly.

"Will do."

I hung up the phone and turned to face the siblings.

"I know how to shoot," Lucy announced bravely, straightening her shoulders. "I dated a cop for like ten minutes."

"Good to know," I replied, glancing at Charlie.

"Don't dismiss me."

I looked back to find her glaring at me. "I'm not."

"Yes, you are."

"I'm glad to know that you can handle a weapon." Even if I had my doubts. "But we have exactly one pistol, and it's mine."

"Oh," Lucy replied, her shoulders slumping. "Right."

"We just need to be patient, baby," I said calmly. "Cavalry is on its way."

"They just want me," Charlie said quietly. "I could just—"

"Don't finish that sentence," I ordered as Lucy's expression fell. "My brothers will be here in a few hours to fly us home. Just have to sit tight."

Time passed so fucking slow. I'd been in tight spots plenty of times before—I'd been leading a unit for Vampire Command for nearly a hundred years—but this time was different. I wasn't surrounded by trained members of my unit or even my brothers. I was holed up with the woman I'd die happily to protect and the man who'd given my brother a reason to live before he'd been killed. The stakes were infinitely higher, and we were fucking blind inside that room.

I paced back and forth, trying not to stare at my watch.

Charlie and Lucy sat on the floor near the bathroom. There were two beds and a nightstand between them and the door, and it still didn't feel like enough. I closed and locked the door between Charlie's room and ours as an extra barrier, but it would only take seconds for them to realize where he was if they made entry and didn't find him inside.

None of us slept.

Lucy used the bathroom three times, mumbling that she was a *nervous pee-er*. If the situation hadn't been so stressful, I would've laughed. Both she and Charlie had put their shoes back on and held their bags at their sides in case we needed to move quickly.

Charlie had run his hands through his hair so many times that it stood straight up like he'd been electrocuted, but he was fully present. For the time being, he'd checked back in. I knew it was because Lucy was in danger, not because he was worried for himself, but I didn't care about the reason. It was a lot easier to keep someone safe when they were actively trying to help.

Around five o'clock that morning, something shifted outside.

"Stay low," I ordered, meeting Lucy's gaze.

She and Charlie huddled together, their knees pulled to their chests.

The sound of carefully placed footsteps sounded along the sidewalk outside our room. There were four pairs. No voices.

Standing in the center of the room, where I could see both points of entry, I checked the magazine in my Glock one last time and then slowly and quietly pulled back the slide.

Lucy let out a shuddery breath behind me.

"Ulf," a familiar voice called. "My mate will castrate you if you shoot."

Relief made my head feel light as I strode toward the exit door.

"It's all right," I said, looking over my shoulder at Lucy.

Her eyes were wide and dark with fear, but we didn't have time for me to reassure her.

I'd barely gotten the door open before the cavalry pushed their way inside.

CHAPTER 5
LUCY

Charlie stood and tugged me up with him as four Vampires crowded into the room. I recognized three of them, but I knew instantly who the fourth was. Zeke's family had arrived.

"I thought you said a couple of hours," Ambrose said as the door closed.

"No fucking airport," Danny replied, barely glancing at us. "Didn't feel like putting it down on the highway."

"Is that where you come in?" Ambrose asked in amusement, looking at the Vampire I hadn't seen in months.

His curly hair had been pulled back in tight braids, and the casual shorts and T-shirts he'd worn in Europe had been replaced with some kind of tactical vest and boots, but I would've known him anywhere.

"Matthias," Charlie said, his voice barely a whisper.

Matthias's head snapped to the side. His eyes were sympathetic as he looked my brother over. "Charlie," he greeted quietly.

"We landed at the property," Chance informed

Ambrose. "Took the helicopter from there. You ready to move?"

"Situation outside?"

"Found five. Assuming they work in twos, there's someone still out there. Nothing we can't handle if the need arises."

"Let's do it."

"Josiah is keeping an eye," Danny said as Ambrose walked my way. "It's going to be a tight fit."

"We'll make it work," Ambrose said over his shoulder as he reached me. He turned back and cupped my cheek in his hand. "Just do whatever we tell you," he said softly. "We'll be out of here soon."

"Okay." I swallowed hard. Sneaking around had been scary, but we'd never actually known for sure if someone was searching for us. We'd just followed Zeke's directions. It was an entirely new experience to know the wolves were at the door. "Give me a gun."

"You won't need it," Ambrose replied.

"You don't know that."

"You think any of us would ever let something happen to you?"

I looked around the room. "Evidence says no," I replied. "But give me one anyway."

Ambrose stared into my eyes for a long moment, then turned. "Who has a pistol for Lucy?"

Chance scoffed, but the brother I hadn't met yet walked toward us and pulled a pistol out of a holster on his thigh. It looked like Ambrose's.

"You know how to use it?"

I wrapped my hand around the grip and the weight of it instantly felt familiar.

"Yes," I replied as muscle memory kicked in, and I checked the magazine. "Thank you."

"Don't shoot me in the ass," the new brother replied.

"Let's move," Chance ordered.

Pulling the strap of my bag over my head and across my chest, I handed Charlie my bat, just in case, and followed the others toward the door. My brother crowded me, not letting me move more than a foot away from him.

I took a deep breath as Danny threw open the door and stepped outside.

"Sorry, Lucy," Matthias said quietly as he wrapped his hand around my arm.

I opened my mouth to ask why the hell he was apologizing as worry filled my chest, but suddenly we were moving. The sun was rising, making the wet pavement practically glow outside, and I squinted as it burned my eyes. My hand grew sweaty around the pistol as I kept my eyes on Ambrose's backpack ahead of me.

The Vampires moved like a well-oiled machine while Charlie and I lurched along, trying to match their pace.

We'd gotten about ten yards from the hotel doorway and were turning a corner when I realized why Matthias had apologized.

Fire engulfed my arm.

Every single point where his fingers touched felt like it was being burned with acid. The breath in my chest felt stuck there as I tried to yank it out of his hold, but his hand was like a vise. Black spots dotted my vision as I stumbled.

"Keep going," he ordered calmly, his head swiveling from side to side. "Try to ignore it."

My mouth filled with saliva, and I fought the urge to vomit as the pain just went on and on. It was probably a good thing that I couldn't seem to catch my breath, because if I had, I would've been screaming. Only Charlie's presence beside me and the knowledge that these

Vampires were trying to protect us kept me from fighting Matthias off.

It only took a few minutes, but it felt like hours later when we heard the helicopter. The blades were still spinning as we jogged toward it. Someone I didn't recognize sat in the pilot's seat, but I barely glanced at him as we bent our heads and climbed inside.

Calling it a tight fit was a joke. Chance got in the front seat while the rest of us piled in the back like clowns in a car.

I let out a whimper as Matthias shoved me into a seat and finally let go of my arm.

Charlie sat on one side of me, and Ambrose on the other, but I barely noticed them as I cradled my arm against my chest.

Someone carefully pulled the pistol out of my other hand.

Then we were lifting into the air. Charlie cursed next to me.

I couldn't even look at him as I curled over my arm. The pain was gone, but the memory of it wasn't.

"Shh," Ambrose soothed into my ear, wrapping his arms around me. He pulled me tightly against his chest, tucking my face in the crook of his neck. "You're okay, Lucy."

I shuddered and pressed closer. Yes. That was what I needed. My hands fumbled with the hem of his shirt until I could slide them under it. The skin against my palms was smooth and warm as I breathed him in.

Shit.

Shit. Shit. Shit.

The helicopter was loud as hell, and there wasn't any conversation as we flew, but at some point, Ambrose set a pair of headphone-things on my head that at least blocked out the noise of the wind and engine. My stomach lurched over and over again, and I could feel Charlie shifting uncomfortably beside me, but I didn't have it in me to check on him. Ambrose's chest felt safe, and I wasn't ready to let go of him yet.

The moment we touched down and someone opened the door, my brother lurched outside, fell to his knees, and puked in the grass.

"Charlie," Matthias called in amusement. "Bad form."

"That was awful," my brother replied, breathing heavily as he wiped his mouth with the back of his wrist.

I looked around as Ambrose helped me step down. We were next to some kind of landing strip. There was a plane parked at one end of it, opposite where they'd parked the helicopter, and across from us was a huge building with another plane parked inside it. Those were the only things visible. We were surrounded by trees as far as you could see.

"Where are we?" I asked as I reached for my brother and pulled him to his feet.

"My family's property," Matthias replied, walking toward us.

I stumbled backward until my back hit Ambrose's chest. His arm came around me instantly, which made me feel a little better, but Matthias was still too close for comfort, even a few feet away.

"I'm sorry," he said with a wince. "It had to be done."

"What the fuck did you do?" I asked, reaching up to grip Ambrose's forearm. He didn't seem like he was going anywhere, but I needed to be sure.

"No one knows you're my mate," Ambrose said, kissing my temple. "And we needed to keep it that way."

"You're not making any sense," I replied, watching Matthias carefully. His hands looked perfectly normal. He wasn't wearing gloves or anything. How the hell had he burned my arm? Was it a Vampire thing?

"It's painful," Charlie said to me quietly. He paused to spit in the grass. "The touch of anyone that isn't your mate is painful."

I stared at him in shock. What the hell was he talking about? If that was true...how many times had I hugged my brother? Held his hand? Ran my fingers through his hair until he fell asleep? How many times had I shoved him or elbowed him or pinched him good-naturedly?

"No, not you," Charlie said quickly. "No. *You* don't hurt me."

"He's your brother, baby," Ambrose said, tightening his arm. "It doesn't work that way."

"My mate says women are fine too," Matthias said sympathetically. "And it fades a bit over time. It's not ever comfortable, but it's never as bad as in the beginning."

I stared at him in disbelief.

I couldn't touch any men who weren't related to me? What the fuck was *that*?

"It could be worse," the new brother said as he strode toward us. "For most mates, I think it's just sustained contact, but Reese can't even brush against someone. She doesn't even shake hands anymore." He stopped a few feet from us. "Hey, I'm Beau."

He smiled gently at my brother, searching his face.

"Beau," Charlie greeted with a nod.

"Chance and Danny," Ambrose said as the other Vampires came around the helicopter. "And Josiah."

We congregated at the end of the landing strip. No one got too close, and I felt a little like an animal at the zoo as they looked us over. I wondered if Charlie felt the same.

"The Boucher brothers," Charlie said softly, a little smile playing on his lips.

"It's good to finally meet you, Charles," Danny said with a grin. It didn't meet his eyes.

"You too," Charlie replied.

"First time on a helicopter?" Chance asked with a chuckle.

"How could you tell?" Charlie asked dryly.

The group laughed, and I felt a little of the tension in my shoulders disappear.

I wanted them to like him, I realized. I didn't really care how they felt about me, but I really needed them to like my kindhearted brother. Zeke wasn't there to make sure that his family treated my brother well. He wasn't there to tell them all about my brother's best attributes or show them how much he loved Charlie.

It was all wrong.

I leaned back against Ambrose. I wasn't sure when he had become my comfort, but I was too overwhelmed to question it.

The Vampires stood around for a few more minutes talking to Charlie and each other, but I wasn't really paying attention to what they were saying. I was too focused on their expressions and body language. Relief filled me when I determined that they were welcoming him in, treating him like one of their own.

"We need to get back," Beau announced finally. "My mate is probably climbing the walls."

Ambrose let go of me to say goodbye to Matthias and Josiah. The two Vampires must've been brothers based on the resemblance. They both had the same brown skin, high cheekbones, and strong jawlines. They also carried themselves the same way. I wasn't sure how to explain it, but I wasn't sure they'd ever slouched a day in their lives. But, while I remembered Matthias's hair in a curly halo around his head, Josiah's fell straight and ended in a jagged line at his shoulders.

Charlie walked over to shake their hands and thank them too. He didn't seem to have any problem touching them, which seemed odd.

I stood alone and tried not to fidget.

It didn't matter that none of them looked at me. It didn't matter that they didn't say goodbye to me before they turned and walked toward the trees. None of it mattered. Charlie was being pulled into the fold. That was all I could've asked for.

"One last ride and then we're home," Ambrose announced as he moved toward me. His hand found mine, and he tugged me toward the plane at the other end of the landing strip.

"Who's flying the plane?" I asked as Charlie and the others followed us, their conversation too quiet for me to hear.

"Danny," Ambrose replied. "Don't worry, he flew with the Wright brothers."

"Didn't they crash?" I asked wryly.

"More than once, I think." Ambrose laughed. "But avionics have come a long way since then."

The inside of the plane was comfortable and smelled like leather, but I still hated it. I couldn't stop thinking about all the plane crashes I'd ever heard about and the fact that they usually happened in small private planes. Flying on a commercial airplane was different. I didn't actually know that pilot, and there was a sense of anonymity and false safety when I was crammed into one with a hundred other strangers.

I sat down and buckled my seat belt while Ambrose watched with a small smile.

Charlie and the others followed us in a minute later. I

looked my brother over as he sat across from me and set his bag and my baseball bat between his feet. The animation in his expression while he'd been talking to the others slipped as he met my eyes. My chest tightened.

I would've let Matthias hug me for an hour if it would've taken away that look of defeat in Charlie's eyes.

"Here, Charles," Chance said as he walked down the center aisle, tossing my brother a little paper bag. "Just in case."

"Thanks," Charlie replied sheepishly as he set the bag on his lap.

An air sickness bag.

"It's *Charlie*," I snapped at Chance. "And he doesn't get air sick unless we're in a helicopter and bouncing all over the place like a frigging ride at the county fair."

Chance raised his eyebrows in surprise.

"It's fine, Luce," Charlie said, glancing at me in embarrassment.

"We good?" Beau asked as he stepped inside the plane.

I was still glaring at Chance. He was such an asshole. I could take it, but I'd fucking end him before he treated my brother like shit.

"It was a joke." Ambrose chastised me quietly.

"Did you think it was funny?" I asked, turning to look at him as I unbuckled my seat belt.

"Good luck with that," Chance grumbled as he disappeared inside the cockpit.

"Knock it off," Charlie whispered.

I ground my teeth as I turned forward in my seat and glared at the wall of the plane.

We'd give them a couple of days, I decided. After that, if I didn't see any change in Charlie or if we just weren't feeling it, we'd leave. Zeke had procured us a couple of fake passports that we'd never had to use. I was resourceful, and Charlie wasn't exactly social anymore. We could find some small town and get lost. It wasn't as if it would last forever. The Bouchers seemed like they were on top of things. They'd stop the assholes going after Vampires and their mates, eventually.

"What's going on in there?" Ambrose asked quietly as he sat down beside me, moving my bag to the floor.

I just shook my head. I'd talk to Charlie later and see what he thought. We didn't have to stay with the Bouchers. We could change our minds at any time.

I refused to think about the mating heat and the fact that everything inside me seemed to still when Ambrose was near. Time and distance would make it fade if we decided to leave. Their brother Beau had walked away. It was possible.

Takeoff in the tiny plane was surprisingly smooth, but I re-buckled my seat belt and tightened it across my hips anyway.

"Almost home," Ambrose announced, smiling tiredly at Charlie. "You guys will be safe there. My parents' property is large and protected. No one will even get close."

"You know, no one *got close* until you showed up," I mentioned dryly. "Maybe you're the problem."

"Just because you didn't see them doesn't mean they weren't close," Ambrose replied, leaning his seat back.

"If they got the drop on Zeke, they're good at keeping a low profile," Beau added. He'd sat down across the aisle from us, his legs stretched out in front of him. "You two got lucky."

"Or maybe they weren't even looking for us," I shot back.

"Well, they weren't looking for Ambrose," Beau said flatly. "Since no one knows he has a mate."

"Maybe they've changed tactics, and they're going to follow unmated Vampires until they find their mates," I said smugly.

"For the next hundred years or more?" Beau asked with a grin. "Seems time-consuming."

I rolled my eyes.

"What's going on?" Ambrose asked me quietly as Charlie closed his eyes and leaned his head back against the seat.

"What do you mean?" I hedged.

"I mean, you'd dropped those guards for a while, and now you're acting like we're the enemy again."

"Maybe I don't like being manhandled and tortured without warning," I hissed, turning to look at him. "Maybe I'm wondering if I screwed up royally trusting any of you."

Ambrose's eyes darkened with remorse.

"Baby, as far as anyone knows, you're just Charles's sister." He reached out and wrapped his hand around my knee.

"Matthias grabbed your arm so that anyone watching would see that you're not mated," Beau added, sitting up and leaning his elbows on his knees. "On the assumption that if you were, none of us would touch you except your mate."

"Matthias is mated to someone else," Ambrose continued. "Anyone with any knowledge of us would know you're not his mate."

I stared at him while the information clicked into place.

"It had to be Matthias, didn't it?"

Ambrose nodded. "Or Beau. But Beau is better in close combat if it came to it. He needed his hands free."

"Because no one else has a mate," I said slowly.

"She's getting it," Beau joked.

"But none of you discussed it," I argued, glancing at Ambrose's brother. "You didn't plan it."

"They're over a hundred years old," Charlie said without opening his eyes. "They all know what the others are going to do before they do it."

Beau huffed. "Accurate."

"I'm sorry," Ambrose murmured in my ear. He gently kissed my temple. "I should've warned you."

"Yeah, no shit," I mumbled.

"If it's any consolation, it couldn't have been comfortable for Matthias either. No one will touch you again."

"Don't make that promise," Beau warned.

My eyes widened. There was no way he'd heard what Ambrose said.

"Our mother is going to hug you," Beau continued. "But it shouldn't bother the bond."

"How the hell—"

"Vampires have really good hearing," Ambrose explained.

"Interesting," I replied, glaring at my brother. "That's something I would've loved to know."

"I can feel you looking at me," Charlie said, his eyes still closed.

"You don't think this is something I would've liked to have known, oh, I don't know, months ago?"

How many times had I whispered to Charlie, assuming Zeke couldn't hear us?

"How good is your hearing?" I asked Ambrose.

"Very."

"Give me an example," I ground out.

"You could've whispered to Charlie in the hotel room next door, and I would've heard you from the bathroom even if both doors were closed."

Frigging hell. I couldn't even remember how many times I'd said something quietly to Charlie, assuming that Zeke couldn't hear me. I was pretty sure I'd mentioned Zeke's ass. I'd warned Charlie not to get attached so quickly. I'd bitched that he was leaving me alone again, even though we'd stopped staying in hostels, and Zeke had paid for nice hotels. I'd bitched about Zeke paying for our hotels. God, I couldn't even remember all the things I'd said. The comments I'd made, believing that they were just between my brother and me, were plentiful and colorful, to say the least.

"He didn't mind," my brother said gently. I looked up to find him watching me. "He thought you were hilarious." He swallowed hard. "He was glad that I had someone who was so protective of me. He wasn't ever offended."

Zeke must've thought I hated him. The things I'd said...well, they hadn't been very complimentary at first. Who could blame me, really? Some Vampire had walked up to us one day, and everything had suddenly changed. Charlie had jumped into that bottomless pond with both feet, but he'd always been the dreamer. I was a pragmatist. I'd seen almost every way that things could've gone wrong. We didn't *know* Zeke. He could've been an absolute creep.

Eventually, he'd worn me down. Surely, he'd known that before he left. By the time we'd parted ways, he'd known how important he'd become to our little family, right? Not just to Charlie, but to me too?

I'd never have the chance to ask him.

Pulling my bag closer, I rested my chin on it. I needed to remember that these Vampires could hear everything. No conversations were private. It put a damper on my plans to discuss with Charlie whether or not we'd bail, but that was a worry for a different moment.

Less than two hours after we'd taken off, Chance spoke over the speaker, telling us that we were getting ready to land. Looking out the window, I couldn't see anything but trees and a small river. There were no signs of civilization beyond a couple of empty two-lane roads.

"How long until we get to your parents' house?" I asked Ambrose as we dropped closer and closer to the trees.

Barf. I looked away from the windows.

"What do you mean?" he asked as Charlie sat up in his seat. "We're landing on the property."

"It's a five-minute walk to the house," Beau explained.

The plane wobbled a little, and Charlie turned green.

"Don't you dare," I whispered to him.

He nodded, the air sickness bag clutched in his fist.

Then we landed with a small bounce, and I was thrown back against the seat as Danny hit the brakes.

"The seat belt was a good idea," I said under my breath as we finally came to a stop.

Ambrose chuckled beside me.

The next few minutes were a little chaotic as Chance and Ambrose opened the door at the end of the plane. Beau was out the door and gone before Danny had even come out of the cockpit. Chance disappeared behind him.

Then Ambrose was reaching for my hand and leading me out into the damp air. It was strangely quiet as we made our way down the stairs. I was used to hearing traffic and noise in the distance. We were in the middle of nowhere, and everything was green. The trees, the grass, the ferns and bushes, *everything*. It felt like the edge of the world. No wonder Zeke and his brothers were so sure that we'd be safe here. I wasn't even sure how anyone would be able to find the place if they didn't know exactly where they were going.

"It smells exactly how Zeke described it," Charlie said to me as Ambrose led us to a path through the trees.

"Like wet trees?" Ambrose asked, shooting him a smile. "Yeah."

"Jesus," I mumbled, looking up through the branches. The trees were so tall that you couldn't even see the tops of them. They must've been hundreds of years old.

"You should've seen it when we first got here," Ambrose said as we walked along the pine needle-covered path. "It was the wildest place I'd ever seen. It took days to reach the closest neighbor."

"Yeah, yeah," I said, glancing at Charlie. His shoulders were so tense, they were up by his ears. "You're old. We get it."

"Each of us has our own little apartment in the house," Ambrose explained, ignoring me. "You can stay in Zeke's, Charlie."

Charlie nodded.

The house came into view, and my mouth dropped open. It was *massive*. Larger than the apartment complex Charlie and I had grown up in. It was a frigging mansion. I'd known the Bouchers were rich—they had their own *plane*—but for some reason I hadn't anticipated the sheer size of it.

"Here we go," I said as we reached the driveway. The gravel crunched under our feet as I let go of Ambrose and moved closer to my brother. His hand found mine when we reached the front porch steps. It was clammy with sweat.

I wanted to tell him that they would love him. That he was the best person I'd ever met, and if they couldn't see that, then they were swamp creatures that didn't deserve to live. I wanted to remind him that these people were Zeke's parents, and if they'd raised the Vampire he'd so quickly fallen head over heels for, they had to have some good qualities.

Remembering that everyone would hear anything I said, I just gave his hand a squeeze instead.

Ambrose led us into the house and almost directly into a large living room. It was less fancy than I'd been anticipating, but it still screamed money from the plush carpets beneath our feet to the wool throws artfully draped over the sofas. I barely paid attention to the décor, though, because standing in the room was a group of people, and I instantly knew who Zeke and Ambrose's parents were.

She was petite and blonde with wide brown eyes. Her mouth was trembling, but it was clear that she was trying to keep her shit together. She was wearing a pale pink sweater set, a long flowing skirt, and no shoes.

He was tall and dark-haired, with the same piercing blue eyes as his sons, whom I'd spent so much time with. Tattoos peeked out of his sleeves and the neck of his shirt. His hair was long and pulled back in a low knot.

A southern belle and a frigging biker. That's what they looked like.

"This is Charles and Lucille Franklin," Ambrose announced, putting his hand on the small of my back.

Charlie was shaking.

"These are my parents, Matilda and Erik Boucher. The couple by the window are Sven and Alice Christensen, basically our aunt and uncle."

"Charles," Matilda said gently, taking a few steps forward. "We're so happy to meet you."

My brother didn't say anything. When I looked at him, he seemed frozen in place.

"Charlie, actually," I said, for him. "He prefers Charlie."

Matilda's gaze met mine, and she gave a small nod of thanks. "Charlie," she said softly. "Hello."

"Zeke asked me to tell you," Charlie said, the words raspy, almost robotic. "Um..." He paused, like he was trying to remember. "I love you. I'll love you long after I'm gone." His voice broke, and he paused. "You once told me that family is worth everything. That the bonds we're born with and the ones we build are worth any sacrifice." He let out a shuddery breath. "*Every* sacrifice. Turns out you were right."

I clenched my teeth together as I watched Charlie. He clearly wasn't done, but he was struggling to finish. The room was silent around us.

"This is my mate, Charlie." His cheeks reddened. "I love him." His voice dropped to a whisper. "Take care of him for me."

I didn't realize that tears were rolling down my cheeks until Ambrose wrapped his hand around the back of my neck.

Charlie wasn't done. He sniffled and raised his chin a little. "And this is his sister, Lucy. She's a pain in the ass, but she means well. Protect her too, I guess."

I let out a bark of shocked laughter.

Charlie looked at me. "He made me memorize it," he said quietly. "Just in case."

"Sounds like Zeke," Chance said from across the room.

"Yes, it does," Zeke's dad agreed. He stepped forward and reached out to shake Charlie's hand.

"Mr. Boucher," Charlie greeted.

"Erik," the man corrected with a sad smile.

As soon as he'd let go of Charlie's hand, Erik nodded at me in greeting. "Lucy."

"Hi," I said, distracted by the way Matilda grabbed both of Charlie's hands and held them. She smiled up at him with tears in her eyes.

"We're so glad you're here," she said, giving his hands a little shake. "So glad."

"Me too," Charlie replied, his voice a little wobbly.

"Ulf," Erik said, meeting Ambrose's gaze over my shoulder.

"My mate," Ambrose said, his hand tightening on my neck.

And then suddenly, every eye in the room was on me. I wasn't especially shy or anything, but it was seriously uncomfortable being the center of attention.

This was supposed to be Charlie's moment.

"We'll see," I said, rolling my eyes.

Someone across the room choked and started coughing.

"Luce," Charlie chastised.

"What?" I glanced around the room. "I barely know the guy."

Chance started laughing. Loudly.

CHAPTER 6
AMBROSE

"Please," my mother said, lifting her hand to quiet us. "Just give me this one night. Everyone is home at the same time. Let me have one dinner where we act like a family and not an army under attack."

We'd been arguing about the next steps for the last fifteen minutes, and we hadn't gotten very far. Chance and Danny couldn't agree on a damn thing. My father wanted to go hunting. He figured if we started at the bottom, we'd eventually reach the top. He wasn't concerned with any collateral damage we could cause in the process. Beau was still holed up in his room with Reese. We hadn't seen them since we'd gotten back to the house, and I thought my mom was being naïvely optimistic if she thought they'd come down for dinner.

I was fucking distracted.

I'd walked Charlie and Lucy to Zeke's room and left them there. I'd thought that Charlie would want to explore by himself, but he hadn't said a word when Lucy walked inside with him. She'd practically closed the door in my face.

I wondered if she was growing more uncomfortable by the moment, or if it was just me who felt like I was going to come out of my skin. The heat was manageable if we were in the same room, but when she was out of eyesight, my body went into revolt. Sweat pooled at the base of my spine as I tried to pay attention to what Chance was saying.

How the hell did Vampires do this shit back when courting a human woman meant that they could only see her for an hour or two a day? The stories of the occasional Vampire kidnapping their mate didn't seem so far-fetched anymore. It seemed crazier to try to stay away.

"Well, at least we know that it's true, no matter what Lucy said," my dad said in amusement. "You still with us, Ulf?"

"What?" I asked, turning to look at him.

"Looking a little warm, son."

"Funny," I snapped, straightening.

"Honey, why don't you go find her?" my mom asked with a grimace. "If it's this bad for you, she must be miserable."

"I doubt it," I replied as the table went quiet. I knew she was there before I'd even turned around.

"Um, Ambrose?" Lucy called, her voice strained.

I was on my feet so fast that the chair behind me skidded across the floor. She looked like absolute shit. The hair around her temples was damp with sweat, and her eyes were dark with pain. The arm that Matthias had held that morning was tucked up against her chest like she was trying to protect it.

"Baby," I murmured, hurrying toward her. "Why did you wait so long?"

The second I reached her, she opened her arms and wrapped them around my neck.

Ignoring my family, I lifted her into my arms and carried her toward the stairs. Her legs tightened around my hips, and her mouth pressed against my neck as I took them two at a time. The entire back of her T-shirt was stuck to her, and she shivered as I rubbed my hand down her spine.

By the time we reached my rooms, she'd stopped shivering, but she didn't loosen her grip. I closed the door behind us and walked straight to the couch.

"This is frigging bullshit," she mumbled against my neck as she dropped her legs so I could sit. Her knees tucked in neatly on each side of me.

"You should've come down sooner."

"I wasn't this bad before," she said with a sigh. "I wanted to be with Charlie."

"It wasn't this bad because we've been together since we met," I reminded her.

She huffed in annoyance. "Well, we're together now, and it's still not going away."

I smiled, glad that she couldn't see my face. "It usually gets worse before it gets better."

"When the hell is it going to get better?"

"After we complete the bond."

"What, so we need to do some crazy Vampire ritual, and then I won't feel like I'm being boiled alive anymore?"

I couldn't hold in my laugh. "I don't think sex is considered a crazy Vampire ritual, but exchanging blood is."

Lucy shot up and glared at me. "Exchanging what?"

"It can't be that surprising."

"I mean, I know Vampires drink blood. That's the whole thing." She paused. "Wait, *you* haven't been drinking blood."

"Yes, I have. I carry it with me."

"Bull."

"Check my bag," I told her. "I've got a small cooler inside."

"When the heck did you drink it?" she asked suspiciously. "I haven't seen you."

"When you were sleeping."

"Oh." She slumped and wiped a hand across her forehead. "So...this isn't going to get better unless I let you drink my blood?"

"And you drink mine."

Her nose wrinkled. "Yeah, *that's* not happening."

"You'll like it."

Gods, she felt good on top of me. Running my hands down her sides, I curved them around the globes of her ass. Perfection.

"And what if I don't want to *complete the bond* or whatever?"

Everything inside me rebelled, and my hands tightened on her ass.

"I don't know," I gritted out. "It will get worse, I think."

"But, *no*," she said in alarm. "I thought we could walk away. Beau walked away, right?"

I wanted to be careful with her. She was my mate. The beginning of our relationship would shape the way we interacted for the rest of our lives. Beyond that, I didn't want to upset her. It was my responsibility to protect her, not just physically, but emotionally as well. It was a lesson that had been drummed into me since I was a child.

But the cavalier way she spoke about the mating bond was like someone dragging rusty knives down my chest.

"Beau practically killed himself when he walked away from his mate." I ground out, holding her in place as she started to pull away. "His mate was married and pregnant. She wasn't even aware of the mating bond because she was so in love with her human husband. Beau sacrificed *for* her. He didn't walk away, Lucy. He tore himself away, *at great cost.*"

"Oh," she breathed.

"So, yes, it is possible to deny the bond. But even if you put a world of distance between us, it would be incredibly painful for both of us." I leaned forward a little. "And I'm not sure that I could stop myself from following you. I'm not even sure that you would get very far before you turned around and came back."

The symptoms she was experiencing were a pretty good indication that she no longer had the option of walking away.

"I wouldn't turn around," she replied stubbornly.

"What was Charlie doing when you left?" I asked softly.

Lucy stiffened.

"I'm guessing you didn't want to leave him, right?" I let out a huff of exasperation. "That was the distance of half a house and about twenty minutes."

"So I'm just stuck," she said angrily.

"We're *both* stuck, baby," I replied flatly.

She shoved at my chest. "Why are you being such an asshole?"

"How am I being an asshole?" I asked, not letting go of her. She may have been pissed, but our points of contact were the only thing keeping the heat from torturing us both.

"You didn't talk to me like that before," she snapped. "You didn't look at me like that, either."

"Sorry," I grunted as she shifted on my lap.

"Oh, yeah, it sounds like it," she said derisively, crossing her arms over her chest.

"Do you have any idea what this is like for me?" I asked, reaching up to grip her chin. "Baby, I'll treat you like delicate china if that's what you need. But you're sitting on my lap, bitching about being stuck with me, and I've been waiting a hundred fucking years for this."

She licked her lips, and I nearly lost it.

"I don't like not having a choice," she said in grudging apology.

"I understand."

"It's not you, it's me," she joked.

The baseline arousal that had thrummed through my veins since the moment I met her seemed to pulse. I struggled to ignore it.

"I can wait as long as you need," I said, the words practically burning my throat. "But please stop questioning the bond. For you, it's a trap. For me, it's fucking salvation."

Lucy's gaze softened. Her arms dropped, and one of her hands reached up to trace the curve of my jaw.

"It's hard for me to wrap my head around that kind of commitment right now," she said softly. "I barely know you."

"The Gods don't make mistakes," I replied, biting her fingers when they reached my lips. "We'll wait to take permanent steps if that makes you more comfortable, but you're meant for me."

Lucy frowned.

"I was made for *you* too," I clarified. "It goes both ways."

Lucy's hips shifted forward, and I wasn't even sure if she'd realized she'd done it, but I couldn't think of anything else. I was notched between her thighs, and the heat of her was making my pulse pound in my ears.

"So what's the point of no return?" she rasped, her

eyes on my lips. She shook her head and met my eyes. "This is getting more uncomfortable."

"The exchange of blood completes the bond," I answered. "I'll take yours, and you'll take mine."

"So we both have to do it?" She shifted on my lap again and cursed. "I can't focus."

"Once I've had your blood, I won't tolerate anyone else's," I explained as I wrapped my hand gently around the base of her throat. Her pulse fluttered under my fingertips. "But the bond won't lock into place until you've had mine too."

"Where does sex come in?" she asked curiously as her hands began to roam over my shoulders and chest.

"That's when we'll exchange it."

"Really?"

"From what I understand, it's incredibly intimate."

Lucy froze. "You've never done it?"

Repulsion must've shown in my expression, because she jolted back in surprise.

"Of course not."

"Not *of course not*," she countered. "Why are you making that face?"

"We don't exchange blood with anyone but our mate."

"Since when?"

"Since always."

"That can't be true."

"Humans can donate without a Vampire biting them." I shook my head.

"But—"

"Do you take a bite out of a live cow when you're hungry?" I snapped.

"Not sure I like being compared to a cow," she shot back.

"That's not what I meant."

"That's what you said."

"I won't ever bite anyone but *you*," I stated firmly, sick of the ridiculous argument.

"Or the reincarnated me," she replied with a shrug. "Right? Isn't that how it works? After I'm dead, someone else will come back with my soul and—"

I cut off her words with my mouth. The thought of her dead made me fucking crazy. She wasn't going to die. Not ever. Horror made my movements jerky as I pulled her closer, tangling my hand in her hair.

It took long moments before I was calm enough to loosen my grip, but at that point, Lucy was as frantic as I was. Her nails dug into the back of my neck, and one of her hands had burrowed under my shirt and was splayed across my chest.

"We're playing with fire," I warned as soon as I had the ability to tear my mouth away.

"Funny," she replied as her lips ran along my jaw. "Because the fire seems to be calming."

"It's an illusion." I groaned as she pulled my earlobe between her teeth and gripped it gently.

I wanted her naked. It took every bit of willpower I had not to strip her there on the couch.

If I got her naked, it would be all over. Any discussion about waiting and any autonomy she had left would be gone. Once we took that step, our future was set in stone. I was under no illusion that I could somehow keep from biting her once I was inside her. Thousands of years of instincts ensured that I would tie her to me irrevocably.

It would happen eventually. I had no doubt. But for now, the possibility that she could leave me seemed to comfort Lucy, and I wasn't going to take that from her.

"Baby, stop," I ordered.

"I don't think I can," she said, almost apologetically. Her thighs tightened as she rolled her hips.

My mouth watered.

"You taste so good," she said, her mouth on my neck. She let out a happy sigh.

I knew exactly how she felt because I was fighting against the same thing. The urge to get closer was overwhelming.

Bracing a hand beneath me, I lifted and turned, dropping her onto the couch.

"Dammit, Ambrose," she hissed, reaching for me. "Come back."

"I'm right here," I assured her, my hands shaking as I reached for her jeans.

Lucy lifted her hips to help me tug them off. Sliding my fingers beneath the waistband of her jeans and panties, I pulled them down her thighs.

"Please," she murmured.

"We should stop," I replied, staring. How the fuck was I supposed to stop once I'd touched her? I knew I would—I wasn't an animal—but I was already dreading the inevitable pain of refusing to follow through to the end.

"Okay," she said, her voice wobbling a little as she pressed her knees together.

When I met her eyes, I knew she'd interpreted my hesitation as the exact opposite of what it was. I was trying to protect her, but all she'd understood was that I'd stripped her and then changed my mind.

"Do you understand how badly I want you?" I asked, pressing her knees apart again.

She let them fall wide, and I struggled to focus on anything else.

"You're right, it's probably not a good idea," she replied hoarsely, but she didn't make any move to sit up or hide herself. Her hands fidgeted at her sides. "It feels like a really good idea, though."

"You want me?" I asked carefully. The words weren't quite right, but she wasn't ready for those yet. I still needed the confirmation that she was mindful enough to make the decision. "Tell me what you want me to do."

"Is this a thing with you?" she asked dryly, trying to hide her embarrassment. "Need me to walk you through it?"

"Is this a thing with you?" I countered. "Too embarrassed to tell me what you need?"

Lucy's mouth snapped shut as she glared at me.

"The question isn't a hard one," I said gently.

"Touch me," she ordered.

Sitting on the edge of the couch, I pulled her leg until her heel rested on my knee, and I had the perfect view of the paradise between her thighs. Using a single finger, I gently traced over the damp skin. It was softer than silk and twice as delicate.

Lucy let out a shuddering breath and tilted her hips up.

"More?" I asked, watching as my finger began to glisten.

"More," she confirmed. "More."

Her thighs began to shake as I dipped in further, using two fingers to gather up the wetness and slide them over her. I'd never gone so slowly in my life, but I couldn't fathom rushing. I was watching my *mate*, her pussy weeping with arousal while I learned every centimeter of her. It felt like a godsdamned miracle.

"More," Lucy ordered as she used her arms to shove herself further down the couch. "Now. More, please."

Looking up, I met her bright eyes as I thrust both fingers inside her, the palm of my hand brushing against her clit with the movement. Her eyes filled with tears an instant before her back arched almost entirely off the couch, and she climaxed.

It was the most surprising and beautiful thing I'd ever seen. Before I realized what I was doing, I'd dropped from the couch and buried my face between her legs so I could drink up every bit of her orgasm. Her hands tangled in my hair and pulled tight as she moaned my name.

I couldn't get enough of her.

She came again, sobbing.

I was breathing her in, unable to force myself to move away yet, when someone knocked on the door.

Rage, unexpected and unwarranted, hit me like a battering ram as I lifted my face. Lucy had thrown her arms over her eyes and was trembling in the aftermath.

"What?" I barked, making her jump in surprise.

"Dinner," Chance called, barely opening the door.

"Another inch and you're fucking dead," I called back.

He laughed and closed it again.

"Could he hear me?" Lucy asked, her arms still over her face.

"No."

"But you said—"

"Our rooms are soundproofed."

"Weird," she grumbled.

Leaning down, I pressed my lips gently against her clit. When she let out a little mewl of welcome, I pulled away again.

"Everyone deserves privacy," I told her as I rose to my feet. "No one can hear us in here."

"The heat is a little better," she said, dropping her arms to look at me.

I let out a sigh. She still had her shirt on. I'd traced

every inch of her with my tongue, but I still hadn't seen her nipples.

"Hopefully, that'll last through dinner," I replied, helping her up. "But don't count on it."

"What do you mean?"

"You remember the first time you got to first base?" I asked, crouching to pick up her sleep shorts. I held them while she stepped into them.

"Vaguely," she replied, setting her hand on my shoulder for balance. I turned my head and kissed it.

"Do you vaguely remember itching for second base once you'd hit first?" I asked, helping with her jeans.

"Okay, so we *are* talking about sex, right?" she said as she pulled her jeans up. "Not baseball?"

"Once you'd been kissed, you wondered what that feeling would be like on the rest of your body," I said, watching as she buttoned and zipped them.

"But I already know what that tongue can do to the rest of my body," she joked.

No. No, she didn't. My hands went for her top, and if she was surprised, she didn't show it as she immediately raised her arms above her head. Beneath the shirt was the small tank top she'd worn to bed, and I yanked it down below her breasts. Her nipples were soft and rosy brown. The moment I pulled one into my mouth, it drew up tight as she gasped. I pinched the other nipple tight and rolled it until it hardened beneath my fingertips.

By the time I remembered that my family was waiting for us downstairs and pulled away from her, Lucy's nipples were bright red and wet from my mouth.

"Dinner," I croaked as I gently pulled her tank top back into place.

Lucy hissed as the fabric brushed against her.

"I'm not hungry."

I laughed at the pout on her face. "Neither am I," I told her while she pulled her T-shirt back on. "But if we don't go down there, they'll know exactly why we didn't."

"Maybe we're talking," she countered. "Getting to know each other."

"Sure," I said easily. "But do you want Charlie to do the first family dinner by himself?"

"Shit, *Charlie*," she hissed, her eyes widening. She raced for the door.

Following her into the hallway and down the stairs, I watched as she straightened her clothes and hair, reaching up to fluff the fringe on her forehead and weave her hair into a loose braid. The relief she felt from the heat was temporary, and I had a sinking feeling that we wouldn't even make it through dinner before she was miserable again and eye fucking me at the table.

Physical contact and intimacy treated the symptoms of the heat, but they weren't a cure. Neither of us would get a reprieve until we'd cemented the bond, and even then, it took weeks or even months before we'd be able to separate for any length of time.

By the time we reached the dining room, everyone was already seated at the table, even Beau and Reese. Charlie must've showered. His hair was combed neatly, and his face shaved for the first time since I'd met him.

"Look at you," Lucy said when she reached him, leaning down to kiss the top of his head. "You smell—" The words seemed like they got caught in her throat. She straightened. "Good," she choked out.

"This is my sister, Lucy," Charlie told Reese. "Lucy, this is Beau's mate, Reese."

"Hello," Lucy replied, sitting in the chair I'd pulled out for her. She glanced over her shoulder and smiled at me in thanks.

"Nice to meet you," Reese said kindly. "Charlie was just telling me about your trip. I've always wanted to go to Europe. That must've been so exciting."

"It was epic," Lucy agreed as I sat down beside her. "Until this one went and found himself a mate. Things got a little boring after that."

Charlie let out an offended huff while Reese laughed.

"I can imagine," Reese said, still grinning. "Lots of time stuck at the hotel, am I right?"

"Bingo," Lucy said. She elbowed her brother.

"Don't pretend you were languishing at the hotel," Charlie replied, elbowing her back. "You did plenty of exploring on your own."

"He's right," Lucy agreed with a shrug.

I looked diagonally across the table and found Chance smirking at me. He wiggled his eyebrows. I glared back. I knew exactly what he was thinking, and I'd fucking kill him if he said any stupid shit. Lucy was having a hard enough time dealing with the mating bond. She didn't need him hassling us about it.

"This is wonderful," my mom breathed, standing at the end of the table. "This is just—"

"It is." My dad nodded and squeezed my mom's hip. "Sit, love."

"Your family really goes all out," Lucy said to me, looking at the large array of food and dinnerware that my mom had arranged across the tablecloth. "Is this normal, or..."

"Mattie wanted to make it special," my dad explained. "Since everyone is home."

Lucy jolted, and her head snapped up to look at him.

"They hear *everything*," Reese explained, widening her eyes comically at my mate.

"Right," Lucy replied. "I knew that."

"You'll get used to it," Reese said as Beau laughed. She scowled at him. "What? I'm getting better."

"Sure you are," he conceded unconvincingly.

"Their rooms are safe," Reese told Lucy conspiratorially. "Just FYI."

"Good to know," Lucy replied. She turned to Charles and smiled at him.

"Charles was telling us that you two grew up in the same apartment building your whole lives," Danny said, changing the subject. "That must've been nice. We moved all over hell and back."

"To be fair, you've lived a lot longer than us," Lucy replied as my mom waved at the table, gesturing for all of us to start serving ourselves. "But yeah, same place."

"I mentioned the courtyard," Charlie told his sister, his mouth twitching.

"That frigging courtyard," Lucy grumbled. "Swear to god, it stunk so bad in the summer it felt like it clung to you after you'd gone back inside."

"Like what?" Reese asked.

"Poop," Charlie and Lucy answered together. They both laughed.

"I don't know what it was." Lucy shrugged. "But you never got used to it."

"Our parents were terrified we'd be hit by a car if we played out by the street," Charlie explained.

"So if we wanted to go outside, it had to be the courtyard," Lucy finished. "I swear, one summer I think the scent burned off all my nose hair."

"Why didn't anyone talk to the landlord?" my dad asked curiously.

"Oh, we did," Lucy said, shooting me a smile when I set a roll on her plate. "They weren't exactly slumlords—"

"They weren't much better," Charlie continued. "It

took forever for them to fix anything. One time our kitchen sink got backed up, and we had to wash the dishes in the bathtub for a month."

"Was it at least rent-controlled?" Danny asked.

"Nope." Lucy shook her head. "But it wasn't a bad place to live, all things considered."

"The tenants were mostly older people," Charlie explained. "We were the only kids there for most of our childhood."

"Olly olly oxen free," Lucy whispered to her brother with a small smile.

Charlie smiled back at her and then glanced around the table. "School wasn't easy for me," he said softly, pressing his lips into a flat line. "Our building was a safe zone."

"Children can be assholes," Lucy announced. She reached for some pasta salad. "Unfortunately for them, I was the supreme asshole when provoked."

My father chuckled.

"She was in more fistfights than anyone else in our elementary school," Charlie said proudly, glancing at his sister. "Picture a little girl in purple overalls—"

"I loved those overalls," Lucy said quietly as she picked up her fork.

"Pigtails with little bows in her hair. Missing front teeth. Absolutely waling on a boy twice her size."

"I'm guessing you're talking about Kirk Shelten," Lucy said, lifting her chin. "That little creep deserved it."

"Is that what his name was?" Charlie joked. "I can't keep them all straight."

"If they didn't want to get humiliated by a little girl, they should've behaved better," Lucy replied simply.

"And then, when the fights started getting a little

more evenly matched, she started training," Charlie told us.

"In what?" Chance asked curiously.

"A little of this and a little of that," Lucy replied vaguely.

"Mr. Wallis was a boxer, right?" Charlie asked her.

"Yeah. Welterweight."

"What about, um...what was his name? Howard? No, Howser?"

"Muay Thai," Lucy replied quietly as she dug into her food.

"Lucy can throw down," Reese said appreciatively.

"Not really." Lucy wrinkled her nose.

"She's underplaying it," Charlie argued.

"How did your parents feel about all these fights?" my mom asked.

Lucy shrugged. "Ambivalent unless they had to take off work to go into the school."

"It usually happened after school," Charlie said, his mood dimming. "But things settled down around ninth grade."

"You were in tenth grade," Lucy corrected. "I was in ninth."

"Right."

"Did you ever train with those guys, Charlie?" Danny asked curiously.

"I tried," he said with a smile that didn't reach his eyes. "I wasn't ever very good."

"Your reflexes got much better, though," Lucy added loyally. "You were always a lover. I was the fighter."

The conversation moved on to other things, but I couldn't stop thinking about Lucy's last comment. Charlie was the lover, and she was the fighter. Why was that? Yes, Charlie was on the smaller side, but that didn't mean anything. I'd known plenty of scrappy men and Vampires who were slight in stature. I understood the disinclination for fighting. Lots of people preferred to avoid confrontation, but defending yourself was different.

Lucy's hand found my thigh about twenty minutes into dinner. Wine was flowing and stories were being tossed around, the latest about when Zeke was ten years old and decided that he was going to run away, but I was having a hard time following the conversation.

It was impossible to ignore the heat licking up my torso.

Lucy's hand tightened on my thigh beneath the table as she let out a strained laugh at whatever my dad had said. Her fingers dug in.

"Where did he think he was going to go?"

"A ranch," Chance and Beau both replied.

"It didn't matter which one," Danny said with a laugh. "He was just determined to get away from us."

"Well, if you didn't torment him so much," my mother chastised.

"We didn't torment him," Chance argued. "At least not any more than Ulf and Bjorn tormented us."

Lucy looked at me in question.

"Our childhood nicknames. Me and Beau."

She nodded in understanding.

"Mom named us, but Dad chose the nicknames," I explained. "Danny's is Arne. Chance is Happ."

"What about Zeke?" Lucy asked.

"Ezekiel was named for my good friend," my dad answered before I could. "More like a brother."

"He was always just Zeke," I confirmed.

"I gave them strong names," my mom said with a sigh. "Ambrose, Beaumont, Chauncey, Daniel, and Ezekiel. But Erik was determined to call them by something different."

"They're fine names," my dad agreed. "There's nothing wrong with nicknames."

"Chauncey?" Lucy asked, looking across the table at my brother, gleefully.

Chance met her stare.

"That fits you perfectly," she said. There was nothing in her tone or the expression on her face to indicate that she was fucking with him...unless you'd seen them butt heads before. I knew with absolute certainty she was trying to goad him.

"I think so too," my mother said happily.

"Knock it off, *Lucille*," Charlie chided, shooting his sister a look.

She gazed back innocently.

As my father and Beau started clearing the table, I made no move to help them. Lucy was still contributing to the conversation, but I'd noticed that her posture had changed the longer we'd sat for dinner. She was very still, her muscles rigid with strain. Oh, she was hiding it well, but I also had the benefit of her nails digging into my thigh.

"Two choices," I whispered into her ear. "You can sit on my lap and alleviate some of this, or we can excuse ourselves."

"I'm fine," she breathed.

"Pick," I ordered.

When she turned to meet my gaze, I made the decision for her. The pupils of her eyes were so wide with pain that the brown around them was just a sliver of color. It was startling, considering the fact that she'd barely fidgeted or given any other indication that she was uncomfortable.

"We're going to skip dessert," I announced, getting to my feet.

"I'd like dessert," Lucy argued.

"It's worse when you try to fight it," Reese said in commiseration, wincing.

"I'm not fighting anything," Lucy countered as she rose from her seat. The trembling in her hands gave her away.

"Luce," Charlie whispered sympathetically.

"If only a mate could get with the program from the beginning," Chance joked, leaning back in his chair. "Things would be so much less dramatic."

Lucy narrowed her eyes. "Charlie fell head over heels for Zeke the moment he met him," she ground out, setting her hand on her brother's shoulder. "I don't think it made anything less *dramatic* for him. Do you?"

Chance's chair dropped forward with a thud.

"Not another word, Happ," my dad ordered as he stepped back into the room. "Lucy, it's nothing to be embarrassed about. Go spend some time with Ulf."

Reese was glaring at Chance in exasperation. I probably was too.

"Charlie?" Lucy asked quietly.

"Go," he ordered her softly. "I'll see you in a bit."

As she turned to me, she let me take her hand and tug her out of the room. We were silent as we headed upstairs. I couldn't wait to get my hands on her, but I knew that she resented the fact that we had to leave her brother behind.

"They love him already," I assured her as I closed the door behind us. "He'll be fine."

"Your brother's a frigging bully," she snapped, letting go of my hand.

"He's a pain in the ass."

"What is his deal, anyway?"

"Who knows?"

"He's been an asshole since we met," she griped, shoving her hair away from her face.

"You really want to discuss Chance right now?" I asked as she tore off her T-shirt and fanned herself with it, pacing across the room.

"I'm pissed. Drama? I can show him *dramatic* if he wants," she said darkly.

I caught her around the waist on her next pass.

"How about you show me something instead?" I asked, pulling her toward me.

"Oh, that feels good." She sighed with relief as I tucked my hands under her tank top. "This crap is really inconvenient."

"Life usually is," I agreed, pressing my lips against her forehead.

"This isn't going to go away, is it?" she asked, leaning into me.

"Never," I murmured against her hair.

"I should probably stop being a little bitch about it, huh?" she asked, her words muffled against my shirt. She tipped her head back. "Charlie was all in from like the first minute."

"It's different for everyone." How many times had I told her that? In some ways, it was convenient that Lucy had seen the mating bond firsthand, but the comparisons she made weren't helpful. Zeke and Charlie's relationship had been different, not better or worse, but their own.

"Still."

"Reese and Beau cemented the bond right away," I told her. "And they couldn't stand each other. So it could be worse."

"They seem to get along fine, now."

"They're obsessed with each other," I agreed. "*Now*."

"It's not like I'd ever get sick of looking at you," she

mused, her cheeks pulling in as she held back a smile. "And I don't mind your company."

"High praise."

"I'm a tough critic," she replied with mock seriousness.

"We'll wait as long as you need."

The playfulness disappeared from her expression. "I never imagined that our lives would go like this," she said. "One day, Charlie and I are quitting our jobs to travel for a year, and the next he's some Vampire's mate. I'd finally gotten my head wrapped around that little curveball when Zeke tells us that there's some conspiracy going on, and he has to leave—which was bad enough—but then he insisted we follow this elaborate plan to get back to the United States if he doesn't come back because we might be in danger."

"You guys have been through a lot," I soothed, pulling her closer.

"Then you show up," she said, reaching up to run a finger down the front of my throat.

"And scare the hell out of you."

"I mean, I did all right," she said. "I got past Danny *and* Chance."

"You weren't expecting me."

"Understatement."

We smiled at each other.

"It's a lot," she said, her smile dropping.

"I know. For me too."

"But you've been looking for your mate, right?" she asked as I shuffled her backward toward the couch. "It couldn't have been that much of a surprise."

"Believe me, it was," I replied as I pulled her down with me. "I was searching for my *brother's* mate. I didn't see you coming."

"Do you think Charlie's okay?"

"I think he's getting a little better every day," I replied honestly. I squeezed her thigh. "But, baby, I think expecting your brother to ever fully heal from this?" I shook my head.

"So he'll just never be happy?" she choked out.

"I don't know." I didn't have much experience with mates who'd lost their other half. It didn't happen often, and those left behind rarely chose to go on without them. "I'd like to think that eventually he'll be able to enjoy some of the things he did before."

"He has to, right?" she asked almost desperately. "All pain fades with time."

I nodded, even though I couldn't imagine it. I'd been with Lucy for mere days, and I couldn't even comprehend going on with my life if she were suddenly lost to me. The memory of the hopelessness and frustration that I'd felt before I'd found her was enough to make my stomach turn. I'd spent my life waiting for her. What was left for me if she was gone forever? All hope lost. All purpose gone.

Perhaps it was different for humans. Their lives and relationships weren't dictated by the quest for the other half of their soul. They found and discarded relationships easily. Fell in and out of love like it was nothing. Maybe that would work in Charlie's benefit. He was human.

"Charlie will be okay," I told her finally. I hoped it wasn't a lie.

CHAPTER 7
LUCY

I nodded, desperately wanting to believe Ambrose. I couldn't accept a world where my big brother was never able to crawl out of the pit he'd fallen into—not without crawling into it with him.

"So...Reese and Beau completed it right away, huh?" I said, trying to distract myself.

"Yes," he rasped, gripping my thighs.

"I mean, that would definitely simplify things." I tugged on his shirt, and he lifted his arms to let me pull it off. It was only fair, considering he'd already seen most of my body.

My breath caught when I took a look at what I'd uncovered. It *couldn't* be, but it *was*.

The tattoo was faded as if it had been there a very long time, but the design of the thick geometric lines was still easily recognizable.

"You have a wolf tattoo," I whispered in amazement, tracing the lines with my finger.

"*Ulf*," he replied in explanation, pushing my hair gently behind my shoulders. "Wolf."

"Holy crap," I breathed. My shock must've been written all over my face because he let me go easily as I climbed off his lap.

Turning around, I whipped my tank top over my head and pulled my hair over my shoulder. Ambrose let out a sound before his hands came out to dig into my sides.

I knew what he was seeing. It wasn't exactly the same —the lines were more delicate, and the design was more intricate—but a geometric wolf stared back at him from the center of my back.

"When did you get it?" he choked out, running his hand over the delicate design.

"When I was twenty," I replied, looking at him over my shoulder.

"Why a wolf?" he ground out, his eyebrows pulled together as he stared at it.

"I don't know," I replied quietly. "I was screwing around with a ruler one day and ended up with the wolf, and I just...knew I wanted it as a tattoo. Charlie and I found a shop. He chickened out, but I was determined."

I remembered the day clearly. I hadn't been able to sleep, and I'd been screwing around with my sketchbook. Mostly, I just doodled to clear my head, but that morning the lines had almost immediately taken on a recognizable shape. I'd spent over an hour carefully finishing it.

"Gods," he whispered, leaning forward to kiss the center of the tattoo.

It wasn't small. The edges spanned almost all the way across my back. When the tattoo artist had originally printed it, he'd scaled it down to only a few inches. He'd been really surprised when I'd explained that I didn't want it smaller. I'd wanted it larger than the original. It was my first and only tattoo, and it took up half of my back.

"Did Zeke see this?" he asked roughly as he gripped my hips and urged me back around.

"I'm sure he did," I replied, running my fingers through his hair. "He saw me in a swimsuit plenty of times."

"And he never mentioned mine?" he asked.

"Not your tattoo, no." He pressed his forehead against my sternum. "But he talked about all of you all the time. He told us that we needed to find you if he didn't come back. He insisted, actually. He made both of us promise that we'd make our way to Oregon."

I paused, remembering those days after we'd realized that Zeke wasn't coming back.

"It was so hard to keep Charlie moving. By the time we got to the Rennos, he was barely even trying to help me. He just wanted to—" The words caught in my throat. "Just lie down and die or something. So I figured it was the perfect time to go back to the apartment and get some things, since I didn't know when we'd be back."

"That's when we found you," he said, looking up at me.

"We were already on our way here," I explained. "We would've met, eventually."

"Inevitable," he said softly, kissing the skin above my belly button.

"I guess so."

"He had to have known," Ambrose muttered, letting out a sigh against my skin.

"Who?"

God, when he looked at me like that, I felt it all the way to my toes. It wasn't attraction, though the heat was evident in his stare. It was something deeper than that. Reverence. Awe.

I'd done nothing to deserve it.

"Zeke," Ambrose replied. "He had to have known when he saw your tattoo."

"It's strange, right?" I asked, looking down at his chest. The similarities to mine were startling.

"Our souls are two sides of the same coin," he said gently. "Not so strange."

I wasn't sure who moved first, but the moment our lips met, it felt like I'd been doused in cool water on a hot summer day. The relief was instant and addicting.

Ambrose had half risen out of his seat to reach me, and he straightened without losing contact. One of his hands cupped my breast, and the other wrapped around my back as he shuffled us away from the couch. I wasn't paying much attention to the change in scenery as I took my time discovering the ridges of his chest and belly. The man had muscle upon muscle. I couldn't even guess how many hours it had taken to sculpt a body like his.

We stumbled to a stop as my ass hit something soft. When I pulled my mouth from his to look around, I realized we were in his bedroom.

He hadn't bothered with the light, but it was just bright enough to make out the bed I'd landed against, a rocking chair in the corner, and a low, wide dresser against the wall under a window with filmy curtains. Moonlight just barely shone through them.

"Mine," he said under his breath, his mouth moving to my throat.

I froze, instinct and something darker making me brace as he sucked the skin into his mouth.

He let go almost immediately, kissing the spot gently.

"Nice room," I said as he gripped my ass and lifted me onto the bed.

"Can I?" he asked, ignoring my compliment. His fingers paused at the waistband of my jeans.

I lifted my hips to help him. Every inch he uncovered tingled with awareness as he bared the rest of me. I'd lost my shoes somewhere in Zeke's room when we'd first arrived, and Ambrose gently tugged my socks off.

"You too," I ordered as he braced my feet on his chest, his hands gliding down my shins to my knees and back up toward my ankles.

"Not a good idea," he growled, lifting my foot to kiss the inside of my ankle.

"I think it's a great idea."

"I think you're not ready to have me inside you."

"Who said anything about being inside me?" I asked, taking in the wide expanse of his shoulders, the light dusting of chest hair, and the tattoo that matched my own. It wasn't as if we had to have sex just because he was naked. There were plenty of other things we could do.

Ambrose just stared at me.

God, he was beautiful. Even when he was looking at me like I'd lost my mind.

A wave of heat pulsed through me, making my breath catch. The feeling didn't seem to be getting any better. Sometimes it was a dull heat, like stepping into a sauna. Other times, it felt like falling into a hot tub that had been set too high. At its worst, it felt like that hot tub water had been injected directly into my veins, boiling me from the inside.

The orgasms earlier had been excellent, but they hadn't come close to satisfying the clawing need that I'd been trying so hard to ignore.

Widening my legs, I clenched my hands in the comforter as Ambrose reached for me, running his fingers gently over my clit before thrusting them inside. I was already so wet that they met no resistance.

"Fuck it," Ambrose said, pulling his hand back. He

pushed the fingers into his mouth and sucked them clean before reaching for the button on his own jeans.

I almost jumped out of my skin when a disembodied voice rang through the room.

"Ulf, we need you downstairs," Erik demanded.

"What the fuck?" I hissed, covering my breasts with my hands as I sat up and frantically searched the room.

"Intercom," Ambrose announced, pointing to a little black square on the wall. Reaching out, he tugged me from the bed and helped me pull my jeans back on. Every inch of my skin was sensitized and screaming at the abrasive denim fabric, but I didn't complain as he hurried me out of the room.

Less than a minute later, we were both dressed and rushing down the stairs. When we got to the living room, Sven and Alice were standing with another man, talking to Ambrose's brothers and parents.

"Finau?" Ambrose barked, slamming to a halt. His arm came out to keep me behind him.

"Easy," Chance said, moving toward us.

"What the fuck are you doing here?" Ambrose asked, glaring at the man.

Beau and Reese came in behind us, and Beau cursed. "Reese, take Lucy out of here," he ordered.

"Fuck that noise," Reese replied.

I moved a little closer to Ambrose.

"You have two seconds to tell me why the hell you're in this house," Ambrose announced, his voice low and menacing.

"They took my mate," Finau replied. Not a man. A Vampire. As I looked closer, I could see the sweat darkening the hair at his temples and the tension around his eyes. I didn't know who he was, but I felt a twinge of sympathy anyway.

"Who did?" Ambrose asked.

"Them," Finau replied frantically, throwing his arm out to the side. "Those men. Whoever they are. The ones Zeke was on about."

"I thought none of you knew why Zeke was killed," Chance replied, seeming to grow a couple of inches as he turned toward the Vampire.

"He mentioned things," Finau said. "Just bits and pieces here and there. We all thought, you know, he was beginning to..." His words trailed off.

"You thought he was starting to lose his mind," Danny finished for him, his voice devoid of emotion.

"It happens." Finau's shoulders slumped.

"Not to our brother," Chance snapped.

"I realize that now," Finau replied apologetically.

"Interesting how that happens," Ambrose said bitingly. "Realizing the truth when you're the one facing the fallout."

"He didn't have proof, and it made no sense." Finau glared. "Who would go after mates? It doesn't happen."

"Until it does," Erik said calmly. "Tell us what happened."

"I came to give you this," he said, grabbing a box off the table behind him. "I found my mate at the airport in Vegas. I—she—we were both on layovers, and we ended up missing our flights. We stayed there for a couple of weeks. I didn't...I didn't think it would matter to wait a few weeks."

Erik took the box from him and carried it back to where he'd been standing. As Finau spoke, he pulled out a pocketknife and sliced the top open.

Mattie let out a noise somewhere between a gasp and a moan when Erik lifted out the contents of the box.

It was a tattered, multi-color quilt with no discernible

pattern. Small bits of formerly blue yarn poked out at regular intervals like little gray bunny ears.

Tears filled my eyes, and I looked behind me, wondering where Charlie was.

He was going to lose it.

"Thank you," Ambrose said, the words practically torn from him.

"I knew he'd want you to have it," Finau replied, lowering his head in a slow nod. "My mate and I decided to drive here. We left Vegas three days ago. Yesterday, she ran into a gas station to use the restroom, and she didn't come back out. When I started to worry, I followed her inside. The attendant was dead behind the counter, and the door was wide open."

"Why do you think this has anything to do with Zeke?" Ambrose asked dismissively.

"I didn't hear them kill the attendant," Finau snapped. "He was alive when I paid for the gas five minutes before. They killed him and took her without making a fucking sound, Ambrose!"

"We believe you," Danny said, shooting a look at Ambrose. "Now tell me everything you remember."'

As soon as everyone was seated, the Vampire told them what time they'd left their hotel, how far they'd gone before they stopped for gas, what cars were in the parking lot when they'd pulled up, the back door of the tiny convenience store that had been left open, the tire tracks he'd found afterward. He described his mate like a goddess come to earth, and from what I gathered, she was barely five feet tall and voluptuous, with olive skin and short black hair. Her nails were painted purple. He seemed to think that was important for some reason, or maybe he was just getting lost in the details because he was so frantic.

Matilda sat close to Erik, barely paying attention as she ran her fingers over Zeke's quilt. I wondered if she remembered how long it had taken her to make it for him all of those years ago. Zeke had told us that every time he found a rip, he'd brought it back to her to mend. A multitude of embroidery stitches were scattered throughout, like little scars that told the story of Zeke's life.

"We were only two hours away," Finau mumbled, rubbing his hands over his face. "Only two more hours. Why the fuck did I stop for fuel?"

"If it hadn't been then, it would've been another time when your guard was down," Chance said, the words and tone not quite comforting.

When Ambrose ordered Finau to take him through the entire thing again, Reese stood up from the couch across from ours and jerked her head toward the kitchen.

Ambrose's hand tightened on my thigh before he rubbed his thumb across the top and let me go. I followed as she, Mattie, and Alice left the room. Instead of stopping in the kitchen, they walked straight out the door. Glancing at my bare feet, I debated for a moment before following. The cold ground felt good on my hot skin as I met them across the lawn under some trees.

"They hear everything," Reese explained. "And I didn't want to distract them."

"We could've gone to one of the bedrooms," Alice pointed out, raising one eyebrow.

"Right." Reese clapped her hands. "Well, we're here now. Do we believe him?"

Matilda scoffed and held Zeke's blanket closer to her chest. "Yes."

"Did you see how badly he's perspiring?" Alice asked. "Yes. He's newly mated. The rest of the story?" She shrugged.

"They'll know if he's lying," Matilda said, reaching out to pat Reese's arm. "Erik and Sven can sense a lie a mile away."

"What does he want them to do about it?" I asked, glancing back at the house. "Why isn't he searching for her himself?"

"I think he has been," Alice replied. "If the story is real, he's been searching for her for over twenty-four hours. He smells like a damn goat, so that fits."

"And if anyone's watching, he led them straight here," Reese added angrily, crossing her arms over her chest.

"Of course he did," Matilda said, moving closer. "Everyone knows that my boys are home. He knew if he came here, he could ask for help. Our home is no secret, Reese. It just feels as if no one knows we're here."

We moved back to the kitchen just as my feet began to grow uncomfortable, and a few minutes later, Charlie strode into the room. The dark half-moons under his eyes seemed more pronounced than usual, but I wasn't sure if I was a good judge anymore. Sometimes when I looked at him, I didn't immediately notice the way grief had ravaged his body, and that scared me. It meant that my mind was starting to automatically see this new version of Charlie as normal.

"I can't believe you have it," he said, walking straight for Matilda. "Can I?"

"Of course," Matilda said, giving the quilt a squeeze before handing it reverently to Charlie. "It's yours now."

"Oh, I couldn't take it," Charlie protested as his hands clenched around the fabric.

"Nonsense," Matilda countered. "Zeke would want you to have it."

"But you put so much work into it—"

"It was Zeke's, and now it is yours," she said firmly. "Have they made any headway in there?"

"I'll be there in a minute, Mattie," Erik called.

Reese let out a breath of a laugh as Alice looked at the kitchen clock.

"It's getting late," she said grimly. "The search won't begin until tomorrow, in any case."

"You're right, as always," Sven announced as he entered the room. He glanced at Charlie and then looked away.

I looked back and forth between them, wondering what that was about, when Ambrose wrapped his arms around me from behind.

"Finau is going to stay in the pool house," Erik told Mattie as he leaned down to kiss her.

"You guys have a pool?" I looked over my shoulder at Ambrose.

"No, but it sounds less pretentious than guesthouse," he replied. "It's just a studio. One room and a bathroom."

"Fancy."

"No one was comfortable with him staying inside the house," Beau said as he pulled Reese against his side.

"Understandable," Alice replied. "His story is plausible?"

"He's telling the truth," Sven confirmed. "The boy is going out of his mind."

Ambrose's arms tightened around me.

No one spoke, but the silence wasn't comfortable. It was weighted, and I wasn't sure that I wanted to know why that was.

"You're going to help him?" I asked finally.

"We have to," Beau replied. "If not us, who?"

"If not now, when?" Danny said quietly.

"Nothing else to get done tonight," Erik said tiredly.

The kitchen cleared out as everyone headed to their respective bedrooms. I followed Charlie as he carried Zeke's quilt up the stairs to his room. Ambrose came along quietly, not willing to let me out of his sight.

When we reached the main room in the suite, I looked around it again. It was similar to Ambrose's room in shape, but the way Zeke had decorated was almost the opposite. Framed movie, music, and video game posters covered the walls. The couch was short and sleek—clearly from a different era—and the rest of the furniture matched it. If it hadn't been for the espresso machine on the counter and the modern posters, it would've felt like we'd stepped back in time.

"I'm exhausted," Charlie announced as he moved toward the bedroom.

I'd heard the phrase so often that it didn't even phase me as I followed him inside. He may be tired, but he'd slept quite a bit already, and it wouldn't hurt him to hang with his baby sister for a while.

"I can't believe that guy brought it back," I said, sitting down cross-legged as Charlie lay down on the bed, clutching the quilt to his chest.

"I know," he said softly. "He considered leaving it with me," he mused, running his fingers back and forth over a spot mended with purple embroidery. "But he said that he hadn't slept without it for so long that he was afraid he wouldn't be able to."

"What a baby," I joked, my heart aching.

"I know, right?" Charlie let out a watery laugh. "Even *I* didn't sleep with a lovey."

"Like our parents would've ever let you," I snorted. Our parents did their best. They were present at least, but they'd never been the cuddly type and hadn't fostered it in us kids either. It was either a miracle or inevitable that Charlie and I had stayed so close as we grew up.

Hell, it was a miracle that we'd been born at all. I wasn't sure our parents had ever been affectionate with each other.

"It took her so long to make it," Ambrose said, leaning against the doorframe. "That he slept with the top piece for almost a year before she'd added the rest."

"Really?" Charlie asked.

"He was obsessed with it," Ambrose confirmed. "On wash day, he refused to play anywhere except the backyard while it hung to dry. Chance used to tease him about being afraid a wild animal would steal it."

"Sounds like Chance," I grumbled.

"He took that thing everywhere," Ambrose said. "I wondered if you had it, but I didn't want to ask."

Charlie nodded. "I have a few T-shirts," he said quietly. "And the dollar coin he carried in his wallet."

"Did he tell you the story of that?" Ambrose asked.

"No, just that it was worth a lot more than a dollar," Charlie replied.

"The one with the lady on the front?" I asked, intrigued. I knew I'd seen it when Zeke had emptied his pockets at some point, but I couldn't remember any significance to it.

"It's one of the first coins ever minted in the United States," Ambrose explained. "My father knew that it was a piece of history, so he held on to it. He told us he won it in a game of cards, but it was probably much more boring than that. Eventually, he gave it to Zeke, and by then, the coins were pretty much obsolete. They'd been replaced by others."

"You're rich," I told Charlie, wiggling my eyebrows at him as I poked him in the thigh with my toes.

"It's not like I'd ever sell it," Charlie countered, shoving my foot away.

"You're wealthy without the coin," Ambrose interrupted, a small smile playing on his lips. "Everything Zeke's is yours now."

"What?" Charlie stuttered, pushing himself up on the bed.

"You're his mate, Charlie," Ambrose replied. "Everything Zeke owned became yours the moment you completed the bond."

Charlie shook his head. "But we weren't married."

"Marriage is a human construct," Ambrose said dismissively. "We follow Vampire law."

"Oh my god," Charlie whispered.

"What?" I asked, glancing between them.

"Our family is wealthy," Ambrose said with a wink. "Zeke was filthy rich."

"He said he always knew what stocks to buy," Charlie said dazedly.

"This is *wealthy*?" I asked doubtfully, waving my arm around.

"In comparison, yes," Ambrose replied.

I flopped down next to my brother. "Well, I want a Range Rover," I ordered imperiously to the ceiling. "With floral seat covers and vents that smell like sunshine." I turned to look at him, and his eyes were still blank with shock. "Also, I'd like one of those castle bouncy houses with the slide. I always wanted those, and no time like the present."

"I'm not buying you a bouncy house," Charlie replied, finally snapping out of it.

"But you'll get the Range Rover?"

"You're such a mooch."

"Better a mooch than a scrooge," I countered. "I want the Range Rover to be white."

"Dream on," he replied drolly.

"G-Wagon?" I asked hopefully.

"Get the fuck outta here." Charlie laughed, flicking me in the forehead.

I grinned back at him. Seeing the real Charlie shining through was such a gift—much better than a Range Rover. Though I'd still love one of those. Who wouldn't?

We hadn't even had a car growing up. I'd learned to drive as an adult.

Ambrose had disappeared out of the doorway at some point, but I didn't think he'd gone far.

"You smell like Zeke," I told Charlie softly, reaching out to ruffle his hair.

"I used his shampoo," he replied just as quietly. "It doesn't smell the same on me."

"Yeah, it does," I argued.

He just shook his head.

"I bet he's really happy we're here." I rolled to face him and curled my hands under my cheek. "He was so insistent that we find his family."

"Do you think he knew he wasn't coming back?" Charlie asked, his eyes welling with tears.

"I think he would've done anything to get back to you," I replied, not quite answering the question. I wasn't sure if Zeke had known that he was going to die, but I had a feeling that he knew it was a strong possibility. He wouldn't have made Charlie memorize the message to his family otherwise. Zeke wouldn't have even put that idea into my brother's head unless he'd felt like he had to.

"I miss him so much it hurts," Charlie confessed. "I don't know how much more of this I can take."

"Just hold on a little longer," I ordered gently, reaching

out to grip the hand he'd pulled beneath his chin. "It'll get better."

"How?"

"I don't know," I replied. "But I *know* it will. You just have to give it some time."

My brother's lips trembled as he nodded.

"I'm the third wheel now," Charlie said. "Is this how you felt when I met Zeke?"

"I was the front wheel," I countered. "Arguably the most important, so I didn't let it bother me that there were two of you following me around."

He let out a watery chuckle.

"It wasn't the same," I said with a sigh. "I wasn't grieving when you met Zeke. I was on an adventure with my big brother."

"We had a good time, huh?"

"The best time." I squeezed his hand. "Do you remember when that bird shit on Zeke in the park?"

Charlie let out a bark of laughter.

"That was the highlight of the trip," I continued, lifting my hand to sweep it down the back of my head, and then putting it in front of my face with an exaggerated expression of disgust. I deepened my voice. "What in the *absolute* fuck?"

I cackled.

"Oh god," Charlie wheezed, crying and laughing at the same time. "He was so upset."

"He was pissed at that bird," I corrected, raising my eyebrows. "It was lucky it had wings and could fly away."

Charlie's entire body shook.

"He wasn't even embarrassed!" I exclaimed. "He was *offended*."

"How...how dare that bird shit on him," Charlie added,

hiccuping. The half laughter gradually turned into gut-wrenching sobs.

I crawled closer and pressed my cheek to the top of his head, my arms pulling him as close as I could get him with the quilt between us. My breath came out in choked gasps as I cried, trying to comfort him.

There was no soothing it. There was nothing I could do or say. My shy, sweet brother had never felt like he belonged anywhere until he'd met Zeke. He'd been drifting through life with me as his only anchor until he'd met his mate. I'd seen the way he lit up in Zeke's presence, like he'd finally found his place, and now that was gone. He wasn't even drifting anymore. He was slowly breaking apart while I watched.

I wasn't sure how long I could keep him anchored.

When I raised my head, Ambrose was standing in the doorway, his gaze soft. He gave me a shallow nod and swung the door mostly closed between us. The light in the main room shut off.

Eventually, Charlie cried himself to sleep, his face pressed against Zeke's quilt. I carefully disengaged from him and pulled the comforter over him before shuffling out of the bedroom. I wasn't sure when I'd ever felt so weary.

The weight of it all was suffocating.

"Hey, baby," Ambrose said, sitting up as I walked toward the couch.

"Have you been here the whole time?" I asked, my voice hoarse.

"I didn't want to go far in case you needed me," he replied, pulling me down to lie beside him. "Did he finally fall asleep?"

"Yeah," I breathed as my body molded into his.

"Good."

"I'm not sure what to do," I confessed.

"You're doing it," he assured me, running his fingers through my hair.

"I don't think it's enough," I whispered tiredly.

"It's enough for tonight." His lips found my forehead in the dark. "You can do it again tomorrow."

It didn't take long before the steady rhythm of his breathing lulled me to sleep.

When I woke up the next morning, I was sprawled out on top of Ambrose, and there was a large wet spot on his shirt where I'd drooled.

"Shit."

"You slept hard," he said in amusement.

Of course he'd woken up before me. Wiping the leftover drool from my cheek, I pushed myself up until I could see over the back of the couch.

"He hasn't come out yet," Ambrose informed me. "But he took a shower a little while ago."

"Great," I mumbled as I stood up and stretched. I really needed to put on a frigging bra. I'd been flitting around without one since the night we'd left the hotel, and it was starting to get annoying. Usually, I preferred to go without a bra, but it wasn't exactly practical. My boobs weren't huge, but they weren't tiny either. The difference when I wasn't wearing one was noticeable. "I need to shower too."

"I wasn't going to say anything," Ambrose teased, still laying back on the couch as he watched me.

I glared and turned my head to the side to smell my armpit. "Still fresh as a daisy," I countered, making his eyes light up as he laughed.

"What would you have done if you weren't?" he asked curiously, sitting up.

"I don't know," I replied, glancing at the closed bedroom door. "Passed out from the stench?"

Ambrose chuckled. "Well, you still smell fine," he said, running his hand over my ass.

"Charlie?" I called.

My brother opened the door fully dressed.

"I'm going to go shower," I said, pointing at the door with my thumb. "Cool?"

"Have at it," he replied with a shooing motion.

Like he hadn't terrified me the night before when he sobbed himself to sleep.

I rolled my eyes and headed for the door, pausing in the hallway.

"Lead the way," I ordered Ambrose. "I don't remember where your room is."

"The wings all look really similar," he replied, taking my hand as he went downstairs. "These stairs are directly across from ours. You just have to go through the living area."

"Right," I said as the sound of voices drifted over from the kitchen.

"We'll be down in a while," he said.

"Who are you talking to?" I asked, hurrying to catch up to him.

"My dad said my mom made breakfast."

"Because it's not weird at all that you have conversations across the house without raising your voices," I said as we climbed the stairs.

"I don't even think about it," he replied. "When I was a kid, I forgot that my mom couldn't hear us, though. Got me in trouble a few times when I was really little, and I assumed she heard me when I went to play outside."

"Yikes."

"Yeah. I only made that mistake twice."

"Twice?"

"The first time, they reminded me that I had to go to her and make sure she heard me. The second time my dad spanked my ass."

I grimaced.

Ambrose shrugged. "It worked. I didn't ever forget again."

"So if I want you to remember something, I should just slap you. Good to know," I said sarcastically.

Ambrose pulled me into his room and closed the door, pressing me against it.

"When I grew up, going outside alone was dangerous. Going outside without either of my parents knowing? Even more so. In my father's eyes, corporal punishment was preferable to a dead son. You disagree?"

"Yeah, yeah," I replied, staring at his mouth. "I hear you."

The tether between us pulled tight as he tilted his head down. But I'd just slept for hours with my mouth open, and I didn't want him anywhere near it before I'd brushed my teeth.

Ducking under his arm, I smirked at his disgruntled expression.

"Shower, remember?" I asked, grabbing my bag. "Point the way."

"Haven't you been in here yet?" he asked, walking through the bedroom to the bathroom.

"I've been using Zeke's," I replied, taking in the space.

The shower was massive and looked like it had been made out of river rock. The light above the shower made everything bright, but the colors and textures in the bathroom were...cozy. I'd been in some pretty fancy hotel bathrooms thanks to Zeke, but Ambrose's was by far my favorite. Everything was spotlessly clean, and I was pretty sure the tile beneath my feet was heated.

"You can use whichever showerhead you want," Ambrose said, gesturing toward them. "Handles are underneath." He walked over to the sinks and opened the cabinet beneath them. "Towels and extra toiletries are in here, but there's also shampoo and soap in the dispensers inside the shower."

"You have dispensers in the shower?" I asked, walking over to peek behind the clear glass wall that only covered half the shower. "Like a hotel?"

"I don't like having a lot of clutter," he replied.

"So if I leave all my bottles and containers everywhere, it'll drive you nuts?" I joked.

"Baby, you can leave your shit strewn across the house."

"That's what you say now," I teased, setting my bag on the floor. "But once you're getting it on the regular, your tune will change. It's all part of the chase."

Ambrose laughed. "If I'm *getting it regular*, I'll care even less about the mess you make."

"We'll see," I mused.

We stared at each other. The more I knew Ambrose, the more I liked him. He was nice. No, he was kind. Nice was surface, kind went deeper. He was thoughtful. He treated Charlie like a long-lost family member. The whole family did, because to them, he was.

He was considerate and attentive, but he recognized when I needed space and gave it to me, like the night before when Charlie and I were talking.

He also wasn't a pushover. When it came to arguments, he seemed to give me a pretty long rope, but the knowledge that he would yank me back was always present.

Plus, he was just ridiculously hot and could do things with his mouth that I hadn't even known were possible.

Ambrose smiled, like he knew exactly what I was thinking, and I looked at his mouth, the canines slightly longer than the rest of his perfectly straight teeth.

His smile widened.

"Stop reading my mind," I ordered with a laugh.

"Stop making it so easy," he replied as he walked away.

The shower was as functionally pleasing as it was beautiful, and I stayed in longer than I'd planned because the hot water was so soothing against the back of my neck and shoulders. We'd been showering in shitty motel room showers for so long, I'd almost forgotten how nice it was to bathe in a place where I wasn't worried about catching some kind of foot fungus. By the time I climbed out, I felt like I'd been reborn.

My clothing options were minimal because I'd had to leave half of them behind when I'd stopped at the apartment in Baltimore. Thankfully, I still had plenty of bras and underwear, four pairs of socks, two pairs of clean leggings, and a couple of clean shirts. I threw on an extra-large shirt screen printed with a cheesing Mona Lisa on the front. I'd need to do laundry soon, but that was a problem for tomorrow.

When I finally left the bathroom, I was slick with lotion, my hair was doing good things, and for the first time in a while, my breasts didn't feel like they had a mind of their own when I walked. I may have been strutting when I found Ambrose leaning against the kitchenette counter, drinking something out of an opaque glass.

"Feel better?" he asked. He threw back whatever it was and turned to rinse the glass in the sink.

"So much better," I confirmed. I moved closer. "Are you drinking blood?"

Ambrose paused for a moment and then gently set the glass in the bottom of the sink before turning to face me again.

"Yes," he replied slowly.

"You don't have to hide it." I glanced at the sink again.

"I'm not hiding it."

"You're only drinking it when I won't see you."

"I only need it once a day. I usually have one at night, but last night I was in Charlie's room with you."

"Oh." I leaned my hip against the back of the couch. "Why do you only drink it at night? Don't you get hungry during the day?"

"We don't need much, as a rule," Ambrose explained. "It's more like a medication. I need a certain amount to keep from getting sick, but my diet is the same foods you eat."

"I feel like this should be required learning," I replied. "So we humans don't look like absolute ass-hats when we're around Vampires."

Ambrose smiled. "But the rumors and the myths are more exciting."

"You're not wrong."

"You never asked Zeke about it?" he asked curiously.

"I didn't know if that was allowed." I wrinkled my nose as his grin widened. "What? I didn't want to offend him. I figured if he wanted to explain it, he would."

"Well, that was very polite of you," he teased.

"Oh, shut it."

"I'm glad you feel like you can ask me."

"Well, I don't care if I offend you," I shot back.

Ambrose let out a bark of laughter. "You ready for breakfast?"

"If you're done in here."

"I'll shower in a while," he confirmed. "I want to get downstairs and see if they've gotten anywhere with Finau's mate."

"Wait," I said, putting my arm out to stop him. "Who *is* that guy?"

"He was in Zeke's unit," Ambrose replied grimly.

"The one he was with when—"

"Yes."

"Oh." I was dumbfounded. I knew Zeke was gone, but no one had even hinted at how he'd died, and I wasn't sure if I should ask. I didn't think knowing would benefit me or Charlie, but it could very well make things harder.

"Zeke was captured," Ambrose said, the words stilted. "And they didn't get him back until it was too late."

"Oh," I breathed.

"If you have questions, now's the time to ask them," he said gently. "But I can promise you that the questions you have are easier to live with than the answers you'd get."

I swallowed hard, searching his face. He'd tell me. If I wanted to know, he'd give me the information, but he really didn't want to.

"I don't have any questions," I replied finally.

CHAPTER 8
AMBROSE

"Absolutely fucking not," Lucy shouted at her brother.

I grimaced and wondered if I should intervene. Charlie should've known better than to tell her in the middle of breakfast, but from the look on his face, he'd been counting on Lucy not wanting to make a scene.

Considering she'd risen to her feet so fast that her chair had crashed over backward, I thought he'd misjudged things a bit.

"I'll be perfectly safe," Charlie practically hissed at her, rising as he widened his eyes in the universal shut-the-hell-up look.

"Bullshit. These guys are frigging commandos, Charles! What the hell do they need you for?"

I tried to hide my wince as Charlie's cheeks pinkened.

"I'm just going shopping with Erik," Charlie said, standing up.

The stubborn, angry looks on their faces were incredibly similar.

"Oh, you're just going to take a little grocery store

trip," Lucy mocked. "Right. After we just snuck back to the United States like a couple of spies, and now you're just going to go flitting around in public—"

Her words trailed to a stop, and I tensed as she realized exactly what Charlie's role in the plan was.

"Fuck that," she snapped, glaring around the table. "What the hell is wrong with all of you? Do you think Zeke would be okay with this?"

My father stiffened.

"Do *not*," Charlie ordered, his fists clenching on the tabletop.

"He made me *promise* him I'd get you back to his family, so you'd be *safe*," Lucy shouted. "What a frigging joke!"

"It's not your decision! You have *no idea* what Zeke would want."

"You're a frigging idiot," Lucy snapped, pointing at her brother. "He wouldn't want this."

"I think I would know better than you," Charlie shot back.

Lucy started laughing, and the sound had me immediately pushing to my feet. The sound was raspy and broken and just shy of hysterical.

"Would you?" she asked, her voice flat. "Would you know better than me, Charlie? Because I'm pretty sure that you've been checked out since the day Zeke left. *I* was the one who made you get out of bed. *I* was the one who spoon-fed you when you refused to eat. *I* was the one who had to carry you into the shower when you weren't even capable of *bathing yourself*. I practically carried you on my goddamn back from Europe, you ungrateful shit."

Charlie's teeth were gritted so tight as he sneered at Lucy that I was worried for a moment that he was about to launch himself across the table.

"That's enough," my dad announced, his voice low.

"Oh, fuck you," Lucy snarled, not even bothering to look at him.

"Baby," I murmured, carefully laying my hand on her back. Things were about to devolve even more than they already had. All three of my brothers were staring at my mate, waiting to see what she would do, and my mother was silently crying.

"You're not doing this," Lucy announced firmly. "They can fuck off with their little rescue mission."

"His mate is missing, Luce," Charlie said, pointing to the end of the table where Finau was staring blankly at the plate in front of him.

"Then *he* can find her."

"He needs help. He—"

"He can fuck off too," she said, her voice suddenly quiet. "They can all go straight to hell."

"Lucy," I said quietly.

"Don't frigging touch me," she hissed, sidestepping my hand. She looked at her brother. "Do not leave this house, or I swear to god, Charlie,"—she looked around the table—"I'll burn the place down before I follow you."

"Lucy," he called as she stormed out of the kitchen.

"I'll talk to her," I said as he dropped back into his chair.

My father stopped me at the base of the stairs.

"Go careful, Ulf," he warned.

"Thanks for the tip," I replied, moving past him.

By the time I reached my rooms, Lucy had already grabbed her bag and was on her way back out.

"Get out of my way," she ordered.

Instead, I stepped inside, closing and locking the door behind me.

"I'm not messing around," she snapped. "I'm leaving."

"Where are you going to go?" I asked, leaning back against the door.

"Who the hell cares? I brought my brother here so he'd be safe, not so you creeps could use him like some kind of bait."

"Aren't you forgetting something?"

"Don't think so," she replied mockingly.

"How far do you think you'd get before the heat got unbearable?"

Lucy froze.

"I'd guess a couple of miles," I continued. "Maybe less."

"Then I guess Charlie would have to take care of me for once," she hissed.

"Charlie's not going with you."

"Yes, he will."

"If you think that using him to lure them out was our first or even fiftieth choice, you haven't been paying attention," I replied. "He came to us and wouldn't take no for an answer."

"And you all thought, *yeah, sure, we'll use the weak, broken guy in our big plan*? What the hell is wrong with you?"

"Your brother isn't weak or broken," I bit out.

"You have no idea what you're talking about."

"What part of *mates rarely survive the death of their other half* didn't you understand?" I asked, taking a step toward her. "The fact that Charlie is still functioning? The fact that he's making an effort to get to know our family? The fact that he wants to do something for someone else... someone he doesn't even know? Your brother is the strongest person I've *ever* met."

"He's still not being used as bait," she screamed at me.

"He needs this," I argued, my voice rising as well. "He

needs to feel useful. He needs to feel like he's doing something to stop the people who killed his mate! Why can't you understand this?"

Lucy's face was red with anger. She was practically vibrating with rage.

"If you let this happen, we are *done*," she spat out. Almost immediately, her back curved, and her arms clutched her stomach. "I will *never* complete the bond. I'd rather let us both burn alive."

My head snapped back like she'd slapped me.

My ears rang.

The inferno in my chest roared.

I reached for the door handle behind me with shaking hands, barely able to flip the lock. I spun and threw it open, hurrying out of the room as I started to dry heave. Keeping one hand on the banister, I moved down the stairs as quickly as I could.

I needed to put as much space between us as I could manage. Every molecule of my body felt like it was screaming as I lurched through the living area toward the front door. I'd barely gotten it open when I heard chairs scraping back from the table.

"Follow him," my dad ordered someone.

Then I was outside and half walking and half running toward the woods.

Gods, the pain was excruciating. Ripping off my shirt, I used it to mop off my face and the back of my neck. Just as I hit the tree line, I stumbled and landed on my knees. Even the breath in my lungs felt like it was burning. I couldn't get enough air.

Every single instinct urged me to go back to the house.

"Ulf," Beau called as he jogged up behind me. "Fuck."

"Give me a minute," I ordered, my own voice sounding unfamiliar.

Digging my fingers into the dirt, I dragged scorching air into my lungs and gagged.

"I'll assume the conversation didn't improve after you'd left," he said awkwardly as he sat down a few feet away.

"You could say that," I ground out, closing my eyes.

I'd never lost control so badly before. The moment she'd said she would never accept the bond, something inside me had snapped. I had to get away from her before I did something unforgivable.

"I understand why she's angry," Beau mused. "I'm not sure that using Charlie is a good idea."

"Would you rather use Reese?" I snapped as the muscles in my back rippled and fire raced down my spine. I needed to go back in the house. Who knew what Lucy was doing in there?

I just couldn't trust myself yet.

"Reese was never an option," Beau replied flatly.

"What?"

"I said Reese was never an option."

"Never an option for what?" I mumbled in confusion. Gods, why was he talking to me?

My heart felt like it was going to beat out of my chest.

She couldn't leave me. I didn't even think it would be physically possible. But if she tried, would I be able to let her? I wasn't sure of that either. The logical side of my brain kept reminding me that mating bonds were sacred and only taken willingly, but thousands of years of instincts urged me to go back inside and start the blood exchange.

I wasn't sure how long we stayed outside. It felt like hours, but it could've been minutes. When Beau realized that I wasn't able to hold a conversation, he stopped talking and just sat with me in silence as I tried not to come out of my skin. It wasn't until Chance came jogging toward us that I had the strength to rise to my feet again.

"You need to get back inside," he called. "Right now."

"What's wrong?" I grunted, the muscles in my back and arms so tight that my entire upper body felt like it was encased in cement.

"Lucy—"

He didn't say anything else before I was hurrying toward the front door. If she was trying to leave, I had to stop her.

When I got back inside, the house was in chaos. Alice was ordering people around, Danny was talking over Chance as they tried to explain something to our dad, and Charlie was yelling.

"What's wrong with her?" he said frantically. "Luce? What the hell is wrong?"

I found her on the stairs. As Charlie reached for her, she reared backward like she couldn't bear for him to touch her.

"Baby," I called, my voice raw.

"Ambrose," she breathed.

When she turned her head, my legs turned to water. Her eyes were so swollen that she could barely see out of them, and her face was wet with a mixture of tears and sweat. She was curled up tightly on the bottom step, her heels to her ass and her arms tucked against her chest. Her bag was in a heap at the bottom of the stairs.

"It hurts," she groaned, her teeth chattering as she rocked back and forth.

"Move," Alice ordered Charlie, pulling him out of the way.

"Stop. She's my sister," he argued.

"She's not your sister right now," Alice chided. "She's Ambrose's mate."

My throat felt thick, but my steps were steady as I made my way toward her. When I was less than a foot away, she used the banister to slowly pull herself to her feet.

She let out a sob as I started up the stairs. I'd barely reached her when I could feel the heat coming off her body. A fever that high would've killed someone who wasn't experiencing mating heat, but even so, I wasn't even sure how she was still conscious. Her hands shook as she lifted them toward me, and the sound she let out when her fingertips brushed my bare chest made me forget the audience we had.

"Come here," I ordered gruffly, pulling her against me.

She held me so tight as I lifted her into my arms, it was as if she was trying to crawl inside me. I took the stairs slowly, my own body not quite recovered yet.

Instead of being doused in cold water, the relief came in small increments. My head stopped pounding. The nausea mellowed. But the heat beneath my skin remained.

"I don't like this," Lucy whimpered as we reached my rooms.

I didn't either.

I'd never heard of the heat reacting that way to a threat that wasn't physical. I'd damn near lost all sense of myself.

"Shh," I murmured, carrying her into the bedroom.

"Don't let him go," she whispered against my neck. "Don't let him go."

"No one's going anywhere right now," I assured her. I could promise her that much. They wouldn't go through with any of it until I was capable of leaving her side. Finau's mate was important, but not at the cost of my own.

151

Lucy wouldn't let go of me long enough to set her down on the bed, so I crawled onto it with her clinging to me like a monkey. It was awkwardly done, but eventually we made it to the pillows.

"Why isn't it getting better?" she asked, her hands roaming. "It usually gets better."

Instead of telling her my suspicion that she'd forced the connection to strengthen when she'd seriously threatened to reject the bond, I just pulled her closer and slid my hands under her T-shirt. When I pulled it off, her torso was covered in large red patches.

I winced as I leaned over her, our torsos pressed together so closely that even air couldn't find its way between us. The cooling sensation that I'd come to expect when we were touching wasn't as evident as it usually was, but the heat did seem to lessen enough that I felt like I could think again.

"I can't control what Charlie does," I whispered in her ear as I ran my hands over anywhere I could reach.

Getting my hands on her did more than treat the heat's symptoms. It cleared the fog in my head enough that I was actually able to speak rationally.

"Yes, you can," she replied, her hands just as busy. I shuddered as her nails dragged down my back.

"It's unfair of you to ask it of me," I countered, lifting my head until we were nose to nose. "He's my brother-in-law. The last link to my baby brother, and you're asking me to potentially sever that connection because you're afraid."

"Of course I'm afraid." She glared.

"He'll be with my father."

"That doesn't fill me with comfort."

"It should."

"Well, it doesn't."

"Baby," I said softly. "You realize that Charlie is immortal, right?"

She scoffed.

"Nothing will happen to him."

"He could get hurt."

"He'll heal."

"He isn't built for this," she whispered. "He'll...he'll be scared, and I won't be there."

Oh.

It wasn't just about the threat to Charlie's physical safety. I should've seen it sooner. Beneath all the anger and the threats, I should've paid attention to the fear in Lucy's eyes. She wasn't just concerned that her brother could die, which was a very thin possibility. She was terrified to let him face it all on his own when she'd spent her life as the protective barrier between her brother and the world.

"He knows that we'll be there," I assured her, smoothing the damp hair from her forehead. "He won't be afraid."

"You can't promise that."

"No, I can't," I admitted. "But I can promise that we won't leave him. We'll be watching the entire time, Lucy."

"I could go too," she said hopefully as tears ran down her temples. "We could go together, and then—"

"No," I cut her off.

"You didn't even listen to me. I'd be just as safe as Charlie—"

"I said no."

"You don't get to tell me what to do."

"In this, I do."

"That's bullshit. I could be just as effective as Charlie as bait."

"No, you couldn't," I snapped.

"That's ridiculous. I—"

"You haven't completed the bond," I said flatly. "You are not immortal. You are a *human*, and your body is frail like a human's. It's out of the question."

Lucy glared at me. "Then let's complete it," she said stubbornly as she jerked her chin up. "Go ahead. Do it."

I stared at her neck for a moment before I snapped out of it.

"Lucy—"

"Do it," she ordered. "Come on. It's what you wanted, right?"

I tore myself from the bed.

"No," she groaned, reaching for me as I stepped out of reach.

"Not that way," I ground out.

"Oh, so now you have conditions?" she complained as she rose to her knees.

"Even if we completed it now, we have no way of knowing how soon your immortality would begin." I ran my fingers through my hair in frustration. It was almost impossible to keep myself from climbing back onto the bed and taking her up on the offer, even though I knew it wouldn't change the fact that she would have to stay behind.

"But, it could, right?" she argued. "It's worth a shot."

"You're not going with Charlie."

"Fuck you," she cried, throwing a pillow at me. It bounced off my chest and fell to the floor.

"Every moment you prolong this, is another moment that Finau's mate is being—" I snapped my mouth shut. No.

"Being what?" she asked.

"She's in danger," I ground out.

"No, that's not what you said." She climbed off the bed. "She's being *what*, Ambrose?"

"Tortured," I replied. The vision of my brother's body in the command morgue flashed through my mind. The dips in the sheet where they'd severed his legs and arms and head. I swallowed back the bile in my throat.

"What?" Lucy whispered.

"You're not fucking going," I roared, taking a step back when she reached for me. "That's the end of it."

She stared at me in frustration, her hands in fists down by her sides.

"Fine," she replied, still glaring. "Fine, I won't go."

I dipped my chin in a nod. Good.

"Could you at least hold me?" she gritted out as her teeth began to chatter.

Fuck.

I reached for her, and she launched herself toward me so forcefully that I fell back a step when I caught her. We didn't make it back to the bed. Instead, I lowered myself to the floor and leaned back against the wall. She straddled my lap and tucked her face into my neck as I ran my hands up and down her spine.

The red blotches were slowly disappearing, but her skin was still hot to the touch.

"You'll look after him?" she asked softly.

"Of course."

"I'm going to go crazy waiting."

Leaning down to kiss her neck, I wrapped my arms around her tightly. "You'll be asleep."

Her body stiffened. "What?"

"In order for me to go," I explained, holding her still as she tried to rear backward. "Aunt Alice will give you something to sleep."

We weren't even sure it would work, but we were willing to try.

"I don't understand," Lucy said slowly.

"She thinks that if you're asleep, I may be able to go with them as long as I'm back within a few hours."

"The heat," she replied.

I nodded. We needed every one of us for the plan to work the way we were hoping, but my ability to leave Lucy behind was in question. Without the bond being completed, we were tethered to each other. It would be as painful or more painful than what we'd just experienced. I hoped—we hoped—that I'd be able to manage it, but I wasn't willing to subject Lucy to that kind of agony. If Alice gave her something to knock her out, she was confident that Lucy's symptoms would be manageable, and in turn, so would mine. She hadn't had enough time to test it, but she believed that a Vampire's symptoms were a direct reflection of their mate's. I wasn't sure how it all worked, but I trusted Alice.

She was going to give the same thing to Reese. Her and Beau's bond had been completed so recently that they didn't want her symptoms to flare back up either. She'd gone through the ringer when Beau had flown to Montana to get us.

"Do you think it will work?" Lucy asked, her hands sliding up into my hair.

"If it doesn't, I won't go."

"You have to." Her grip tightened. "You have to go if Charlie's going."

"Okay," I replied. There was no use in arguing, especially now that she'd finally accepted that Charlie was going through with it. Without asking, I knew that Lucy would rather be in pain than let Charlie put himself in danger without someone she trusted watching his back. And I was the only one she trusted.

Turning my head, I pressed my lips against her temple.

She trusted me. That was something. She wanted me. That was something too. We were getting somewhere.

She leaned back so that we were face-to-face. "Sorry I told your dad to fuck off."

My lips twitched as I held back a smile.

"And that I threatened to burn your house down."

"Forgiven," I replied.

"That easy, huh?"

"That easy."

"Do we need to get back downstairs?" she asked, resettling herself on my lap, like she couldn't help herself. Her core nestled more snugly against me, and I nearly groaned. The erection I'd been walking around with for days throbbed.

"We can take a few more minutes."

She nodded. "It got really bad," she whispered, like she was telling me a secret. "The minute you walked out the door, it got really, really bad."

"I know," I whispered back, wrapping my hand around the side of her throat so I could run my thumb along her jaw.

"Where did you go?"

"Just outside. I wasn't far."

"It felt really far."

"Would you really walk away?" I asked. The question felt like pulling the pin on a hand grenade, but I couldn't stop myself from asking.

Lucy was silent for a long moment.

"I'm not sure I physically could," she confessed.

That didn't reassure me.

"Would you really want to?"

"No," she breathed, dropping her head until our foreheads touched. "No, I don't think so."

Finally, some fucking progress.

"What's your favorite memory?" I asked her, running my fingers through her hair. It was so silky that it slid easily through my fingers, even as the waves wrapped around them.

"My favorite memory?" she asked, frowning. "Why?"

"Because we don't know enough about each other."

Lucy rolled her eyes. "Um..." She looked up at the ceiling. "Maybe when Charlie got his first bike, and he was so excited because he climbed on it and just took off. He didn't need my dad to teach him or anything. He just pushed off with his feet and figured out the pedals on the fly. It was so cool."

"Yeah?"

"Or maybe the first time he trained with me. He was so proud of how hard he'd hit the bag that he turned to make sure I was looking, and the bag swung back and knocked him onto his face." She chuckled. "Pride goeth before the fall—literally. What's yours?"

It was very telling that Lucy's favorite memories were of Charlie.

"The last time my brothers and I were here together," I said after a moment. "We sat out back half the night talking around the fire. That's a good memory."

"I thought you'd say something cheesy, like the moment you saw me," she joked, the tension at the sides of her eyes relaxing a little.

"That's in the top ten."

"Oh no. You can't backpedal now."

"Top ten is good," I argued. "I've lived a long time, you know."

"I'm aware of that, yes."

"Top five, even," I joked, staring into her warm brown eyes. "I'll never forget it."

"*This* is my mate?" she said, deepening her voice in mock disgust. "Well, all right. I supposed she'll do."

I laughed at the absurdity of it. "More like, holy Gods, there she is."

"Oh, I'm *so* sure."

"And then it was, I wonder how long before she'll let me see her naked."

"Not long, apparently."

"And then I thought, I'll never be alone again, and my mate is the most beautiful woman I've ever seen."

"Now I know you're full of shit."

"Why?"

"I'm far from the most beautiful woman you've ever seen," she scoffed. "I mean, yeah, I'm all right, but I'd never win a beauty contest."

"Why the fuck do you say that?"

"It's just the truth."

"It isn't," I insisted. How the hell had she made it to her age without realizing what a knockout she was? "I'm not exaggerating. You're the most gorgeous woman I've ever laid eyes on. There isn't a single thing I don't like."

"Beauty is in the eye of the beholder, I guess," she replied lightly. "I'm not complaining. Actually, you know what? You're right. I am the most beautiful woman you've ever seen. Worship me." She jokingly arched her back and stretched her arms out at her sides, making her breasts strain against the lacy bra she was wearing.

"I plan on it," I assured her, dropping a kiss between her breasts.

"Shit, that feels good." She sighed, reaching for my head so she could hold me in place. "More."

I traced my tongue along the outline of her bra, reveling in the salty taste of her skin. I wanted to consume her. I wished we had hours to play, not minutes, but eventually I lifted my head.

"We have to go back downstairs, don't we?" she asked.

"They've given us enough time."

Lucy nodded and got to her feet. "The heat isn't as bad as it was, but it still hurts."

"I know." It felt manageable for the moment, but just barely. I didn't know how we could maintain the distance between us for any length of time. I knew she was hoping that things would take a more human course, slow and steady, but I didn't think either of us would be able to hold out.

"It's like an empty feeling," Lucy said as she walked over to put her shirt back on. "Is it like that for you too?"

"Not exactly." I'd left my shirt on the stairs and had to get a clean one out of the dresser. Shit, my hands were still grimy from when I'd been outside. I went in to wash them, and Lucy followed me to the bathroom door. "It's more like pressure in my chest," I explained, meeting her eyes in the mirror. "Hot pressure."

Lucy pressed her lips together and nodded thoughtfully. "We're delaying the inevitable, aren't we?"

"Yes," I confirmed. "But there's nothing wrong with that. We have time."

"Except we don't," she argued as I took her hand, and we headed for the main part of the house. "Because even if you find that guy's mate, it won't be the end, right?"

"Probably not."

"And you're half useless while you're dealing with the mating bond."

"The symptoms won't just magically disappear once we cement it," I explained as we moved down the stairs.

"I'm not sure if it matters whether we have or not, I'll still be distracted."

"You know that's not true," Alice argued from the couch in the living room. I'd known she was there from the sound of her knitting needles clicking together before I'd even seen her. "Without the mating cemented, you're not truly immortal."

"What does that mean exactly?" Lucy asked, glancing between us.

"He's hard to kill now," Alice said, looking up from her project. "Not impossible."

"It wouldn't be impossible to kill me even after my immortality begins," I argued. "Someone could take my head."

"Take your—" Lucy's mouth snapped shut as she went a little green. Then the blood drained from her face. "Zeke."

"Vampires can survive a lot of abuse," Alice said, setting down her needles and yarn. "But before they're mated, they can still be killed by any number of things."

Lucy's hand tightened around mine until her nails dug into my skin.

"That's enough," I ordered Alice.

"Keeping her in the dark won't do you any favors," she shot back as she walked away.

"How does this work?" Lucy asked, shaking her head. "I think I missed something."

"When mates cement the bond, *both* become immortal. Before that, the same things that would kill humans could kill Vampires if the injury was severe enough."

"But I thought..." Her words trailed off. "I guess I didn't really think."

"It's a discussion for another day," I told her, lifting her hand to my lips. "Let's go find the boys."

We found my father and brothers sitting around the table with Charlie and Uncle Sven. Finau was missing.

"Did you tame the beast?" Chance joked as we entered the room.

"Fuck off and die, Chance," Lucy said easily. "Charlie, can we talk for a minute?"

Charles stood and followed her outside. I watched through the glass doors as she led him across the yard and stopped beneath the old oak tree out back.

"Have you finalized anything?" I asked, staying on my feet. Where the hell was Finau?

"I'll take Charlie to Goodman's tonight after dinner," my dad began. "That puts us a few hours behind schedule, which is a problem, but it can't be helped if we want you with us. Lucy needs more time to settle if the medicine is going to work."

I nodded.

"You're sure that you don't want to stay back?"

"If I can make it, I'm going," I confirmed.

"My mate already placed Charlie's tracker under his collarbone," Sven noted. "I'll monitor it from here while I keep watch over the women."

"You won't be the only one here." It was half order, half question.

My father shook his head. "We've got six on the perimeter. When we leave, two will move closer to the house."

"The four of us and Finau will monitor the situation from the ground," Danny announced. "We'll stay on Charlie for as long as we can, keep in close contact with Sven, and use his tracker if they slip past us."

"We don't move in until they get him to wherever they're staged," Chance said firmly. "Or the whole mission goes to shit."

"We all agreed on that?" Beau asked, looking around to meet each of our gazes. "Because things may get messy before that."

My lower stomach twisted with worry, but I nodded. "As long as it doesn't look like Charlie's about to lose his head."

"He says he can take it," Danny said doubtfully. "I don't like this."

"It's the best we have in the limited time we were given," my father reminded us.

"Matthias and Josiah will be there to take care of Dad so we can follow Charlie," Beau added.

"You think that'll be needed?" I asked my dad.

"They'll bring in enough to overpower me. We'll need to make them believe they have."

"Don't—"

"I won't let anyone near my neck," he assured me drolly. "I'm coming home to my mate tonight."

CHAPTER 9
LUCY

"**W**hy aren't you nervous?" I asked Charlie as my knee began to bounce. Ambrose had left us only a few minutes earlier, and I was already having a hard time focusing on my brother. I'd been adamant that Charlie hang out with me until dinner, but my body's response to the distance between me and the Vampire was already beginning to annoy me.

"There isn't anything they could do to me that would be more painful than losing Zeke," Charlie replied, his fingers drumming on the arm of the couch.

"Don't underestimate these people, Charles," I ordered.

"I'm not," he assured me. "But I'll have the Bouchers watching the whole time. They'd never let anything happen to me."

The words coming out of his mouth should've been comforting to some degree, but something in his tone was wrong.

"What was that earlier?" he asked before I could grill him. "The mating heat?"

"On steroids," I confirmed.

"It never happened like that for me," he mused.

"Ambrose tells me it's different for everyone," I mumbled. "I think it's getting worse because we didn't immediately fall into bed."

"You haven't—"

"Don't ask, and I won't answer that question, you weirdo," I warned.

Charlie smiled. "Probably for the best. So what are you waiting for?"

"I barely know him."

"You know him better than I knew Zeke."

"That's not saying much. Zeke smiled at you, and you were like, lead me anywhere, and let me adore you."

"You're not far off," Charlie agreed. "Best thing I ever did."

"Still?" I asked curiously. "Even now?"

"I'd feel this a thousand times, a million times, if it meant that I had Zeke for even a day. It was worth it."

"See, I don't know if I feel that way," I replied, leaning back on the couch. "I like Ambrose, and he's hot as hell."

Charlie laughed.

"But tying myself to him for all eternity seems like a big step."

"Do you think you'd ever leave him?" Charlie asked softly, watching me intently. "Not a knee jerk reaction because he pissed you off, but actually leave him? Can you imagine ever being without him again?"

I tried to picture it, going back to my life in Baltimore, doodling in my notebook in the mornings, going to some boring corporate job that paid well enough that I could save up for another trip, eating takeout in front of the TV alone. The thought was depressing. Somehow, in the past couple of days, I'd grown used to having Ambrose near.

Of course, I wouldn't be totally alone. Charlie would probably come with me when it was safe to go home, but for the first time in my life, I wasn't sure if his company would be enough. It was a sobering thought.

"I don't have to make the decision now," I said, waving him off.

"Alice said it will only get harder to leave. She's only known two Vampires who didn't cement the bond with their mates, but neither of them had formed relationships before they were separated."

"Alice is just full of information," I grumbled.

"Luce, I'm serious."

"So am I."

"You're both safer once the bond has been cemented," Charlie huffed, glowering at me in exasperation. "Stop stalling. You know you'll do it, eventually."

"It's very strange having your brother pushing you to have sex with someone." I shot back. "You know that, right?"

"It doesn't have anything to do with sex," Charlie argued.

"Oh, I beg to differ."

"You're such a child."

"And you're a busybody," I replied, getting to my feet. "When did that happen?"

"Go find your mate," he grumbled, waving me off.

"Don't leave without saying goodbye first, okay?"

"I'll see you at dinner."

"Promise."

"I promise I won't leave without saying goodbye," he said, making a face. "Go."

I wandered out of his room and down the stairs slowly, thinking about what he'd said. He'd made some good points. I was pretty convinced that Ambrose and I would complete the bond or cement the bond or whatever it was called—eventually. Even though rationally I thought it was too soon, I couldn't ignore that down deep, I knew that I'd never want anything else. Even if I walked away, even if it was possible, I knew with absolute certainty that I'd never find another partner that came anywhere close to making me feel the way Ambrose did. I'd never find another smile more attractive. I'd never be drawn so strongly to someone else's body. I'd never feel as comfortable as when he listened to me talk. I'd never find anyone else who understood my bond with Charlie and respected it.

He'd never once questioned when I was a mother hen. He'd never seemed exasperated or annoyed by the way I babied my older brother or made decisions based on how they would affect him. He just rolled with it, accepted it as fact, and made accommodations if needed.

If I'd found him on the street and built a relationship with him over time, I didn't honestly believe that I'd ever have reason to question whether or not we fit.

We belonged together in a way I hadn't anticipated.

As I crossed the empty living area and made my way up the stairs toward his room, I contemplated what Alice had told us. Once we'd completed the bond and become true mates, both of us would be immortal. Even if they weren't sure when the immortality began, it was possible that it would happen immediately.

He could potentially be as safe as Charlie when he went to rescue Finau's mate.

And I would never have to leave Charlie behind, another person for him to mourn forever.

By the time I opened the door to his rooms, my decision had been made.

I wasn't sure what I'd been waiting for, really. I'd

never been one to back away from something scary or unknown, but the past couple of months of keeping Charlie safe had made me infinitely more cautious of everyone and everything.

Ambrose wasn't in the little living room or bedroom, but I could hear the shower running. I followed the sound into the bathroom and paused as I caught sight of my mate.

Mate.

Mate.

I'd never felt any kind of way about the word husband, but the word mate felt like it resonated through my bones.

Ambrose was rinsing his hair, his eyes closed and his head tipped back into the spray. He looked like a frigging shampoo commercial. I let my gaze travel down his body. Scratch that, he looked like a frigging porno.

"Are you going to get in or just watch?" he asked, his eyes still closed.

"How did you know I was here?"

"I heard you open the door," he replied, tilting his head down to meet my stare.

The bedroom and bathroom doors had been left open. He'd heard when I'd come into the suite.

"I'm enjoying the view," I replied, toeing off my socks.

"Is that right?" One of his hands dropped to his waist, and my mouth watered as he gave his erection a slow, firm tug.

"I mean, another shower couldn't hurt," I mumbled. I *had* gotten really sweaty after our fight.

Ambrose grinned. He watched intently as I stripped off my clothes, his hand still absentmindedly stroking his erection. God, he was incredible. I had a hard time looking away long enough to pull my shirt off. Every inch of his body was muscular and covered in a light dusting of hair a few shades darker than the hair on his head.

I stepped into the shower slowly and closed the few steps that separated us, my skin already tingling.

"Did you need me?" he asked, pulling me into the spray. His mouth immediately went to my shoulder, his tongue swirling over the skin before he let it go with a pop.

"No," I replied as his hands swept up my sides and back down again. "I just thought I'd see what you were doing."

He hummed as his hands swept higher, teasing the bottom of my breasts.

"You were hoping to see me in the shower," he teased as he dragged his lips up my neck.

"I mean, I wasn't opposed to it." I let out a squeak as his hands cupped my breasts, his thumbs swiping firmly over my nipples.

"I'm done now. So if you're still unsure," he whispered into my ear, pinching my nipples between his fingertips. "I need to get out of here before things go any further."

My hands had found his biceps at some point, and almost involuntarily they dug in like I could hold him in place. He was still trying to give me the time I'd asked for. Even now, even when I'd stripped and walked into his shower, he was still trying to respect my wishes.

"I'm not unsure," I replied as his lips slid down my jaw.

He lifted his head to look me in the eyes. His blue irises were so vivid they burned, and his pupils were wide with arousal.

"Are you *sure*?"

The anxiety about our connection disappeared like a puff of smoke. There were plenty of things left to be afraid of—whoever was hunting Vampire mates and what they would do when the Bouchers caught up to them, my brother's ability to ever be happy again, starting an entirely new life in Oregon—but I wasn't afraid of this. Of him.

"I'm sure," I confirmed.

I expected him to sweep me into his arms and fuck me against the wall or something—I'd been kind of counting on it—but he didn't. Instead, he did something even more diabolical.

He frigging bathed me. His soapy hands traveled every centimeter of my body, from my hair to the spaces between my toes. By the time the water rinsed away the last of the soap, we were both breathing heavily, and the heat beneath my skin pulsed in steady waves.

"Come on," he ordered softly, leading me out of the shower. His hands were never still as he toweled me off and then himself, and mine weren't either. I traced his trapezius muscles, ran my fingers over the tattoo lines on his torso, wrapped my hand around his erection, and explored his testicles and the space behind them.

I wanted to know his body as intimately as I knew my own, discover every secret.

"Gods," he sighed, tipping his head back as I ran my finger over the head of his shaft, circling the opening.

We barely made it into the bedroom before his mouth met mine, his tongue sliding inside like it had always meant to be there. I gripped his ass and cupped his testicles in my hand as his fingers pinched my nipples hard and then soothed them with the lightest of touches. The insides of my thighs grew wet as he ushered me to the bed, groaning into my mouth.

"What do you want?" he asked, pushing me onto my back, my legs dangling off the side of the bed.

"Your mouth," I replied quickly. I was past the point of embarrassment or self-consciousness. He'd seen and touched every piece of my body already.

Mewling, I arched off the bed as he took my nipple between his teeth and bit down just hard enough to sting before sucking it into his mouth, thrumming and laving it with his tongue. It was incredible. His hand moved up to pinch and rub and soothe my other nipple until I was writhing, reaching for any piece of him I could grab hold of.

When his mouth trailed down my body, I pulled my heels to the edge of the bed and let my knees fall wide, reaching for his head.

I gripped his hair in my hands, and he chuckled as he leaned down to delicately kiss my clit and blow gently against the heated skin.

"More," I ordered, lifting toward him.

I was past the point of teasing. Past the point of waiting.

I gasped and cried out when he stopped messing around and pressed his mouth against me, his tongue thrashing at my clit until I was on the edge and then thrusting inside me. I ground against his mouth as I keened, letting out a sob of relief when he moved to my clit again.

He did it over and over until I was ready to tackle him and ride his face until I came. My nails dug into his shoulders and scratched along the back of his neck as I tried to hold him in place.

Little black dots danced in my vision, and my throat ached from my scream when I came. I shook with aftershocks as his tongue pressed steadily against my clit and two fingers, then three slid inside me.

"Oh my god," I rasped when he finally lifted his head. His fingers left me with a slow curl.

Ambrose swiped his hand over his mouth and smiled softly.

"You taste so good," he said so quietly I barely heard him.

I pushed myself up and scooted away from him before moving to my hands and knees. He watched me intently as I got closer, his hands reaching for my back, then curving around my ribs.

He was salty when I licked the tip of his erection and then sucked him into my mouth. A past relationship had cured me of interest in blow jobs years before, but I wanted Ambrose in my mouth. I wanted to taste him and feel him against my tongue and the back of my throat. Any associations I'd connected to the act weren't applicable with my mate. I wanted to know him in any and every way I could.

One of his hands tangled in my hair as the other slid down my back and between the cheeks of my ass, gently playing over the skin there until I squirmed.

It wasn't like any other experience I'd ever had. I needed more, more, more. I couldn't imagine a way that we could get close enough. I burned, addicted to him and what we were doing. My clit throbbed.

"Come here," he ordered gruffly as he tugged me away by my hair.

As I kneeled on the edge of the bed and met his eyes, my hair still tangled in his fist, I'd never felt more myself. Powerful even.

"May I have you?" he asked, tipping my head back until our lips were nearly touching.

The words were heavy. Weighted. And though I wasn't sure why, I knew they were important.

"Yes," I rasped.

He groaned as his lips crashed down on mine, and he crawled onto the bed with me in his arms. I wrapped my legs around his waist and mewled when his erection tapped against my swollen clit. Our chests brushed, the hair on his abrading my nipples as he pressed me into the bed.

"Ulf," I whimpered, canting my hips as he ground against me. "Please."

Leaning up on one arm, he cupped my cheek in his palm as he shifted his hips and pressed in, the head of his erection notching just inside me before pausing.

"My mate," he whispered, his eyes crinkling at the corners as he kissed my chin.

"Almost," I whispered back as I arched my neck.

The sound that left my mouth when he rammed inside me was something between a scream and a growl, unrecognizable to my ears. When he began to move, I held his face in my shaking hands, so overwhelmed that I needed the sight of him to keep me grounded.

"You're so perfect," he grunted, his eyes on mine. "Everything I've ever wanted."

I gasped as he twisted his hips a little on the next thrust, hitting the spot inside me that made my entire body throb with pleasure. The heat was like hot lava in my veins, and every inch of flesh he touched sent out waves of cool relief, the mixture of pain and pleasure so intertwined that it was impossible to keep them separate in my mind.

Sex was fun, and it felt good, but I'd never experienced anything like Ambrose staring into my eyes as he pressed himself inside me over and over again. Calling it sex was a misnomer. What we were doing was transformative. It turned us from two single people into a single entity. I was him and he was me.

I came so hard that I didn't have the breath to make a sound, but when it faded, the arousal just crested higher, like I hadn't orgasmed at all.

I stared at Ambrose in alarm. Something was wrong.

"It's okay, baby," he said softly, pulling me with him as he leaned back until I was in his lap, our bodies still connected.

"Ambrose," I whimpered, rolling my hips as the pleasure intensified. I was getting close again already, the feeling so acute that my skin broke out in goose bumps.

"That's it, love," he said, his hand on my hip guiding the movement while he thrust in counterpoint. "That's it."

As I came a third time, his fist tugged my head back, and his teeth sank into my neck.

White noise filled my ears as I stared blindly at the ceiling, the sensation going on and on with no respite. I couldn't think or breathe even as he lifted his thumb and gripped it with his teeth. It wasn't until he shoved that same thumb into my mouth and I closed my lips around it that my eyes fell closed, and I sucked.

My pussy clenched as a new wave rushed over me, and by the time he lowered me gently back to the bed, I was sobbing with relief and exhaustion.

The mating heat had all but disappeared except for a cozy sense of warmth.

Ambrose kissed my mouth. My cheeks. My temples and forehead. My nose.

"That was..." I sniffled and searched for a word that would fit.

"Beautiful," he whispered against my skin. "Fucking beautiful."

"It was...*a lot*," I replied, raising my tired arms to run them through his hair. "But beautiful works too."

"I'm yours," he said as his lips drifted lazily down my neck and over my collarbone. "And you're mine."

The certainty of that sunk in to the tiny places inside me—the ones I kept hidden and refused to look at—like a balm.

He was still hard inside me and eventually began to move again. The next round was languid and intimate, our gazes never veering from each other's faces as the pleasure built, and we came again. It wasn't as overwhelming as the first time, but almost better for it.

Once the urgency was gone and the bond between us pulled taut like an unbreakable steel wire, we'd made love.

It was hard to get dressed afterward and nearly impossible to follow Ambrose down the stairs to where the family was gathered in the kitchen.

I'd accepted that Charlie was going to go on this rescue mission, not because I'd been convinced of its merits or because I thought that he needed to do it. No, it was more basic than that. I'd finally realized that I didn't have a choice. He was going to go whether I liked it or not. I couldn't stop it, and I couldn't expect Ambrose to stop it either. That wasn't his responsibility.

I was woman enough to realize I'd been outmaneuvered.

Now that we'd completed the bond, it occurred to me that I was potentially as immortal as Charlie, but I didn't even mention it. Logically, I knew that bringing in two inexperienced humans was an even worse idea than bringing in just one. If I was there, the Bouchers' focus would be split between us. I'd only make Charlie less safe.

Dinner was a pretty quiet affair, and I could barely

choke down my food. Everyone around the table was distracted. Reese sat with her head resting on Beau's shoulder, their chairs pulled so close together that there was no space between them. Alice and Matilda talked about random things, cool as cucumbers. They didn't seem concerned at all, and that gave me a weird kind of hope.

"You have to eat, baby," Ambrose chastised, nodding at my plate.

"I'm not very hungry."

Ambrose let out a small sigh and nodded, leaning over to brush his lips against my temple.

Fifteen minutes later, I was gripping his hand as he led me to a room I hadn't even known existed. I paused at the threshold.

It looked like a hospital room. There were two uncomfortable-looking beds in the center, with IV poles and machines set next to them. A large stainless-steel sink hung from the wall in the corner. Shelves and cabinets of supplies lined the walls.

Alice strode past us and went directly to the sink, washing her hands brusquely with a little scrub brush while she hummed under her breath.

Reese and Beau came in behind us. He was murmuring to her soothingly, but I couldn't understand what he was saying. She didn't want to be here.

I looked at Ambrose as Reese assured Beau that she didn't need to be sedated. She argued that she could hack it. That she'd rather just wait in a different room, fully conscious. Ambrose shook his head at me and led me over to one of the beds.

"You can climb up," Alice said, not unkindly. "If you'd be more comfortable, we have gowns to change into."

I looked down at my leggings and T-shirt. I'd picked

an old Rolling Stones shirt that was so thin it was almost transparent. "No, I'm good in this."

Now that the moment was fast approaching, I felt myself beginning to panic. My hand tightened around Ambrose's. He was going to leave. He and Charlie were going to leave, and no one knew what would happen. I would be stuck there, unconscious, and I wouldn't have any idea if something went wrong.

"Breathe," Ambrose whispered, turning to cup my cheek in his hand. "If it doesn't work, it doesn't work. We'll adjust, and I'll stay close."

My mind spun with horrific scenarios, so many that I couldn't even articulate that I wasn't afraid for myself or what the heat would do when we were separated. That was so far down the list that it didn't even matter.

A thump sounded behind me, and I jolted, spinning to look.

Beau physically lifted Reese and dropped her onto the other bed while she cursed at him.

"Last time she was in here," Ambrose explained as he gently helped me onto the bed. "Beau was hurt and having surgery. She's just dealing with some bad memories."

"Beau was hurt?"

Ambrose nodded as I lay back. He carefully covered me with the thin blanket, smoothing out any wrinkles.

I tensed as Alice walked between the beds and started messing with the machines.

"She knows what she's doing," Ambrose said, bracing his arm on the bed as he leaned close. "Alice has been taking care of Vampires and their mates for more than a century."

I glanced over my shoulder at her, but she wasn't paying any attention to us.

"You'll take care of him?" I asked, wrapping my hand around his wrist.

"You know I will."

"And you'll be careful," I ordered.

"Of course."

"I think this was maybe a bad idea," I said as my heart started pounding so hard I could feel it at the base of my throat.

"It's not," he assured me. "By the time you wake up, we'll be home."

Alice carried over a little kidney-shaped bowl of supplies and perched on the bed opposite Ambrose.

My hands started to tremble.

"I'm just going to get your IV started," she said, smiling. "That's how I'll administer the sedation. I'll be here the whole time, monitoring you and Reese. All right?"

"Okay," I replied, letting her lift my arm with blue-gloved hands.

"I'm thinking," Ambrose said softly, distracting me from the little wet wipe that Alice scrubbed along the top of my hand. "When I get home, we should hole up in my rooms and spend a few days in bed."

"I'm not opposed to the idea," I replied, wincing at the sting of the needle.

Ambrose smoothed my hair back from my face gently. "It's going to be fine, baby."

"This is just saline," Alice said, patting my arm as she stood. "I'll add the sedation in a few minutes once I'm done with Reese."

I let out a long breath.

"It should only be a few hours," Ambrose said.

Both of our heads turned as Charlie came rushing into the room.

"Oh good," my brother said with a relieved smile. "I'm not too late."

"For what?" I asked as he walked toward my bed. "I'm not going anywhere."

"Har har, you're hilarious," he replied with a smile. "I brought you a lovey."

My throat tightened as he flicked out Zeke's quilt and tossed it over me. The scent of Zeke—and my brother—drifted through the room, masking the smell of antiseptic.

"You didn't have to do that," I said, my hand going immediately to one of the little embroidered scars.

"I know," he said as he stood next to the bed, straightening the quilt. "But I thought—I don't know—that it would be comforting or something."

"It is," I choked out, nodding. "Thank you."

"I'll be fine," he said with a little wave of dismissal. "And we'll get Finau's mate back, which is the most important thing."

"*You're* the most important thing," I countered.

Charlie glanced at Ambrose meaningfully.

"Yeah, him too," I grumbled jokingly.

The truth was, I was worried for them both, but less for Ambrose. I knew all about his history because Zeke hadn't skimped on the details while talking about his brothers. Ambrose had been successfully putting himself into dangerous situations and then getting himself out for a very long time. This was just another Tuesday for him.

"Okay, I think we're ready," Alice said. "Say your good nights. This shouldn't take long."

I met her eyes, and something like understanding passed between us.

Charlie immediately leaned down to give me a hug as I stared wide-eyed at Ambrose.

"Sleep good," Charlie said. "Love you."

"Love you too. Don't be an idiot."

He laughed as he leaned back up.

Ambrose moved in next, brushing his lips over mine once, twice, then pressing them more firmly. I closed my eyes and inhaled the scent of his skin as my eyes watered.

It would be fine. They were going to be fine. They were sedating me so that Ambrose could help Charlie. It was a good thing. I was doing my part, even though it felt like the opposite.

"I'll be here when you wake up," Ambrose promised, still leaning close. "Relax."

My eyelids grew heavy.

"Be careful," I ordered, forcing them as wide as I could.

"I will."

I pressed harder against the quilt, trying to ground myself, trying to keep myself awake. I had other things to say, but I couldn't think of them, and then it was too late. I couldn't keep my eyes open anymore. As they slid shut, I felt Ambrose's lips against my forehead.

That's when I felt the strange lump beneath the embroidery. Something was inside the quilt. My fingernail caught on the edge of it, and I opened my mouth to tell someone.

Then nothing.

Nothing.

Nothing.

The room grew warmer.

Warmer.

Hot.

Hot.

HOT.

Somehow, in the suffocating darkness, I remembered that I had to stay silent as I burned. There was a reason for

the heat. The little lump pressed against my fingernail. I
focused on that as I burned from the inside out.

CHAPTER 10
AMBROSE

"It's time," my father said, standing in the doorway.

Lucy was out. It had taken less than a minute for her to fall asleep. I ran my hand down her arm and rose to my feet, following Charlie and Beau out of the room as Alice put little oxygen cannulas in the women's noses.

Now it was time to see if the sedation had worked.

Danny and Chance were fully prepared when we walked into the armory, and they immediately moved to help Beau and me get ready.

I changed into black trousers and a long-sleeved black shirt, waiting for the familiar warmth as the minutes passed. Chance handed me a vest and helped me with the straps. He tossed me a thigh holster to put on. Then a shoulder holster. Extra magazines that I stuffed into my pockets. A small med kit.

I moved over to the wall and chose my pistols and rifle. Each of us had our own preferences, and there were already open spaces where Chance, Danny, my father, and

Sven's choices had been. Grabbing more magazines, I loaded them all and put them in my holsters.

My skin itched, but it was the lack of heat that was starting to bother me.

We left the armory and strode through the house, stopping briefly to kiss our mother.

Fifteen minutes since I'd seen Lucy, and there was still nothing. I forced myself not to run back and check on her again. She was fine. Alice was with her. If something had gone wrong, she would've already come to get me. The lack of heat meant that the sedation was working, nothing more.

In the garage, we paused with my father and Charlie. Finau stood fidgeting by the cars. He was already dressed and armed to the teeth.

"Don't get yourself killed," Chance ordered, pulling my dad into a backslapping hug. "We'll be close."

"Not too close," my father ordered. "Or we're fucked."

"We've been doing this a minute, old man," Chance countered as he let go.

Danny was next.

I turned toward Charlie. "There's no way for you to do anything wrong," I told him as he stood, pale and tense. "They'll take you. Don't try to get back to my dad. He'll be down by the time they've got you, all right? The sooner you leave with them, the faster Matthias and Josiah can get to him."

"We've gone over this," he replied, nodding. "I remember."

"It's worth going over again," I said, reaching out to squeeze his shoulder. "It'll be easy to forget when you're in the thick of it. You're going to want to help him, but the best thing for you to do is leave."

"I got it," he said, glancing toward my father.

"We'll never be far," I told Charlie, bringing his attention back to me. "Even if it feels like it. You won't see us, but we're there, okay?"

Charlie nodded.

"They won't expect much fight from you—"

He scoffed.

"That's a good thing," I assured him. "The more you fight them, the greater chance of you getting hurt before we find Finau's mate."

"She has a name," Charlie said, his chin rising a little. "It's Evelina."

"Evelina," I conceded. "Keep yourself safe until we find Evelina. Cower if you have to."

Charlie looked away, embarrassed, and I shoved his chest. He looked at me in surprise.

"You're playing a role," I told him firmly. "They think you're weak? Let them. Play into that."

"We know the truth," my father said gruffly, with a nod at Charlie.

My stomach was in knots as we parted.

Chance and Beau climbed into one car with Finau, Danny, and I climbed into another, and my father and Charlie climbed into a third. Uncle Sven stood outside the garage as we pulled away, watching us go.

We were counting on a whole hell of a lot with the plan we'd thrown together, like the assumption that the fuckers were still in town. That they'd go for Charlie. That they'd bring him to wherever they were holding Finau's mate. That she wasn't already dead.

It was all we had.

We didn't have enough information. Vague theories about who was in charge and why they were targeting mates were all we had to go on. Searching for Charlie had taken priority above researching, and we were feeling it now.

"How is it?" Danny asked as we took the long way to town.

"Fine," I replied. The heat was barely flickering under my skin.

"She's okay," he said, his eyes on the road. He reached up to tap his earpiece. "We'd know if she wasn't."

"Yeah."

We rode in silence until we'd hit our mark and parked the car two blocks from the grocery store. Holding my coat closed, I followed Danny into a pawn shop owned by the father-in-law of one of the Vampires currently patrolling our property.

"Through the back, first door on the right," the man said quietly as we moved through the store. He didn't look up from what he was doing. "End of the hallway is the exit door."

"I've got cameras," Matthias announced in my earpiece. "Erik and Charlie just parked."

Danny and I hurried toward the exit door, dropping our long coats in the hallway. Just outside was a fire escape, and we climbed until we reached the roof. The sun had almost set as we crouched and made our way to the edge.

Across the street, my father was talking to Charlie as they walked toward the store. Beau had warned them not to park too close to the front doors. We needed them to be visible for as long as possible before they went inside.

"Inside," Josiah announced.

"We're in place," Danny replied.

"In place," Beau confirmed.

Then came the worst part. The waiting.

185

Goodman's was an old mom and pop that had been around almost as long as we'd lived in Oregon. A larger grocery chain had bought them out about twenty years before, but they'd known that the community was loyal, so they'd left the name and the employees alone while they stocked the shelves with their merchandise. It was one of those rare takeovers that had worked out for everyone.

Tonight, it was working out well for us. Few people knew that the manager of the store's sister was a Vampire's mate, and that worked to our advantage. As it grew later and people came outside with their groceries, we watched as the parking lot emptied out but for a few cars.

"Employees are going out the back," Josiah confirmed.

We still had half an hour before the store closed, and we couldn't control all the variables, but it was a small town. Most people wouldn't try to slide in right before closing because they knew that meant the employees would have to stay later. It was a courtesy that worked in our favor and made the gray minivan that parked right out front even more conspicuous.

"Hold," Danny said as we stared at the van.

It could've been a mother with a last-minute need. We waited.

Two men climbed out of the front of the van. Three out of the back.

"We're a go," Matthias announced.

"We've got another," Beau warned. "Hold."

Another car pulled into the lot and parked a few rows away from the van. Three more men climbed out.

All humans. Thank the Gods.

"We've got eight," Chance announced.

Danny scoffed and shot me a look. "Only eight?"

I smiled grimly. If we hadn't planned for this, eight men would've ended up in the county morgue. My father was going to be insulted that they'd only sent that many.

I stared at the front of the store where the men had disappeared. If we were really fucking lucky, they wouldn't notice that there wasn't anyone at the check stands and my father and brother-in-law were the only people inside.

"Moving to cameras inside," Matthias announced. "We have visual."

Absentmindedly, I rubbed at the back of my neck. It was hot to the touch as my body started to recognize that I'd been away from my mate for too fucking long.

"Engagement," Josiah announced grimly. "One, no, two down. Erik's a fucking beast."

"Where is Charles?" Beau demanded.

"In the meat section," Matthias answered. "He's crouched behind the refrigeration section in the middle. Fuck, there are mirrors. Worst possible hiding place."

"They want him," Chance replied grimly. "It's fine if they know where he is—"

"Erik's been hit," Josiah interrupted. "Another bogey down."

"He doesn't know how many there are," I said tightly. It was one of the flaws. He wouldn't know how many they'd sent, but he had to make it look believable when they were able to take Charles. He could kill some of them —but not all. He was playing a guessing game.

"Five left," Danny replied.

"Erik's hit again," Josiah announced.

"They're converging," Matthias said quietly.

"Another down."

"Four," I murmured to myself.

"Erik is down," Josiah said.

My stomach jolted like I'd been punched, but I held myself perfectly still. This was the plan.

"Steady," Matthias ordered sharply through the earpieces.

"Another down," Josiah announced.

"Tell us what the fuck is happening," Chance ordered angrily.

"Humans are making their way over. Erik is fully down. He's saying something to Charlie—no audio. Charlie is shaking his head," Josiah replied. "Contact! One on Charlie, two on Erik. Motherfuckers. Kicking Erik. Charlie's up."

My pulse pounded.

"Knife," Matthias said grimly.

I braced my hands on the edge of the roof.

"They're going for Erik. Who's closest?" Josiah said tightly.

"Wait," Matthias said. "Charlie just knocked one of them out. The kid can fight. Why did no one tell us the kid could fight?"

"Lost interest in Erik," Josiah announced. "His two are too busy trying to contain Charles."

The training. Charles had downplayed how much he'd learned. I felt a smile pull at the corners of my mouth.

"He's fighting like hell," Matthias said, his voice filled with respect. "Shit. He's down."

"They're bringing him out," Josiah announced.

"Dad?" Danny asked.

"Left him," Matthias replied. "Too busy carrying Charlie and the human he knocked out."

I hesitated, wanting to get a look at Charlie as they carried him out, but I knew it would be a mistake. We needed every second if we were going to be on the ground in time to follow them. I had to trust Matthias and Josiah's account of what had happened.

If he still had his head, Charlie would be fine.

Following Danny, we jumped off the roof, landing on top of a trailer. From there, it was easy to hop down to the tractor unit and then to the ground. We hit the car at a run, and I'd barely shut the door before the engine was running, and Danny pulled it onto the street.

We idled at the intersection.

"Charlie's in the van," Matthias announced. "Repeat: Charlie is in the van. They're ditching the car."

Danny turned on his blinker as the van passed us and then pulled easily onto the street behind him.

"You think he's still out?" I asked, watching the back window. The only people visible were the driver and passenger.

"Hopefully, he's playing possum," Danny replied.

"We've got Erik," Josiah said through the comms. "Getting him to Alice. We'll call in a clean-up on the way."

"How is he?" Beau asked.

"He'll be fine. Two chest, one stomach. It'll hurt like a bitch when he wakes up, though."

Knowing that our father was fine and out of danger, it was easier to focus on what we were doing. We followed the van onto the freeway and fifteen minutes later took an exit as Beau and Chance took our place.

Heat pulsed beneath my skin, but it wasn't as distracting as usual. Instead, it was oddly comforting.

"Charlie just put his hand up to the back window," Chance said, laughter in his voice.

"He flipped us off." Beau snickered.

Charlie was awake and okay. That was a relief.

Danny and I hopped out of the car we'd been driving and into a new one that Uncle Sven had stashed that morning. He'd left the night before and spent all night parking them in different directions. I wasn't sure how he'd known where to put them. Something about possible routes and the odds of which would be used. Minutes later, we were pulling onto the freeway ahead of the van carrying Charlie.

Keeping his eyes forward, Danny puttered along in the slow lane, letting them pass us. Two exits later, Chance, Beau, and Finau disappeared.

Danny sped up and moved to the middle lane, gradually catching up to the van.

There were enough cars on the road that another pair of headlights was nothing to think about, and we settled in. Thirty minutes later, the boys joined us again in a different SUV, and we took the next exit. This time, we just circled around and got back onto the freeway without switching cars. It was dark enough that they wouldn't have noticed us with the others between us.

"Really hoping they're not taking us across the state," Danny said after we'd been on the road for an hour.

"Looks like you're getting your wish," I replied, nodding at the van as it exited the freeway.

Uncle Sven's voice came through the earpieces as we took the next exit. He was monitoring Charlie's tracker. Following his directions, we made our way through the town. The goal was to follow close enough that we wouldn't lose them, but far enough away that they never saw us. It was an intricate dance that included pulling over more than once so we wouldn't cross paths.

Eventually, he announced that the van had pulled into a garage.

I cracked my neck from side to side as we parked one block over and climbed out of the car.

"Almost done," Danny said quietly, slapping me on the back.

"Lucy's going to be pissed if anyone messes up my pretty face," I joked. The heat inside me flared, and I sucked in a breath. It still wasn't bad, and if mine wasn't bad, hers shouldn't be either. Uncle Sven would've let us know if there was anything happening at the house.

"She doesn't care what you look like," Chance said, his voice coming from somewhere near the building to our left. "It's your dick she needs."

"For a second there, I thought you *weren't* being an asshole." Beau scoffed. He was further ahead than Chance, but not by much.

"Everyone quiet," I ordered.

If there were Vampires in that garage, even the smallest noise could alert them. Hopefully, we'd only be dealing with humans, but we couldn't count on it.

"Only camera is on the north side," Josiah announced. "Move to the others."

We stepped carefully as we moved between buildings. Danny and I came in from the east side while Beau, Chance, and Finau took the west and south.

"Erik is fine," he continued. "Currently being fussed over by Alice and Mattie. Woke up on the way to the house, cursing a blue streak."

The building wasn't large by anyone's standards, but it did have a pretty good-sized yard surrounded by a chain-link fence. The whole area was well lit, which was a bit annoying. We had to scale the fence and move to the darkness closest to the building one by one while Josiah kept an eye on the north door.

The windows were cloudy, but light still filtered out of

the rooms that were occupied. One in particular looked promising, and I noted where it was so I could check there when we finally got inside.

"Got the blueprints," Matthias announced in our earpieces.

When we paused, I wiped my sweaty palms on my trousers and pulled on my gloves. The long-sleeved shirt and vest were saturated, and I fought the urge to pull them away from my skin.

"South entrance goes directly into the bays, three side by side. Sixty by thirty. Two offices and a bathroom along the north wall. East and north entrances go directly into the bays, west entrance into the office."

"They've got four exit doors?" Chance asked dubiously, his voice barely audible.

"Guess they need to be able to run," Josiah replied. "Idiots."

"Set," I breathed as we reached the east door. I reached out and found the knob turned easily. I held it as we waited.

"Set," Beau whispered.

"Set," Finau said. I nearly jolted with surprise. It was the first time he'd spoken since before we'd left the house, and I hadn't even remembered that he had a comm.

"Execute," Matthias ordered.

When we entered the building, there were four men sitting off to the side, closer to the northern door and between us and the offices.

Chance opened fire from across the room before I could, and two dropped instantly. A third tried to run, and I hit him in the thigh. He tripped over a chair and fell with a crash. The van was parked in the center of the room, and I headed straight for it, even though I had a feeling no one was there. Throwing open the door, I found smeared blood, but no Charlie.

Someone had taken down the fourth man while I searched, and we cleared the rest of the room quickly. The man I'd hit in the thigh was moaning on the concrete floor, and I stopped long enough to tie a tourniquet around his thigh.

"You take this off, you'll be dead before you can call for help," I told him flatly. His face had already been mangled. His nose was broken, and one of his eyes was almost swollen shut.

He gasped and glared at me.

"Ulf," Beau called.

I rose back to my feet and met my brothers at the far edge of the room.

The bathroom was clear, and so was the office on the left. Taking a deep breath, I slammed my boot against the locked doorknob and watched in satisfaction as it flew open.

Danny stayed outside the door to make sure there weren't any surprises, while Beau, Chance, and I moved inside with precision built from years of working as a team.

Charlie was tied up on the floor. The ropes on his ankles were tied with a short lead to the ones on his wrists, and his back was curved so sharply that I winced as I hurried over to cut him free.

"How many?" I asked as I pulled the gag in his mouth down his chin.

"I saw three, but I heard four," he replied, letting out a low groan when I cut through the ropes, and the pressure on his joints disappeared.

I helped him to his feet and turned to find my brothers untying a woman on an office chair in the corner of the

NICOLE JACQUELYN

room. She was dirty and had a split lip when they pulled the gag off, but she didn't seem to be any worse off than that.

"We're getting you out of here," Chance said, crouching in front of her. "Are you hurt anywhere?"

The woman shook her head.

Her gaze went from Chance to me, then to Charlie, then to Beau.

"Sorry," Beau said as he carefully cut the ropes that held her arms to the chair. He glanced over his shoulder. "Where the fuck is Finau?"

Chance's head snapped up from looking at the ropes on her ankles.

"We haven't seen him," Charlie said, looking toward the doorway.

"Finau, check in," I ordered into the comm.

"Looks like Finau's comm is offline," Matthias reported grimly.

"What the fuck?" Chance asked as he rose to his feet.

"Sorry again," Beau said gently as he reached for the woman's legs.

"Why do you keep apologizing?" she asked hoarsely, rubbing her wrists.

I took a few steps closer to get a better look, just as Beau wrapped a hand around her ankle.

The woman didn't even flinch.

Staring, I looked her over. This woman wasn't Latina. Even sitting, I could tell that she wasn't five feet tall, and her body would've been considered more muscular than curvy by anyone's definition.

"Your mate sent us to get you," I told her, hoping for a reaction. Hoping I was remembering wrong.

Her hazel eyes shifted between Chance and me, then down at Beau. "What are you talking about?"

194

"Finau," Chance said, his body perfectly still. "Billy Finau."

She stared at us, relief turning into confusion. "I don't know who that is."

"She isn't sweating," Charlie noticed.

"Fuck," Chance barked, making the woman flinch back in her seat just as Beau pulled the ropes from her ankles.

I'd barely blinked when suddenly the woman was out of the chair, and Beau was staggering backward. She jumped and slid over the desk, landing behind it, her hand wrapped around the beer bottle that had been lying on the top. Without flinching, she hit it against the edge of the desk, making it into a weapon.

"Whoa," Chance said, raising his hands, a knife still held in one. "We're not going to hurt you."

"What the fuck is going on?" she asked.

Danny stepped into the room, his eyes wide.

"I know you," the woman said, staring at my little brother. "How do I know you?"

"No fucking clue," Danny replied, moving forward slowly. "You planning on using that?"

She looked down at the broken bottle. "If I need to."

"How far do you think you'd get?" he asked, stopping at the other side of the desk.

Understanding hit me with the weight of a boulder.

"You'd be surprised," she said, still staring.

"You remember where we met, yet?" Danny asked, his mouth curving upward.

"Fuck, fuck, fuck," Beau muttered as he looked at me.

There was no other explanation for the look on his face or the feeling in the room—a mixture of tension and electricity.

"Oh no," Charlie breathed.

"No one here is going to hurt you," Danny said, flipping his pistol around so he could offer it to her. "Take it."

She didn't question it. Reaching out, she plucked it from his hand.

"Bullseye," she said slowly.

Chance shifted, and I glanced over to find him watching her, his gun half raised.

Danny shook his head at her.

"The gun shop," she said, her eyes searching his face. "That's where I saw you."

"I haven't been there in almost a year," Danny replied.

"I know." She licked her lips. "You came in with another guy. He looked like you, but his hair was shorter."

Danny cleared his throat. "My brother Zeke."

She looked around the room and then back at Danny, the question clear.

"He's not here," Danny explained. "These are the rest of my brothers. Ambrose, Chance, Beau, and Charlie."

Her gaze stopped on Charlie.

"Zeke's mate," Danny said softly.

The woman's head slowly turned back to Danny. "You're Vampires?"

"Yes."

They stared at each other.

"I'm your mate," she said, the words hesitant.

"Yes," Danny confirmed.

"Shit," she whispered, dropping her arm to her side. The gun dangled loosely in her grip.

When what we'd all suspected was confirmed out loud, the room erupted into movement. I jogged for the door and picked up speed until I reached the garage bay. The man I'd put a tourniquet on had pulled it back off and bled out on the floor.

"Fuck," I roared, kicking the body.

"If she's Danny's mate," Charlie said worriedly. "Then where is Finau's—"

"It was a fucking misdirect," Chance barked as he raced down the hallway. "She's never met Finau."

That's when I heard Sven's voice in my ear.

"Breach," he reported grimly. "Breach. Breach. Breach. Get the fuck back here."

CHAPTER 11
LUCY

There was fire everywhere. In every direction. Licking up my arms and legs. Pouring down my throat.

"Wake up now," a firm voice ordered. "Lucille, wake up."

I opened my eyes and choked, gasping for air.

"There you are," Alice said grimly. "You with me?"

"Where's Ambrose?" I rasped, rolling my head to the side to look around the room. My limbs felt heavy and hot. So hot.

Matilda was helping Reese out of the other bed.

"He'll be here soon," Alice said, helping me sit up.

I swayed in the bed. The room was spinning.

"Look at me," Alice ordered, her face suddenly in mine. "Better?"

"What's going on?" I asked groggily, rearing back.

"It's time to wake up."

"Where is Ambrose?" I asked again, looking over at the door.

"He'll be back soon," she said. She gripped my hand in

hers and held it firmly as the top of it started to sting. A few moments later, the room seemed to sharpen around me.

"Better," Alice said as she threw the quilt and blanket off my legs. "You need to get up."

"What the hell is going on?" I asked, twisting in the bed to drop my legs off the side.

Ambrose had told me more than once that he'd be there when I woke up. There were no windows in the little makeshift hospital room, so I couldn't even tell what time it was. How long had I been unconscious? It felt like it had been days, but I knew that couldn't be right.

Matilda and Reese strode through the room without looking my way. They paused for a moment before they disappeared out the door.

"Let's go," Alice said, tugging me off the bed.

My feet tingled as I set them on the floor. I planted them stubbornly. "Where are we going?"

"Upstairs," she said, glancing at the closed doorway across the room. "Right now."

I fisted the quilt in my hand and dragged it with me as Alice pulled me toward the door. On the way, she lifted something from the foot of Reese's bed. My stomach lurched when I realized it was a pistol.

"What the fuck is going on?" I asked, pulling my hand from hers so I could roll the quilt into a ball that was easier to carry. I didn't want to drag Zeke's blanket across the floor. It was in bad enough shape as it was, but for some reason, I couldn't bear to leave it behind either.

"Something went wrong," Alice replied grimly.

"Ambrose?" I asked, searching her face. "Charlie?"

"Everyone is fine," she replied as she started to move. "They're on their way back."

"Then what do you mean, something went wrong?" I followed along behind her.

"We're the target," Alice spat as we hurried toward the stairs. "Finau was bullshit. It was all bullshit."

Distant gunshots sounded outside, and I flinched.

"Al," Sven called as he hurried toward us, his hands full.

"How many?" she asked as she paused to let him catch up. I wasn't paying attention and almost ran right into her.

"Not sure," he replied. "Matthias and Josiah are outside with the others, but neither of them is answering their comms."

"How much time do we have?"

He paused for a moment, tilting his head a little. Then he spoke, and not to us. "She's here, and I'm looking at her."

He focused on us again. "An hour until help arrives. How long until Erik is up?"

"Longer than that," she said with a sigh. She tipped her head back, and he leaned down to kiss her.

I looked over the weaponry in his hands. "May I?" I asked.

He nodded, his eyebrows raised.

Slinging the quilt over my shoulders like a scarf, I looked over the weapons. I pulled a pistol and a box of ammunition from the box he carried, then what looked like some kind of club. I tested the weight of it and put it back.

"Take your time," Alice sniped sarcastically.

Sven huffed in amusement.

I lifted another, but it wasn't right either, and I put it back. I looked up at Sven.

"You don't have brass knuckles, by any chance?"

"Doubt they'd fit you if I did."

"Who the hell do you think you'd be using brass knuckles on?" Alice asked.

"Whoever I needed to." I looked up at Sven and lifted the ammunition, shaking the small box. "Thanks."

He nodded, and I turned back toward Alice.

"I'll see you soon, love," she called to Sven as she strode toward the stairs that led to Ambrose's room.

He replied in a language I didn't understand.

"I really wish you'd tell me what's happening," I said nervously as I followed her up, and a fresh burst of gunfire went off outside.

"Can't you hear it?" she asked dryly. "Finau lied. I don't know if he was working with the humans by choice or by chance, but I suppose it doesn't matter now."

"Where are we going?" I asked as she turned in the wrong direction.

"Beau's rooms."

"Why Beau's?"

She threw open the door. "It's me."

"You didn't, by chance, bring more ammunition for this rifle, did you?" Reese asked as she did something with the long gun on the kitchen table.

"Didn't know you needed it," Alice replied.

"I guess this will have to do."

"Why are we in here?" I asked as Matilda moved away from the window.

"Our window faces the front of the house," Reese replied, barely glancing at me. "I can watch the front door."

"I'm headed back downstairs," Matilda announced.

"We'll be fine up here."

"Wait." I glanced around, still trying to get my bearings. I was holding an unfamiliar pistol, Finau had lied,

Ambrose and Charlie were okay, there were people shooting outside—I felt like my head was going to explode.

"They lured the boys out of the house," Reese told me as Alice went to the left side of the window and peered out. "So they could come here, I guess."

"How do you know?"

Reese smirked as distant gunfire answered for her. She shook her head. "They figured it out when Finau's earpiece went offline and the men on the perimeter called in at almost the same time. I'm not sure how many there are, but we have to keep them out of the house until the boys get back."

"We've got an hour," Alice said flatly. "At least."

"An hour's not so long," Reese whispered to herself. Her hands were shaking.

I looked at the window. "But who's watching the back door?"

"Sven," Alice replied.

"Okay, but what about the garage?"

"I can see that from here," Reese said.

Information raced through my mind. "Where's Erik?"

"Downstairs in the guest bedroom. Mattie's with him."

"Is he okay?"

"He's fine," Alice barked impatiently. She inhaled slowly through her nose and out through her mouth. When she spoke again, her voice was calm. "He's unconscious."

"Couldn't you give him whatever you gave me?" I asked hesitantly. "You know, whatever woke me up."

"No," she said, her eyes on the window. "You were asleep to keep the heat bearable. There wasn't anything physically wrong with you. Erik's asleep while he heals."

"What happened to him?"

"He was shot," Reese answered for Alice. "But he's going to be fine."

"How do you know so much?" I asked Reese.

"I'm guessing Mattie was more forthcoming when I woke up," Reese said, rolling her eyes and shooting a look at Alice.

"Reese," Alice called, her voice low.

My heart pounded as Reese lifted the rifle and moved to the window.

"See him?" Alice asked. "At the tree line."

"I see him."

Slowly, they both reached for the window, gripping it on each side without moving into view. Inch by inch, it crept upward until it was halfway open, and a cool breeze flowed into the room.

"Can you make it?" Alice asked quietly.

"Only one way to find out," Reese answered. Bracing the rifle against her shoulder, she changed position slightly.

I'd been around guns plenty of times, but for some reason, I jerked in shock when the sound crashed through the room the moment she fired.

"Good?" Alice asked.

"Lower mid-section," Reese replied. "I didn't account for the drop."

"You will next time," Alice ordered or consoled. I couldn't tell. "He's down?"

"Yes." Reese's hands began to shake as she lowered the rifle and stepped back from the window.

"It's just adrenaline," Alice told her, looking out again. "Oh shit."

"Yeah," Reese whispered.

"Well, get back here," Alice ordered.

Once again, Reese raised the rifle and moved into position.

"What?" I asked.

Neither answered.

"What? What's out there?"

"More," Alice replied emotionlessly.

"How many more?" There was no way to look out the window without putting me in sight. Stumbling back, I flicked the light off.

"Thank you," Alice said, her face barely illuminated by the moonlight. "Should've done that sooner."

"How many more?" I asked again.

"Too many," Reese gritted out, a tear rolling down her cheek.

"Not too many," Alice corrected. "Find the closest one, or whichever you're sure you can hit."

Reese nodded. A few seconds later, she fired again.

"Why aren't you shooting?" I asked Alice.

"Bad shoulder," she replied darkly. "Can't hold a rifle. Can you shoot?"

"A pistol," I replied, my voice rising with hysteria.

What the fuck was even happening?

Reese fired again and then reeled backward.

"Someone saw me," she hissed.

Alice nodded. "Let's go. Chance's room is on the opposite side. We'll run."

I was first out the door, but I didn't head for Chance's room. Instead, I threw the door open to Ambrose's room, tossed Zeke's quilt on the couch, and grabbed my bat from where I'd left it against the wall.

"What the hell are you doing?" Alice called.

"I'll be right behind you," I called back.

I took a deep breath, sucking in Ambrose's sent for good luck or something and then turned and hurried down the stairs. Alice and Reese had already disappeared up the opposite stairs, but I paused in the living area and looked at the front door.

Alice and Reese were picking off the men who headed to the front, but there were too many. Sven was covering the back door, and I thought he probably had better odds. Somewhere in the bowels of the house, Matilda was with Erik and a shotgun.

If I was going to do anything to help, the front door was where I needed to be. I was no good with a pistol for the kind of shots Reese was taking, but if they came through the front door, I could help with that. Maybe.

It was locked. I could see the way the dead bolt was pointing. That would give me a few extra seconds if someone made it onto the front porch.

Crouching, I hurried into the living room where a row of three windows with filmy curtains let the moonlight in. Pulling one back as slowly as I possibly could, I looked out. There was no one near the porch. Yet.

Praying that no one could see me, I reached through the curtains and slid open one of the windows a few inches. Then I moved to the next and the next. I didn't open any of them much, just enough that I could shoot through the screen if I needed to. A rifle shot came from somewhere above me, and I jumped, backing away. All of them were opened exactly the same amount, so I hoped that at first glance, you wouldn't even notice that any of them were open at all. It helped that all the lights in the house had been turned off. It was actually lighter in the yard because of the porch lights and the moon.

I looked around the room and rushed to the couch, sliding it across the floor so that I had a barrier between me and the front door. I moved a chair too, so the couch wouldn't look out of place.

"What are you doing?" Matilda hissed from the darkness behind me. I nearly shit myself.

"Watching the front door," I replied, my voice barely a whisper. "Go back with Erik."

"Are you out of your mind?"

"I have a pistol," I replied dumbly. I figured I shouldn't mention the bat unless I wanted her to really think I'd lost my mind.

Gunfire sounded too close for comfort outside, followed by a rifle shot from above us.

"Go," I whispered, making a shooing motion. "I've got this."

I didn't have it in any way, shape, or form, but I was determined to fake it until I made it, and at the very least, go down swinging. There was very little room for fear, probably because of the adrenaline racing through me, mixed with the burn of the mating heat. It hurt like hell, but it was also strangely comforting, like having Ambrose with me.

Reese's rifle went off again. Again. Again.

They had to be getting closer to the house.

Laying the bat across the couch, I moved into place, kneeling below the first window, only my eyes and forehead above the frame. My palms were sweating as I checked to make sure the pistol was loaded and pulled back the slide. Carefully, I rested the barrel on the windowsill, flicked off the safety, and waited.

My pulse was pounding in my ears so loudly that I didn't hear the first man until he came into view at the top of the porch steps.

I lifted the pistol off the windowsill. Aimed.

He was three steps in when I fired. The bullet hit him somewhere in his torso, and he spun toward me.

I fired again, hitting him in the crotch.

He went down like a sack of potatoes, screaming, and fell off the porch.

I swallowed the enormous amount of spit in my mouth, trying not to gag as I waited for the next one.

I hit him in the chest and belly because he'd turned toward me right away. He dropped in a heap on the porch, and I had to keep looking at him as I waited for the next one.

All the while, Reese fired from upstairs. I hoped she was hitting her marks because I felt like I was going to hyperventilate. I didn't want to shoot anymore. I didn't want to watch any more men fall. I didn't want any of it.

I hit another as he came onto the porch, but he disappeared back off of it before I could shoot again. Which meant there was a wounded man who knew where I was shooting from.

I moved to the window at the opposite end. I could see the stairs better, but I didn't like being in the line of fire from anyone in the yard. I glanced toward the front door.

I just had to keep them from the door.

Two men rushed the steps, and I panicked, shooting the pistol until I was out of ammunition.

I hadn't thought to bring a spare magazine, only the extra ammo. Throwing myself to the side, I hid against the wall between the windows and the door as I ejected the magazine and reloaded it with shaky hands. I wasn't sure how many bullets I dropped, but it was too many. It was taking me too long.

I'd barely gotten the magazine loaded back into the pistol when light from the moon was blocked by a large shadow outside the window.

Rolling onto my side, I pointed toward the window and fired.

Glass shattered and fell everywhere. I was covered in it. But the shadow dropped.

My relief was short-lived when someone shot at the door. Bang. Bang. Bang. The door rattled as I scrambled toward the couch, keeping one eye on the windows. One of them was basically just a frame now, an easy entrance.

When the door flew open, I screamed and fired.

The man stood there for a moment and then dropped in a heap. I couldn't even tell where I'd shot him.

"Lucy," Matilda called.

"I'm fine," I called back. "Stay there."

"The hell I will," she said from somewhere behind me as I scrambled for the front door. I slammed it closed, but the lock and doorknob were absolutely mangled.

"The sideboard," she said, racing toward me. She heaved the long cabinet down the foyer a foot before I'd even gotten a hold of the other end.

Someone must've been looking down on us, because I wasn't sure how we managed to get the heavy cabinet wedged in front of the door before anyone else had made it onto the porch.

Reese's rifle sounded again.

Okay, maybe the person looking down on us had been Reese.

"Did you do that to my window?" Matilda asked, breathing heavily as we snuck over to the couch.

"Charlie will reimburse you," I said, crawling across the floor to where I'd left the box of ammunition. I clutched it to my chest and half-crawled, half-scooted back to her. "He's filthy rich now, apparently."

Matilda scoffed, but her lips turned up in a little smile.

"How much longer do you think we have?" I asked. It felt like we'd been at it for hours, but I knew that couldn't be right because Ambrose would've been there already.

"Half an hour," Matilda replied. "Fifteen minutes if we're lucky."

I nodded as we watched the windows.

"How's Erik?"

"He's going to be livid when he wakes," she replied softly. "But otherwise, he'll heal."

"That's good."

"Do you—" She stopped and shook her head.

"What?" I asked. "Do I what?"

"It's nothing."

"Come on now," I teased gently, my voice trembling with nerves. "If you can't ask me now, when could you? We're practically besties at this point. We've moved furniture together."

"Do you think Charlie would be offended if I let him know he could call us Mom and Dad?"

If I hadn't been staring so intently at the windows, searching for any hint of a shadow, my mouth would've dropped open in shock. It was the oddest time to think about my parents, but I couldn't stop the memories that flashed through my mind.

Dad pointing at the door, a silent order for us to leave for school even though we'd begged him to stay home. I'd been suspended later that day when the boy who'd been threatening to beat up Charlie actually attempted it. I'd jumped on his back and choked him until he passed out, falling like a tree with me still dangling off his back.

Mom brushing us off when we tried to tell her that Charlie's teacher wouldn't stop the kids from harassing him. That she'd made him stand in front of the class for an hour while she taught because she said *he'd* been disruptive in his seat.

Dad picking Charlie up off the bed he'd made on my floor and carrying him crying out of the room because he said Charlie was too old to be sharing a room with his little sister.

Mom ignoring my scuffed cheek and elbows, rat's nest hair, and dirty clothes because some kids had ambushed us on the way home from school. Charlie's nose had been bleeding. She hadn't noticed that either.

"I don't think he'd be offended," I replied flatly, pushing those memories away. "He'd probably like that."

"And what about you?" she asked.

Was that a shadow? Why was it so quiet outside? The hair on my arms prickled.

"What about me?" I breathed, trying not to spook myself.

"Would you be offended?"

"Of course not," I replied, rolling to my knees.

Something was about to happen. I didn't know what, but I knew.

The other two windows shattered as bullets sprayed into the room. I threw myself on top of Matilda and put my arms over my head as we cowered at the end of the couch. Something stung my ankle, and I jerked my legs back. It felt like it went on forever, but it had to be only a few moments.

As soon as it stopped, I dragged myself off of Matilda and looked at her. She nodded silently. She was okay.

We both turned toward the window, and Matilda racked the shotgun.

She shot the first man dead center. It was gruesome and fucking disgusting the way the closely grouped balls tore through him. She was racking the shotgun again when the second man came through. I shot twice and hit him once as we backed away.

Matilda shot him again and then snapped the shotgun

in half, pulled two more shells out of her pocket, and reloaded.

I shot the next man three times.

Then there were too many to count.

I couldn't hear anything as they came in the window, every sense almost muffled as I fired and Matilda fired beside me.

They didn't shoot back, and that was almost scarier because I knew what it meant. They didn't want to kill us.

I shot until the bullets ran out, and then I threw the pistol at the closest man, hitting him in the face. He didn't go down, but it gave me enough time to grab the bat where I'd left it on the couch.

Matilda and I worked our way backward as she fired.

Then, from the top of the stairs, came a rifle shot, and the next man went down.

Another.

Another.

They just kept coming through the fucking window. There were so many of them. They had to step over the men who had already fallen, and sometimes they stepped right on top of them. It was heinous and terrifying. Reese just kept shooting, and Matilda just kept reloading and shooting again, but eventually one of them got close.

I swung the bat so hard that when it bounced off his shoulder, it reverberated in my arms. I took aim again as he reached for me and hit him in the side of the face that time, knocking him out cold.

All the while, the room rang with gunfire.

Bang. Bang. BANG. Bang. BANG.

Matilda let out a whoof sound, and I glanced at her.

Blood bloomed on the front of her housedress.

I lost my fucking mind.

Screaming so loud that I drowned out everything else,

I ran toward them, my bat braced over my shoulder. I hit the first one in the throat, and while he was clutching it and trying to draw in air, I swung for the next one. He lifted his arm to block it, and I heard his forearm snap as he screamed. Then I reached the one who'd shot her.

We both knew he wasn't going to shoot me because he wasn't sure who I was, but that didn't mean he was going to let me hit him, either.

Reese was still firing, but her shots were limited now that I was in the middle of everything.

I swung the bat, and he ducked, taking it on his shoulder as he rushed me.

The air in my lungs left in a whoosh when his shoulder hit my chest, but I didn't let it distract me. As he tried to lift me off the ground, I arched and threw my weight backward, throwing off his center of gravity. We both fell to the floor in a heap, and I landed half on and half off a still-warm body.

"Little bitch," the man spat, reaching for my throat.

Twisting, I elbowed him in the side of the face and tried to drag myself out from under him.

He gripped my hips like a vise as he tried to crawl his way up my body.

Reaching for him, I dug my thumbs into his eye sockets as he screamed.

Still, Reese fired from the top of the stairs.

How many of them could possibly be left?

It didn't matter if I didn't get this beast off of me.

When he let go of my hips to try to push my hands away from my eyes, it was all I needed. I dug my feet into the carpet and swiveled my hips out from under his body. I felt my leggings sliding down my ass as I pulled my legs out from under him. His fingers dug into my wrists as they pulled my hands from his eyes.

But now my lower body was free, and he was fucking blind.

Throwing my body sideways, I lunged onto his back, my arms screaming as they twisted in his hold. He was still yelling and cursing me as I yanked them away and wrapped them around his neck.

"Lucy," Reese screamed.

Bang.

Heavy weight landed on the lower half of my body as I tightened my arm around the monster's throat. Something wet was running down the inside of my thigh.

I ignored it.

The monster gagged and scratched at my forearms as I wrenched his head back as far as I could.

When he went limp, I readjusted my grip.

Then I snapped his neck.

My entire body slumped with relief.

All of a sudden, the house was strangely silent.

"Reese?" a deep voice called from somewhere.

"Beau!" Reese called back frantically.

"Lucy?"

I'd know that voice anywhere. A flare of heat emanated from my chest, instantly making me lightheaded.

Ambrose.

I opened my mouth to call back to him when everything went black.

CHAPTER 12
AMBROSE

Leaning forward, I tried to ignore the fire racing through my veins and stared out the windshield as Danny flew up the driveway. Every porch light and spotlight outside was on, and the front yard was littered with bodies. We'd lost contact with Sven seven minutes ago. Until then, his contact had been sporadic at best.

I felt like I was going out of my mind. I could hardly focus.

"Oh my god," Danny's mate whispered from the back seat as she got a good look at the carnage.

"Faster, Danny," I ordered, my hand on the door handle.

Beau's SUV skidded to a stop ahead of us. He and Chance jumped out, running toward the house.

"I'm coming with you," Charlie announced.

"No. Keep watch," I ordered when the car had slowed enough for me to jump out.

"Fuck, Ambrose!" Danny shouted in alarm.

The front windows were fucking *gone*.

I jumped over a body at the base of the stairs. Gods, there were so many of them on the porch that I had to step on a couple as I raced for the door. I shoved against it and got nowhere.

"Lucy?" I yelled. I slammed against the door again, but it still didn't budge.

Fuck. I hurried to the windows.

"She's in here," Chance called.

I hadn't thought it was possible, but the sight that greeted me as I climbed inside was far worse than what I'd seen outside.

Chance was crouched in the middle of the floor. Beau and Reese were kneeling further away. There were bodies everywhere. Blood and Gods knew what else painted the walls, the floor, the furniture.

"Where is she?" I barked.

"Here," Chance said, shifting to the side.

My heart stopped.

Lucy was lying face down on top of a body, her pants pulled halfway down her ass. Another large body covered her legs. Her hair was still in the braid she'd been wearing when I left her, but pieces had fallen out and pooled on the floor. Her arms were covered in blood.

"She's breathing," Chance said as I scrambled toward them, tripping over the mess. "I can't tell where she's hurt, so I didn't want to move her."

"Get him off her," I ordered, falling to my knees.

"Mom," Beau called. "Mom, can you wake up for me?"

I looked to the side where my mother was lying flat on her back, motionless.

There was so much blood.

"Beau?" I called out, brushing Lucy's hair away from her face.

"Gut shot," Beau called back. "Alice!"

"I'll find her," Reese said, pushing herself quickly to her feet.

"Stay here," Beau argued. "I'll get her."

"Lucy?" I called gently. "Baby, can you open your eyes for me?"

Chance grunted as he pulled the body off of her lower half. "Fuck."

"What?" I asked, looking at her.

"She's bleeding."

"Where?" I brushed my hands down her body, gently pulling her leggings back into place.

"I can't tell," Chance said frantically. "It's a lot of blood, Ulf."

"I'm getting her up." We couldn't figure anything out while she was still draped over the body beneath her.

Lucy didn't stir as I rolled her onto her back. Her skin was so pale it was practically translucent.

"Thigh," Chance said, reaching for her. He wrapped his hands around it as I rose to my feet. We carefully carried her out of the room, stepping on anything that was in our way.

Reese barely glanced at us as she tried to put pressure on my mother's wound. It didn't seem to be making much of a difference, since it looked like the blood had mostly stopped already.

Forcing myself to look away, I carried Lucy through the kitchen to the hospital room.

Inside, Alice was just finishing up stitching a horrendous slash across Sven's throat. He was out cold.

"Alice?" I called as we laid Lucy on the bed. Chance climbed on with her, his hand still gripping her thigh.

"I'll be right there," she replied, her voice rough. She turned to face us, and her eyes were dark with fear.

"Sven?"

"It wasn't complete," she said as she rushed to the sink. She quickly started scrubbing the blood from her hands. "The old fool made it back into the house. Lucy?"

"Thigh," Chance replied.

"How bad?"

"Bad."

"Baby," I whispered, brushing Lucy's hair back from her face. "Baby, wake up."

"All right, let me see what we have," Alice ordered Chance as she tugged a pair of gloves on. She grimaced when he let go.

"Alice," Reese bellowed from the living room.

"Go tell her that I'll help Mattie when I'm able," Alice ordered Chance. "And please tell her that a gut wound won't kill your mother, will you?"

"Do you know where Beau went?" Chance asked as he strode for the door.

"I sent him outside to find Matthias and Josiah." Twisting, she grabbed a pair of shears off the little rolling table between the beds and began cutting Lucy's leggings off. Beneath them was a large hole.

I looked at it with foggy detachment.

I'd seen hundreds of bullet wounds. Thousands, maybe. It was familiar, that hole.

"Ambrose," Alice bellowed.

I looked at her in surprise.

"Stay with me, kid," she ordered.

I nodded.

"Start an IV," Alice said briskly.

"Right," I said, my fingers tangling in Lucy's hair as I pulled my hand from her cheek.

I reached for the supplies as Alice mumbled to herself. "No exit. Didn't hit the bone. Where the hell is it?"

Setting out the supplies I'd need, I looked at Lucy's

arms. I wasn't even sure where to place it. She was covered in blood and scratches. Reaching for the wipes on the cart, I froze when Alice called my name.

"I don't care if she's your mate," she chided. "Go wash and glove."

Fuck, I needed to get my head right.

I half-ran and half-stumbled over to the sink and began to scrub. Lucy would be okay. There was no other possibility. The Gods wouldn't be cruel enough to take her when I'd just found her. I scrubbed harder. The Gods wouldn't take Charlie's sister, not after he'd lost his mate.

"Gloves," Alice shouted.

I grabbed a towel to dry my hands and turned back toward the bed just as Matthias and Josiah stumbled into the room.

"How bad?" Alice barked.

"Two GSWs," Josiah replied. "Side and shoulder." He helped his brother lower to the floor.

"You'll have to get in line, sweetheart," Alice replied, all business. "Where the hell have you been?"

Matthias let out a choked laugh. "Taking care of the stragglers."

I pulled on a pair of gloves.

"Josiah, you're good?"

"Pretty much." He limped toward the bed.

"Scrub," Alice ordered him. "Take over for Ambrose."

"Lucy?" Matthias asked, leaning over to see the bed.

"Gunshot to the thigh," Alice replied as I reached the bed and leaned down to kiss my mate's forehead. "It's still in there."

"I can start the IV," I said, leaning back up.

"You'll sit there and make moon-eyes at your mate," Alice countered. "You're in no shape to be any help."

I nodded and pulled the gloves back off so I could lay

my bare hands on her skin. I swallowed against the lump in my throat as I carefully pulled a piece of hair away from her neck and set it behind her.

"Damn, Ambrose," Josiah said with a whistle as he began to clean her arm. "Your woman's a fighter."

I nodded, staring at Lucy's face. She was so out of it that her eyes weren't even fully closed. A sliver of white was showing between her lids. The round cheeks that I loved so much hollowed out because of the way her jaw hung slightly open.

It felt like I couldn't get enough air into my lungs.

"There you are," Alice mumbled.

Lucy jerked.

Josiah lifted Lucy's hand and sniffed it, letting out a noise of surprise.

"Was she shooting?" he asked Alice.

"Wake up, baby," I whispered, putting my face close to hers. "Open those pretty brown eyes for me."

"Best she's not awake for this part," Alice said dryly. "And yes, she was."

"No shit?" Josiah asked.

"No shit," Alice replied. "More than half those bodies in the living room are hers. Porch too."

"Fucking hell," Matthias said tiredly from his place on the floor.

"You should've seen Reese," Alice said, amusement in her voice. "That girl can shoot too."

"She had the rifle? We saw the bodies outside." Josiah asked as he laid Lucy's arm gently on the bed. "You need anything?"

"I've got it," Alice replied. "Clean and bandage those cuts on her arms."

"On it."

"Reese had the rifle," she confirmed. "Used the upstairs windows."

"Smart," Matthias mumbled.

"I used to be good with a rifle," Alice said as she dropped the bullet she'd pulled out of Lucy's leg on top of the rolling cabinet.

"Uncle Sven said you were a better shot than him," Josiah said as he crossed the room.

"Easily," Alice agreed, glancing at her mate.

"You want me to check him?"

"No, he'll do," Alice replied. "Lucy's arms first."

I didn't move from my place at her side, so Josiah worked around me. Once the blood was cleaned off her arms, the wounds were easier to see. Across the top of each of her forearms were four deep gouges with familiar spacing. Josiah laid his hand on top of them so I could see where his fingernails fell. I nodded.

Someone had scratched her, and they hadn't been fucking around.

The bottoms of her forearms were worse. Little bits of glass were embedded in the tender skin there, one of them so deep that it would need stitching once Josiah pulled it out.

"Alice," my dad called, carrying my mother into the room.

"Josiah, get the extra gurney," Alice ordered.

He rushed across the room and set it up in less than a minute.

"She's still out," my father said as he laid my mother down.

"For the best," Alice replied. "I'll get to her next. Then Matthias."

"I'm good," Matthias said faintly. "Jo, call Adira. Tell her I'm—" His words drifted off.

Lucy's eyebrows pulled together in a frown as her eyelids fluttered.

"It's okay, love," I said, running my thumb over her cheek.

"Almost done stitching," Alice said as my father set his hand on my shoulder.

"Lucy?" Charlie called, running into the room. "Oh no."

"It's a fucking party in here," Alice snapped sarcastically.

Charlie ignored her as he rushed to the foot of the bed. "Is she okay?"

"She'll be fine," I replied firmly.

"What happened to her?" Charlie asked as he began to cry. He wrapped his hand around her foot.

"She was shot," Josiah replied when I couldn't seem to get the words out. "And she's got some good scratches on her arms."

"Oh god," Charlie choked out.

I knew he loved her, but I needed him to shut the fuck up. I was hanging on by a very thin thread. When Josiah and Alice spoke, they were matter-of-fact. They didn't get emotional. They just did what needed to be done. The way they moved around the room was habit, comfortable, businesslike. That's what I needed. I couldn't take on Charlie's worry. It felt suffocating.

My father's hand tightened on my shoulder.

Lucy woke up with a cry when Josiah pulled the large piece of glass from her forearm. She shot up in bed so fast that none of us were able to stop her before her fist swung for his throat.

"Lucy," I yelled, catching her around the shoulders as she lunged for him.

She froze and turned toward me. "Ambrose?"

221

The sight of her big brown eyes nearly brought me to my knees.

"Hey, baby," I replied as she went limp in my arms.

"Fuck," she breathed. Her entire body shuddered.

"You sleep through me digging a bullet out of your thigh, but wake up when this one pulls a puny piece of glass from your arm?" Alice asked. She shook her head and strode toward the sink. "No sense."

Lucy let out a painful sounding laugh and then groaned.

"Get her something for the pain," I ordered Josiah.

"She nearly took my head off," he said as he walked toward the cabinets along the wall.

"You're back," Lucy croaked when she caught sight of Charlie at the end of the bed.

"Told you I'd be fine," he replied tightly, shaking her foot a little.

Before I could warn him not to jostle her, Lucy inhaled sharply.

"Your mom?" she asked me, her eyes filling with remembered dread. She looked up at my dad.

"She'll be fine," he assured her gently. "Immortal, remember?"

"I...She..." Lucy's face fell, and she began to cry in great, wrenching sobs. Her chest heaved with each breath she took.

"You're okay," I soothed. "It's over. Shh. You're okay, love. Everyone is okay."

Josiah came over and carefully leaned over the bed so he could reach her arm. A minute or two after he'd administered the pain medication, her sobs slowed to a gradual stop.

"What the fuck?" I yelped as her body relaxed completely against me.

"Just the pain meds," Josiah said over his shoulder as he hurried to the sink. "And she's probably exhausted. Did you see what she did out there?"

I held Lucy for a few minutes, relishing the feel of her breath on the base of my neck.

My father stood at the head of my mother's bed, smoothing his hand over her hair as Alice and Josiah got to work.

"Should someone help him?" Charlie asked, staring at Matthias's prone body on the floor.

"He's next," I told him as I finally laid Lucy back down on the pillow. "He's mated. He'll be fine."

"Oh, good," Charlie said faintly.

"How's it going in here?" Chance asked from the doorway.

"Working on your mother," Alice replied. "Go away."

Sven began to cough.

"Erik?" Alice glanced over her shoulder at her mate.

"I've got him," my dad replied, crossing the room.

"Ulf," Chance called, grimacing when Alice shot him a glare over her shoulder. "You should come see this."

I stared at him blankly. He wanted me to leave my mate?

"I can stay with her," Charlie said hesitantly. "If you..." He glanced between me and Chance. "Just until you get back, if you want."

Chance nodded.

Gritting my teeth, I leaned down and kissed Lucy's cheek, breathing her in. She was safe. She was asleep. Her brother was there. I could leave her for a few minutes.

I followed Chance out into the house, and the first thing I noticed was the smell. Death had a distinctive smell, and violent death even more so. Beau and Reese were standing in the kitchen.

"We didn't want to get in the way," Reese explained, glancing past us. "How's everyone doing?"

"They'll live," I replied flatly. "Where's Danny?"

"He left," Beau said, pointing with his thumb. "The woman wanted to go home. Insisted."

"His mate."

"Yeah."

"Did he find out why she was in that garage?" I asked.

"She said she had no fucking clue," Chance answered. "Last week, a couple of guys ambushed her in her driveway. Took her to the garage. She couldn't figure them out. They fed her, let her use the facilities, didn't hurt her. They just seemed to be waiting."

It didn't make any sense, but I didn't have the headspace to try to puzzle it out. "What am I supposed to be looking at?" I snapped. The whole night had been an epic clusterfuck, and I just wanted to get back to my mate.

"I told you it could wait," Beau chastised Chance.

"We need to clean up the bodies," Chance argued. "They're starting to fucking reek."

Reese messed with something around her neck, and when she pulled it toward her face, I realized it was a kitchen towel. She covered her nose and mouth with it and gestured toward the living room.

When we reached the edge of the mess, she stopped.

"Walk us through it again, baby," Beau said gently.

"We started there." She pointed toward my wing. "In Beau's room. Lucy and Alice met Mattie and me up there after they'd woken us up. I made a few shots out that window."

She paused, and Beau slid his hand down her back. She leaned into him and continued.

"They saw me, so we changed rooms." She pointed to the opposite wing. "We used Chance's room. Lucy said she was right behind us, but she never came up." She looked around the room. "She stayed down here."

"Best guess," Chance continued. "She opened the windows. See how the frame is open a few inches, each one? It's uniform. So she posted up at the windows."

"There were so many outside," Reese said, her voice muffled. "Too many. Your mom had gone down to protect your dad, but the three of us knew it was only a matter of time before they reached the front door. I couldn't stop all of them."

I looked around the room. The couch and one of the chairs had been moved, making a barrier between the living area and the front door. She'd found a defensive position.

"She took out all but one on the front porch," Beau said.

"With a pistol," I breathed.

"Glass outside on the porch. *She* shot at least one of the windows out."

"I didn't see Lucy when she was shooting. When I came to the top of the stairs, she was literally throwing her pistol at one of them." Reese let out a watery laugh.

"Did she hit him?" I asked, my gaze roaming over the bodies.

"In the face," Reese confirmed. "It knocked him back enough that she was able to get the bat off the couch."

"That fucking bat," Chance said, shaking his head.

"They just kept coming," Reese whispered. "I was doing my best, but with Mattie and Lucy down here—"

"You did great," Beau said.

"Then your mom got shot." Reese stumbled over the last word. "And Lucy went crazy, like the Hulk or something. She started in with that bat and took two guys down before she got to the shooter. He caught her, though. He tried to lift her off the ground, but Lucy threw herself back, and they both went down."

My chest felt like it was about to cave in. We'd believed a fucking liar and left our mates without enough protection. Vulnerable. And now Lucy, my mother, Sven, and Matthias were paying the price.

"They wrestled," Reese said as she gingerly picked her way through the room. She came to a stop where I'd found Lucy. "He was on top of her, but somehow she managed to wiggle out." Reese shook her head. "I'm not sure how she did it. I was still trying to stop the men coming in through the window. One second, she was under him, and the next, she was on his back with her arms around his neck. I shot that one as he came up behind her." She pointed to the body that Chance had dragged off Lucy's limp body. "And he fell on her legs."

"Look at this, Ambrose," Chance said, crouching down by the body that Lucy had been laying on top of. He pointed.

The man's eyes were nearly gouged out of his head, and his neck was broken.

My mate had broken the man's neck.

Good.

"Watched her do it from the window," Chance said, rubbing his hand over his mouth. "It was clean, Ulf. Precise."

I nodded and lifted the dead human's hand and checked the nails. They were bloody. He was the one who'd scratched her forearms.

I rose to my feet, my boots crunching on the broken glass all over the rug.

"You did good," I told Reese, turning my head to look at her. "Thank you."

She let out a little hysterical laugh.

Chance shook his head and pushed to his feet.

We gazed around at the bodies around us. Some of them were mangled from my mother's shotgun. Some had huge exit wounds from Reese's rifle. A lot of them had smaller bullet wounds from Lucy.

Silently, I made my way over to the front door while my brothers followed, and Reese walked back to the kitchen.

"I wonder who did that," Beau said, gesturing to the sideboard pushed against the door.

"Sven?" Chance asked as he moved toward it.

"Could be."

I helped him scoot it back against the wall where my mother kept it. The door had been shot to hell, and it swung open once the cabinet wasn't holding it closed anymore.

"Leave it," Beau ordered as I pushed it shut again. "I'll figure out a way to keep it closed."

I stepped away from the door. With the windows wide open, it wasn't like the door would keep someone out anyway. "What happened to the security? Anyone know?"

"I found two outside and sent them home," Chance replied, leaning tiredly against the wall. "The others are either dead or taken."

"Fuck." There should've been more than enough of them to hold the property, but we hadn't imagined an assault of that size.

"We'll deal with it tomorrow," Beau said as he walked back toward Reese.

I went back to Lucy.

Charlie was sitting on the edge of the bed, holding his sister's hand. She was so still.

"Alice," I called, looking at my mate's pale face.

"She'll be okay," Alice replied without turning around.

She and Josiah were still working on my mom. "We got to her in time."

I looked around the room. Everyone else who'd been injured was mated and immortal, but there was a very real chance that Lucy's immortality hadn't locked into place yet. She had to have known that when she'd decided to make her last stand at the front door.

Charlie smiled wanly at me as I rounded the bed. He'd pulled a light blanket over her. I should've done that. I doubted she'd be happy when she realized how many people had been in and out of the room while she'd been half naked and getting her thigh stitched up.

"Has she woken up?" I asked.

"No," he replied. "But her temperature's been rising. It's good you're back."

"Fucking heat," I said under my breath. The thing I'd found so incredible, the first link between us, had become an albatross. She needed to heal without that shit ravaging her body further.

Carefully scooting onto the bed, I aligned my body with hers and pulled her head to my shoulder.

"I shouldn't be surprised," Charlie said conversationally, the tears from earlier gone as he rubbed his thumb over the top of her hand. "That she decided to go all *Rambo*, I mean. She's been like that our whole lives— protective to a fault."

"She was in the most danger."

"I doubt she considered it," he said, meeting my eyes.

"How are you holding up?" I asked. The dark circles around his eyes had never really faded, but they seemed more pronounced.

"Glad that Erik is over there pacing," Charlie said ruefully. "I bet you don't even think about it, but watching him fall was..." He swallowed hard. "I'm human. Wounds like that are fatal. You were right about the instincts. I fought."

"Did a hell of a job too," Josiah commented from his place by my mother.

Charlie's head shot up, and then he looked at me sheepishly. "I keep forgetting you guys hear everything."

"You did great," I assured him, remembering Josiah's and Matthias's voices in my ear. Part of me wished I could've seen it. "They would've taken his head."

Charlie shuddered.

"They didn't because of you."

"They were *there* because of me," Charlie replied drolly.

"Done," Alice announced, using her arm to wipe the sweat from her forehead. She stepped away from the table, pulling off her gloves. "Take her to bed, Erik. Josiah can help with the IV."

Josiah snapped off his own gloves as he nodded. He grabbed the IV pole and followed behind my father as he carried my mother like a bride out of the room. The back of her head was crusted in blood from where it had pooled around her on the floor.

Charlie made a little sound in the back of his throat, but when I looked at him, his face was blank.

"How's she doing?" Alice asked, looking Lucy over.

"Just asleep, I think."

"It's good for her," she said plainly. She paused and pressed her lips together before she looked at me. "I saw what she did. We wouldn't have made it until you got here if she hadn't. Stupid, but brave."

I nodded. The bravery had been apparent since the moment we met.

Alice glanced over at Matthias and sighed. "One more."

She walked over to the bed my mother had been on and stripped the linens before wiping it down. By the time Josiah came back into the room with Chance, the bed was ready.

"Put him up there," Alice ordered as she strode toward Sven. She looked him over and checked his IV. Picking up a scalpel, she made a small cut on her wrist. Smoothing his hair from his face, she set her wrist against his mouth.

I looked away as Sven began to drink.

Josiah and Chance lifted Matthias from the floor and carried him to the bed.

"Gods, why is he so heavy?" Chance griped. "Does he carry bricks in his pockets?"

Josiah grunted. "His mate can cook," he grumbled. "I'm going to tell her to stop."

Charlie laughed.

"Hey," I said quietly. "You can head up to bed if you want. I'll stay with her."

Charlie shook his head. "I'll stay." He looked around the room. "You think I could pull a chair in, though? My head is pounding."

"Go ahead," Alice answered for me as she washed her hands. "Grab two, would you?"

"You need to sleep when you're done," I protested as she crossed the room. She looked ready to drop.

"I haven't slept without Sven since we were mated," she replied as she pulled on another pair of gloves. "I will not start tonight." She looked at Chance and Josiah. "Well? What are you waiting for? Start cutting these clothes off."

I turned back toward Lucy while Charlie left the room. Her breath was coming out in small puffs of air, steady and regular. My hands began to shake.

Things could've gone so differently.

Down near the end of the bed, something caught my eye. The blanket had a small, dark spot. At first, I thought it was a fly, and it took me a second to remember that I wasn't in a field hospital. Leaning up, I looked closer.

It was blood.

Carefully, I climbed out of bed and walked down by Lucy's feet. When I pulled back the blanket, I found her white sock covered in blood.

We'd missed it.

Peeling the mangled sock away, I found a deep gouge.

"What?" Alice demanded, looking at me over her shoulder.

"She's got a graze on her ankle," I replied.

"Clotted?"

"No."

"Can you stitch it?"

I nodded.

Charlie came back with a couple of chairs as I scrubbed again. A few minutes later, I'd grabbed all the supplies I needed and started to clean the wound.

I'd trained as a medic so long ago that it was a distant memory, but I'd used the skills so often that I'd never gotten the chance to get rusty. It was a different beast altogether to stitch up my mate's soft skin. Focusing on the wound and not the person was harder than I'd anticipated.

Thankfully, Lucy slept through it.

I wasn't sure how Alice had doctored her mate over the years. My hands were shaking by the time I was through.

I spent time once she was bandaged, searching her entire body for anything else we'd missed. When I was through, I climbed back into bed with her.

By the time Alice was done with Matthias and he'd

been carried away, Josiah was taking him home to be with his mate, Charlie was asleep in the chair, and my eyes were burning and heavy.

Alice walked over and dimmed the lights. "Try to get some rest," she ordered.

"I should go check—"

"Your brothers and Erik will keep an eye on things," Alice said as she sat down beside Sven. "Rest, or you'll be no good to her when she wakes."

"Look who's talking," I replied, curling my arm beneath my head on the bed above Lucy's pillow.

I closed my eyes and focused on Lucy's breath against my throat.

"This was a close one," Alice said to Sven. "But don't worry, I'll be happy to remind you daily that I saved your ass again." She paused. "Rest, my love. I'll be right here."

Clenching my jaw, I tipped my head down until my lips rested against Lucy's hair. It had been *too* close. If they'd made it fully into the house, we would've lost them all.

Beau and I wouldn't have been far behind them.

CHAPTER 13
LUCY

The room around me was so dark that I couldn't see my hand in front of my face. For the first time in a while, I didn't feel like I was burning alive, but when I tried to move, pain exploded in my leg.

I gasped, reaching for it, when my hands were caught in a strong grip.

"Don't touch it," Ambrose ordered gently. He let go of my hands and moved away from me. A second later, light filled the room.

We were in Ambrose's bed, and he looked like shit. Still, seeing his face so close to mine was like coming up for air.

"You're awake." He smiled.

"What..."

I wasn't sure what to ask first. Where was Charlie? What was wrong with my leg? Why the hell were my arms wrapped with gauze? What had happened?

The last question answered itself when the gunfight downstairs came back in little flashes.

"Your mom?" I asked, holding my breath.

"She's fine," Ambrose said, leaning closer. "Currently pissed that Alice has her on a liquid diet for a few more days."

"She was shot," I argued. "It was really bad."

"Immortal, baby," Ambrose said slowly. "Remember?"

Oh, yeah. That made sense.

"Everyone is fine," Ambrose continued.

"Good," I replied, lowering myself back down to the pillow. "That's good."

I was having a hard time processing the memory of what happened.

They'd just kept coming.

"Hey," Ambrose called, reaching out to run his thumb along my jaw. His face appeared above mine. "How are you feeling?"

"Probably better than you look," I replied.

He'd gone from a five o'clock shadow to a full beard, but it didn't mask his newly sunken cheeks or the hollowness in his eyes. His hair was a mess, and it looked like he'd thrown on the clothes he'd found. The sweatpants he had on were lime green.

"It's been a long thirty-seven hours," he said ruefully.

"I've been asleep an entire day?"

"And then some," he replied. "You needed it. Alice says sleep is the great healer."

"I thought that was God."

He just shrugged.

"What's wrong with my leg?"

"You were shot in the thigh."

"I think I would've remembered that," I argued. When the hell had I been shot? I'd been on my feet the whole time.

"Alice said you probably didn't notice because of the adrenaline."

I let out a huff of breath.

"You have a graze on your ankle too."

I was pretty sure I knew when that one happened. It was when they'd shot out the windows.

I stared at the ceiling. My entire body felt heavy and weak.

"You want to get up?"

The moment he said it, I realized I really did need to get up. My bladder felt like it was going to burst. I nodded, and he moved around to help me sit on the edge of the bed.

"What's wrong with my arms?" I asked, looking down at the bandages. Someone had put me in a T-shirt I didn't recognize, and there was so much gauze that it looked like I was wearing a long sleeve shirt under it.

"You had some cuts from the window glass." Putting his hands on my hips, he braced me as I stood.

My leg didn't feel as bad as it had when I'd first moved it. I was in nothing but a pair of panties, and there was a wide bandage taped near the inside of my thigh and another on the outside of the opposite ankle. Instead of the sharp pain I expected, it felt more like a dull throbbing as I hobbled into the bathroom.

Ambrose hovered in the doorway.

"I've got it from here," I told him.

"Are you sure?"

I glanced at the toilet three feet away. "I think I can make it."

Reaching up, he rubbed his hand over his jaw and then smiled ruefully. "I'm having a hard time letting you out of my sight."

"You're not watching me pee."

"I'll turn my back."

"You'll shut the door," I retorted. I gestured at it,

making something on my arm twinge. I barely held back a grimace. "I'll be right out."

He sighed and closed it between us. Turning, I headed over to do my business.

"Stop listening at the door," I called out.

"I'm not," he called back.

"Bullshit!"

"I have good hearing, remember?"

I felt my cheeks heat as I tried to ignore his presence. When I was done, I shuffled over to the sink and jolted at the sight of myself in the mirror. Someone had brushed my hair and pulled it neatly into a low ponytail, but my fringe was wild on my forehead, and my cheek had a large yellowing bruise. Looking down, I turned my arms back and forth. The bandages were clean, like they'd just been changed.

"Lucy?" Ambrose called.

"I'll be right out!"

I washed my hands carefully so I wouldn't get the bandages wet and then shuffled back out of the bedroom. When I got there, Charlie was sitting on the end of the bed.

Relief rushed through me so hard that I swayed.

"Nice of you to wake up finally," he greeted, looking me over. "Have a good nap?"

"That's bold, coming from you," I replied, moving to the bed. "You're good?"

"Well, I've been worried out of my mind for the past two days, but yes," he said as I gingerly sat down near the pillows. "How are you feeling?"

"Like someone ran me over with a Zamboni."

"Close enough," he said with a small smile.

"Why are you looking at me like that?"

"You *dated a cop for ten minutes*?" he asked, raising an eyebrow.

It took me a moment to understand what he was referring to.

"I may have gone back to the gun range without him," I replied as Ambrose walked back into the room.

"Did you live there?" Charlie asked dryly.

"No, I didn't go for long." I didn't want to talk about it anymore.

"Then how the hell did you do all that?"

"Once you know how to load and fire, it's not hard." I shrugged.

"Oh, please," he shot back. "I saw the aftermath. You—"

"They were practically on top of us, Charles," I snapped, my voice high and weird. "It doesn't take a whole lot of skill when you're that close!"

The amusement in Charlie's eyes disappeared. "I'm sorry, Luce."

"It's fine," I replied flatly.

"Hey, baby," Ambrose called. "You up for a little trip?"

"Oh, sure," I spat, spinning on him. "How about we go back to Europe? I had so much fun there the last time."

Charlie jerked with surprise, but Ambrose just watched me steadily.

"I was thinking we could walk down and see Alice so she doesn't have to come up here."

"Definitely," I said, dropping my feet to the floor. I ignored the pain in my thigh and stomped toward him.

"You want some pants?"

"Not if they look like yours." I glared.

The asshole laughed.

"She's always like this when she's sick," Charlie said.

"I'm not sick."

Ambrose got me some baggy sweatpants and helped me step into them. They were very loose in the waist, but that was fine because it meant they were also very loose in the legs and didn't put any pressure on my wounds.

I complained as we left Ambrose's rooms. "Should I really be walking?" I asked, letting him tug me along slowly. "It seems like a bad idea."

"She wanted you up last night, but you were sleeping," he replied.

"That seems way too soon."

"She's pretty good at what she does," Charlie said from behind me.

"Good to know," I mumbled.

We took the stairs slowly, setting two feet on each one before I moved to the next. As a result, there were people waiting for us by the time we reached the bottom floor.

"How are you feeling?" Erik asked, watching me intently.

"Like shit. How about you?" I replied flippantly.

After a moment, he smiled. "Better."

That's when I remembered he'd been shot too. Shit. I didn't have time to apologize for being a jerk when Reese moved in for a hug.

"Holy shit, dude," she said, squeezing my waist. "You've been asleep a long time."

"It was an exhausting day," I replied, patting her back.

"Understatement of the year." She pulled back and looked into my eyes. "We did it."

"Barely."

"It counts," she said firmly.

"I'm taking her to see Alice," Ambrose said, wrapping an arm around my shoulders.

Erik and Reese backed out of the way as he led me toward the hidden hospital room. When we got there, I got a nasty sense of déjà vu, but it wasn't Reese in the bed next to the one I'd been in. Instead, Alice's large mate lay there, still as a rock, his face pasty white. His neck was wrapped in white gauze.

"Oh, good. You're awake," Alice said from her place in a chair beside him.

"Sven?" I asked, looking back at the Vampire.

"He's still recuperating," she said firmly as she stood. "It takes time. Let's take a look at those wounds."

I walked over to the other bed and stood beside it. Untying the knot at my waist, I let the sweatpants fall to my feet.

Alice raised her eyebrows. "Well, that's one way to do it." She walked over to wash her hands as Ambrose knelt down to help me step out of the pants.

"How are you feeling?" Alice asked over her shoulder.

"Sore."

"I'll bet. That bullet was a tricky bugger."

My stomach flipped at that.

I stood very still while she took off the tape and uncovered the wounds on my legs, my chin high as I stared at the wall. As she poked at those, Ambrose began to unwind the cloth around my arms.

"Healing nicely," Alice said. "Your immortality hadn't solidified yet, but if I had to guess, I'd say it *had* started."

"How long will it take?" Ambrose asked quietly.

"You know I can't answer that," Alice chided. "But I don't think it will be long. A week, perhaps?"

"How will I know?" I joked. "Is someone else going to shoot me?"

"Don't say that," Ambrose snapped.

I looked at him in surprise and accidentally got a good view of my arms. They were covered in fresh pink scars. Four on each arm were oddly uniform. Some of the others were still scabbed over. Near my elbow, a row of six neat stitches ran in a straight line.

"Shit."

"That's what you get when you go wrestling around in glass," Alice said.

My stomach pitched again, and I pushed that memory away.

"Stitches on your arm can come out today," she announced. "I want the ones on your legs to stay another day, maybe two."

As she stood, I looked down at my legs. There were stitches along the inside of my thigh, a few inches above my knee, and another set low on my ankle, almost on the top of my foot.

As she pulled a little cart closer to the bed, I went somewhere else in my head. I stared at the gray sink in the corner, watching as a little bead of water lost its grip and ran slowly down the inside edge. Then another and another.

"All done," Ambrose whispered in my ear, kissing the spot below it softly.

Alice put smaller bandages over my stitches to keep them dry, but left the rest of my healing cuts uncovered.

"You'll do," she said, pausing with her hands full of wrappers. She searched my face.

"Thank you," I rasped. I wasn't sure what she was looking for. I wasn't even sure how I felt. Everything felt just slightly out of focus.

"Let's get some lunch," Ambrose said as he helped me pull the sweatpants back on. "Want me to bring you something, Alice?"

"I'd appreciate it," Alice replied as she walked to the trash can.

I tried not to look at my arms as we left, but it was

nearly impossible. The scars were everywhere. I'd never be able to hide them without wearing a long-sleeved shirt. Vanity had never been one of my vices. I looked like what I looked like—it was the reminder that I dreaded never being able to escape. I'd remember that heinous night every time I got a look at my own skin.

"I don't want bone broth, Erik," Matilda snapped just as we reached the kitchen. "I want a piece of toasted bread with burrata, tomatoes, pesto, and basil on top."

"I told you she was angry," Ambrose said jokingly as we rounded the counter.

I froze.

Matilda stood in the center of the kitchen with my brother and Erik, wearing some kind of classy blue silk robe. Her hair was pulled into a loose French braid, and she didn't have any makeup on.

She looked completely fine. Healthy, even.

Visions of her hand pressing against her dress as blood crept out from behind it battered me. The sound was first, she'd dropped the shotgun, and then seconds later the thud when she'd fallen onto the hardwood floor. The sight of the soles of her bare feet lying askew as I'd shifted and wrenched on that man's neck.

I couldn't stop them. They played in a loop. I jerked, trying to distinguish between what was happening in the present and what had happened before.

"Lucy," she called, hurrying across the kitchen. "There's my girl."

Before I could brace for it, she'd wrapped her arms around me, her head going to my shoulder. I lifted my hands and patted her gingerly on the back. After a moment, I began to hug her back.

"You had us worried," she said quietly, her hand smoothing down my ponytail.

"*I* did?" I choked out. I swallowed against the urge to cry.

"You've been asleep so long," she replied as she pulled away. "I'm so glad you're feeling better."

Was I feeling better? I didn't remember feeling bad in the first place. I didn't even remember when I'd lost consciousness, but I must've at some point because eventually, I woke up.

"Come eat," Erik said gruffly.

"I'm not hungry," I replied, looking over at Matilda.

She grinned. "You're sweet," she said. "But you haven't had anything in days. You need to have something, even if it's small. I'll stop complaining and be a good girl."

Erik made a noise, and when I looked at him, he was gazing at his mate in a way I hoped I never saw again. No one's parents should go around throwing those kinds of looks at each other.

I planted myself on a stool next to Charlie at the counter while Ambrose went over to make me a plate.

"Do they hurt?" he asked quietly, looking at my arms.

"Not really," I replied, dropping them to my lap under the lip of the counter.

"They'll fade," he murmured sympathetically.

"It doesn't matter."

"They looked a lot worse before—"

"I don't care, Charlie," I snapped.

The kitchen went silent.

"They're fine. They don't hurt, okay?"

"Lucy?" Ambrose called questioningly.

I wasn't sure why I was so angry, but I *was*. The longer I was awake, the higher the wave of rage built. The large kitchen felt like it was pressing in on all sides.

"Mm," Matilda said with mock cheerfulness. "Broth. My favorite."

"Come sit here, Mom," Charlie said, patting the seat next to him. "You can at least pretend it's a meal."

My vision darkened at the edges.

"Do you think Charlie would be offended if I let him know he could call us Mom and Dad?"

My heartbeat thundered in my ears.

"Baby?" Ambrose rounded the island and moved toward me.

"I'm fine," I said, sliding off the stool. I backed away.

"What's wrong?"

"I said I'm fine," I gritted out, still backing up.

"Lucy, stop," he ordered as I bumped into the kitchen table.

"You stop," I shot back, making him freeze. "I said I'm fine, all right?"

"You're clearly not."

Bang.

Bang.

Bang.

BANG.

My hands were over my ears in an instant.

I could see Ambrose's mouth moving, but I couldn't hear him.

"Safe," he repeated as my ears stopped ringing. "You're safe, love. You're safe."

I started to laugh, my eyes watering.

"Lucy, come here."

"I'm safe?" I asked doubtfully. "That's what you want to go with? That's the big declaration you want to make *now*?"

"It's over," he said softly.

"No, it's not," I argued, staring at him in disbelief. "It'll never be over."

"We'll find them," he assured me.

"Who?" I threw my arms in the air and immediately regretted it. "Because I killed"—my voice cracked—"a lot of them, and they just kept coming. Waves of them. Like frigging zombies."

"We'll cut off the head of the snake," Ambrose replied. "That's how we'll stop them."

"You don't even know who that is," I screamed. "You don't know anything!"

"That's because we were searching for Charles," Ambrose countered. "Now that we know he's safe, we can research. Talk to contacts. Get to the bottom of it."

"Oh, he's safe?" I hissed. "Like I was safe?"

Ambrose's expression fell.

"You left me here unconscious," I said. "I woke up to Alice telling me that everything had gone to shit and gunshots going off outside. Do you have any idea what that was like? I'd been worried about you, not me!"

"I know," Ambrose ground out.

"I wasn't prepared," I screamed, my hands shaking. "I wasn't—you said I would be safe here!"

"I know," he repeated, his eyes darkening.

"I wasn't safe! None of us were safe!"

"I know," he croaked, taking a step forward.

"I laid there, burning, thinking that I was keeping *you* safe, and—"

"What?" Ambrose breathed, his eyes widening in shock.

"Oh, yeah," I snapped. "That sedation? Couldn't move. Couldn't wake up. *Still burned from the inside out.*"

"No."

"You didn't feel it?"

"I—yes," he sputtered, his brow drawn in confusion. "But it wasn't so bad that—"

"Well, I'm glad it wasn't so bad for you," I shot back. "But it didn't even work, and you left me here *helpless*. What if Alice hadn't been able to wake me up in time? What then? Do you have any idea what that was like?"

"Lucy," Charlie called in warning as Ambrose's face lost all color.

I ignored him as the heat inside me roared to life again at the worst possible moment.

"You fucked me, and then you *fucked* me," I spat. "I told you to let that asshole find his own mate. *I told all of you.*"

Ambrose just stared at me in shocked silence.

Suddenly, the rage left me almost as quickly as it had come, and all I was left with was a hollowness. None of it mattered. They'd made a bad call, and things had gone to shit. There was nothing to do about it anymore. We couldn't change the past.

Matilda set her mug down and moved toward us.

"I watched you die," I choked out. "I—there was so much blood. You fell down and your feet—"

"Come here, sweetheart," she said, pulling me into her arms.

I felt like a little kid as she shushed me and smoothed her hand over the back of my head.

"You be angry if you need to," she said. "Get it all out. He can take it."

"He left me all alone," I whispered, squeezing my eyes shut. "It hurt."

"I know. I know he did."

"I was supposed to be safe here," I replied. "If I'd known, I could've prepared myself."

"No one can prepare themselves for that," she soothed. "But I understand what you mean."

"You were dead," I whispered.

"Sorry," she teased gently. "You're still stuck with a mother-in-law. You can't get rid of me that easily."

I let out a choked laugh.

"I want you to remember three things for me," she said, rocking me from side to side. "Can you do that?"

I nodded against her shoulder.

"One, there are a lot of things in this world that are unpredictable, but Ambrose is not one of them. He'd protect you with his life, and he'd never willingly put you in danger. That's not how he was raised, and it's not how he's built. He loves you."

I jolted, but she held me tight.

"Two, he will always be your sounding board," she said softly. "He's the rock that you'll crash against, the meadow you'll relax in, the wind that pushes you along. But please remember that he feels things as deeply as you do, and be careful which words you use when you're hurt or angry."

Shame made my throat tight.

"And last," she said with a sigh. "You were incredibly brave."

I tried to pull away, but she wouldn't let me go.

"You may have been scared—I was too—but I'm so glad you were there next to me. We wouldn't have made it without you, Lucy. You held them off until the boys got back."

"So did you."

"I did," she agreed. "But without you, they would've overpowered us. It's not an opinion. It's a fact."

"Can you remember those three things?" she asked, pulling away to look at my face.

"I'll try."

"Good." She reached up and wiped the tears from my cheeks with her thumbs. "Charlie's agreed to call me Mom, so you will too."

I snorted.

"Hey, you didn't make me that offer," Reese complained from somewhere behind me.

I turned to find her and Beau standing at the entrance to the kitchen. A few feet away, Alice leaned on the door-frame leading into the hospital room.

"Of course, the offer is for you too," Matilda replied with a smile.

"Good," Reese said firmly. She looked at me. "I feel it all too," she said sympathetically. "I just prefer to yell at Beau in our rooms."

I nodded and glanced over at the table. Ambrose was sitting in one of the chairs, his elbows on his knees, head in his hands.

Agony was in every line of his body.

I'd wounded him. Remorse hit me like a slap in the face.

I was angry at what had happened. It wasn't fair. I'd spent my entire life fighting. When did I get a break? I was so *tired*.

But what I'd ignored during my outburst was that I wasn't even mad at Ambrose.

I knew, deep in my bones, that he would never let anything happen to me if he could help it.

He'd die for me without hesitation.

The same way Zeke had gone back into the viper's nest to keep Charlie safe.

The same way I'd looked at the front door that night and known that I had to protect that entrance, even though I'd probably die in the process.

Ambrose and I were the same. A matched set.

I moved toward him and slid my hands into his hair.

Without hesitation, his arms encircled my hips, and he rested his face against my stomach.

"I'm sorry," I whispered. "It wasn't your fault."

"It was," he argued, kissing me through my T-shirt. "But I swear it'll never happen again."

"We'll stop them," I said, tipping his head back.

"Fuck yeah, we will," Chance said as he strode into the kitchen. "You're done yelling now, right?"

I opened my mouth to say something when he hummed and wagged his finger at me. "I saved your life, so you have to be nice to me."

I gawped at him.

"Unfortunately true," Ambrose said as he rose to his feet. "He put pressure on your thigh until Alice could help you."

"Why didn't *you*?" I asked in confusion.

"I was too busy carrying you out of the pile of bodies." He winced as he realized what he'd said.

I tried to remember those moments, but it was just a blank spot in my memory.

"You were out of it," Chance said, stuffing a piece of bread into his mouth. Pesto dropped down his chin. "Don't worry, I won't ever touch you when you're conscious."

I stared at him, waiting for him to realize—

"You know what I meant," he snapped uncomfortably.

I laughed. I couldn't help it. He'd walked right into that one himself.

"Food," Ambrose ordered quietly.

I tipped my head back to look at him, and he immediately dropped a soft kiss on my lips. "Never again. I promise."

I nodded.

Alice had disappeared into the room with her mate again, but I thought about her as the rest of us sat down around the table to eat. She had to have known that the sedation hadn't stopped the heat. She'd been monitoring us the entire time. So why hadn't she called the men back? Had she understood the look I'd sent her? Had she known that I wouldn't have wanted her to call Ambrose back, no matter how bad it got? Maybe it wasn't as simple as that. Maybe she'd just made the decision alone, knowing that they had a better chance of coming back safely if Ambrose and Beau stayed with the group.

I didn't think I'd ever ask her. What was done was done, and she was paying for it, anyway. Her mate still hadn't woken up.

I looked around the table. Someone was missing.

"Wait, where's Danny?"

CHAPTER 14
AMBROSE

"When I suggested staying in bed for days, this wasn't exactly what I meant," I grumbled.

Charlie had carried over Zeke's projector, and a film that wasn't holding my attention played against the wall. Bags of junk food littered the comforter, and Lucy was currently bent nearly in half so that her head rested on my stomach. It would've been nice except for the extra person in our bed.

"I love this part," Charlie said, pointing at the wall. "She doesn't take his shit."

"He says that," Lucy joked. "But you should've seen him with Zeke. That guy could've told him his shirt was ugly, and he smelled like dog poo, and Charlie would've just smiled and nodded."

"I would not," Charlie retorted. "And Zeke would've never told me that, anyway."

"True," Lucy said, gently nudging her brother with her foot. "And I'd never let you smell like dog poo."

"I *can* take care of myself, you know," Charlie mused, his eyes on the movie.

"Really?" Lucy joked. "Let me know when you want to start."

Charlie scoffed.

I would've loved some one-on-one time with Lucy, but I couldn't be angry that she and Charlie wanted to spend time together after all that had happened. My family had dealt with trauma on a smaller scale my entire life. The males had gone on dangerous missions, fought in wars, and seen the worst of humanity firsthand. My mother had lived through the Civil War, buried three children, and watched as her sons left to fight armies across the world—and even we were shaken.

They had come into our home. Our sanctuary. The one place in the world that should've been safe.

"I forgot how much I dislike the main characters in this," Lucy said conversationally. "Neither of them is very bright."

"They're sweet," Charlie countered.

"Whatever you say," Lucy hedged.

"They overcome so many obstacles," Charlie insisted, pointing.

"Obstacles of their own making," Lucy shot back. "If they'd just talk to each other, half of their issues would be resolved."

"You're the worst person to watch a movie with," Charlie grumbled, rolling off the opposite side of the bed with a thump. "I'm leaving."

"You don't have to leave," Lucy argued, lifting her head. "I'll pretend I like it." She laughed. "Stay."

"It's two in the morning," Charlie replied. "I'm going to bed."

"Let's watch a different one! Ambrose doesn't mind," she said, elbowing me in the gut as she boosted herself up. "Right?"

I just looked at her.

Charlie snorted. "I'll see you tomorrow. Not too early." He pointed at her. "I'm sleeping in."

"Yeah, we'll see," Lucy replied, dropping back down with a sigh.

She paused the movie, and we lay there quietly, listening as Charlie left my room and shut the door behind him.

"Thanks for being such a good sport," she said, carefully rolling to face me. "I think he needed some sister time."

"I think *you* needed some brother time," I countered, running my hand over her hip.

"That too."

"How are you feeling?"

"Physically? Sore. The stitches on my ankle itch, and it feels like someone donkey kicked my thigh. Emotionally? It's a crapshoot."

My lips twitched.

"The overwhelming rage is gone," she said with a shrug. "At least for the moment. That's good, right?"

"It'll come back." I squeezed her hip. "All of it will come back. You'll deal with it, and you'll feel better for a while until it comes up again."

"Oh, great," she grumbled.

"You survived a traumatic thing," I reminded her. "Give yourself time to sit with it."

She nodded. "I'm sorry for what I said in the kitchen earlier. I wasn't even mad at *you*."

"It would be okay if you were."

"It's not like you knew it was going to happen."

"I should've listened to you."

"Before or after I threatened to burn down your

house?" she asked dryly. "I wasn't exactly a pillar of logic at the time."

"Finau was believable." Just the thought of him made rage build in my chest. "He had to have a mate somewhere. That kind of thing is hard to fake."

"Maybe they did take his mate," Lucy said softly. "Maybe they told him that if he helped them, they'd give her back."

My hand froze on her hip. "That would explain it."

"I still hope he dies a horrendous death," she said. "But it would make what he did understandable."

"I'd do anything to get you back," I confessed. "I'll still kill him if we ever find him."

Lucy smiled sadly. "I think you'd have to get in line. Your dad might beat you to it."

"I could take him," I boasted, completely full of shit.

"Yeah, okay." She rolled her eyes and made a face.

"I thought you were calling them Mom and Dad now, not *my* mom and *my* dad."

"Is that weird for you?" she asked, scooting up so she could lay on the pillow next to me.

"Not at all. Is it weird for you? You didn't have to, you know."

"I'm pretty sure your mom wasn't taking no for an answer," she replied wryly. She smiled. "It isn't weird for me, which is weird. Does that make sense?"

"Yes."

"Our parents weren't terrible people or anything," she said, tucking her hands beneath her cheek. "They provided for us. We never went without, even when things were tight. They just...didn't know how to be parents. My dad grew up in a group home, so he really never had that kind of family life, you know? And my mom's wasn't much better. I think my grandma tried, but she'd been through so much trauma in her life that she never really recovered."

"You don't have to explain," I assured her, cupping the side of her neck so I could feel her pulse against my fingers.

"My grandma on my mom's side actually escaped Europe during the Second World War."

"Oh?"

Lucy nodded. "She was only like thirteen or fourteen, and family lore says she went over the Alps to Switzerland and eventually made it to the United States. I don't remember which country she left, but Charlie could probably tell you. From what little my mom said, she wasn't an easy woman to live with." She lifted her head. "Could you grab my bag?"

"Sure."

I went and got her bag from the top of my dresser and set it next to her on the bed.

"So...remember when I told you I had to go back to Baltimore?"

"Hard to forget."

"Well, this is why." She unzipped her bag and pulled out a file folder, a binder, and a small cigar box and set them between us. Opening the file folder, she shuffled through the papers. "Birth certificates and my parents' marriage certificate. Both of our diplomas from high school and college." She neatly packed it away. "Boring."

I smiled.

"This is the good stuff." Sitting up cross-legged, she pulled off the rubber band that held the cigar box closed. Inside was an assortment of random tiny trinkets that she pulled out one by one.

"Are those teeth?" I asked, leaning to get a closer look.

Lucy laughed. "Yeah. The first one each of us lost. Actually, it's my second one. I think I swallowed the first one."

"You went back to Baltimore for your baby teeth?"

"Not just my baby teeth," she replied loftily. "This is the penny my dad wore around his neck. He said it was the first money he ever made, for pulling weeds, and he felt so rich that he couldn't make himself spend it. He carried it in his pocket for a long time, but eventually he just drilled a little hole in it so he could wear it around his neck."

She pulled out a gold ring with three diamond chips inlaid on the band. "My mom's wedding ring. Dad didn't wear one.

"This is a ticket for the first film festival Charlie and I ever went to. We thought we were so cool because we didn't have to go with our parents." She waved a little ticket and placed it back inside. "This is the only patch Charlie ever got in Boy Scouts. He only lasted a month before he lost interest. Between you and me, I think he didn't like it because I couldn't do it with him."

"Unsurprising."

"Right?" She let out a little laugh. "This little guy sat on my parents' nightstand. I have no idea why, since neither of them were Buddhist."

Every small trinket had a story behind it, something that only she or Charlie would know or remember, and with each item she pulled out, her expression grew a little softer. As pragmatic as Lucy was, she'd still considered these bits and pieces of her past worth going back for.

"This," she said, pulling the binder over. "Is everything else."

Inside was a scrapbook of sorts. The front page was a photo of her and Charlie when they were around five or six years old. Charlie was standing behind her, his little arms around her waist as he lifted her a couple of inches off the floor. Lucy's expression could've best been described as terrified as she stared at the camera.

"He did that for years," she said with a snicker. "He thought it proved that he was stronger than me or something." She flipped the page. "This is my parents on their wedding day."

"They're young." Lucy's parents didn't have the glow that you'd normally see in a wedding photo. They were both smiling, but there was something about the way they held themselves, like they were uncomfortable in front of the camera or with each other.

"We got my dad's eyes," she said, looking a little closer. "Mom's nose and hair, though."

"You both have his eyebrows too," I said, pointing.

"How can you tell?" she asked dryly. "My mom barely has eyebrows."

She turned the page again, and there was a photo of what had to be her mother as a child, standing next to a woman who looked vaguely familiar. I leaned a little closer, trying to place her.

I let out a breath of surprise when recognition finally dawned.

Slowly, I pointed to the woman. "Your grandmother?"

"Yes. Her name was—"

"Anna," I said softly.

The memory of that same face, but smaller, softer, with wider eyes and a shy smile, made my chest ache.

"How did you know that?" Lucy asked, her brows pulled together in confusion.

I cleared my throat. "I was there," I said quietly, still looking at the stern woman in the photo.

"Where? What are you talking about?"

"I was part of the team that led her and other children through the Alps," I explained, looking up into my mate's bewildered eyes. "There were four of us. I remember her because she carried one of the younger ones on her back." I stopped.

I didn't want to take out that memory and examine it.

"She escaped from Austria," I said, tapping my finger on the photo.

"You were *there*?" Lucy asked, like she couldn't quite grasp what I was telling her.

"The United States hadn't joined the war yet," I explained. "So our hands were tied. We did what we could." I glanced down at the photo again. "It wasn't enough."

"You saved my grandmother's life," Lucy said slowly.

"I was part of a larger network," I argued, unwilling to take on full responsibility.

"Oh my god," she whispered, looking down at the photograph. "That's insane."

"Improbable," I agreed.

"Everything is connected, isn't it?" she said, shaking her head. "Like a giant spider web."

"The world is smaller than we realize."

"You *saved* her," she said softly, reaching out to cup my cheek. "How many did you save?"

"Not enough," I rasped.

I didn't like to think of that time. The misery, the fear, the inability to fight for what we *knew* was right. So many people had suffered. So many had died.

"You're incredible," she whispered, running her thumb along my cheekbone.

"She wore a dark-brown coat," I said, uncomfortable. "And a dark hat with a little bobble on the top of it. She was tough. Quiet. They were *all* quiet."

"I can't believe you remember her."

"I remember them all," I replied. I pulled my face away and rose from the bed, gathering the food wrappers and garbage.

"We don't have to talk about it," Lucy said, handing me a half-eaten sleeve of crackers.

"I don't like to think about it," I replied, taking the wrappers out to the garbage in the kitchenette. When I came back into the room, she'd stuffed her treasures back into her bag.

"We could've finished looking," I told her.

"Another time," she said, carrying the bag back to the dresser. "You okay?"

"I'm fine." I shook my head.

"We all have things we'd rather not revisit," she replied, walking toward me. She wrapped her arms around my waist. "I just want to say one thing."

"All right."

"You saved my grandmother, not knowing that eighty years later you would kidnap me from a hotel room. How cool is that?"

I chuckled. "Pretty cool."

"You still look like shit," she muttered.

"I'm fine."

"Oh crap," she breathed. "You need blood. That's it, right? When's the last time you had it?"

"You were there," I replied dryly.

"I thought you needed it every day?"

"You needed it more."

"Well, I'm good now," she said, tipping her head ridiculously far back. "Do your thing."

I choked and started coughing.

"What?" She jerked her chin down.

"I'm fine," I said, herding her toward the bed. I turned

off the light and unplugged the projector on the way, blanketing us in darkness.

"This is part of it, right?" she said as I threw the crumb-covered comforter off the bed. I wasn't about to sleep in that shit, and with the heat keeping our body temperatures higher than normal, we wouldn't need more than a sheet anyway.

"Part of our relationship?" I asked.

"Yeah. The whole mates thing."

"Yes, it's part of it."

"Well, then." She crawled across the bed and flopped onto her back. "Get to it."

"Part of it," I clarified, slower as I got in beside her. "Just like anything else. You're healing. I can wait."

"I'm practically healed," she argued, rolling toward me. "I've eaten...a lot. I've showered. I'm good to go."

"As tempting as that sounds..." I joked. To be honest, it did sound tempting. Very fucking tempting. I'd been ignoring the craving since the night before, instincts urging me to feel her skin between my teeth and her blood in my throat to assure myself that she was alive, but I wasn't an animal. I wasn't going to die if we waited a few days. She'd lost a lot of blood, and her body was still recovering.

Lucy huffed and pressed herself against my side. "What if I told you that *I* need it?"

"Is that what you're telling me?"

She was quiet for a moment. "I thought I was going to die," she said softly. "And I'd never see you again."

"Baby," I whispered back, turning to face her.

"And you'd be left here without me." The words were so soft that a human probably wouldn't have heard them.

"I would've been right behind you," I replied, tipping her face up so I could see her eyes.

"Don't say that."

"It's the truth."

"No, you don't get to do that."

"Get?"

"I forbid it," she snapped.

"There would be nothing left here for me." It was the truth. Until we had children—if we had children—there wouldn't be any reason to stay. I loved my parents and my brothers, but without my mate, I would be a shell of the person they knew. I'd seen it happen.

"Stop it."

"Do you want me to lie?"

"About this?" she snapped again. "Yes!"

"Okay, fine," I replied flatly. "I'd miss you for a week or two, and then I'd get on with my life."

Lucy rolled her eyes and stretched up to pepper kisses over my chin and jaw. She slid her hand under my shirt and raked her nails softly over the skin on my back.

"You've still got stitches in your leg," I reminded her as I turned my head and captured her lips with mine.

"Can't even feel them," she lied against my mouth.

We stripped each other slowly, taking our time rediscovering all of the spots that made each other moan. Lucy loved when my beard brushed against the bottom curves of her breasts. I almost lost it completely when she fisted my hair in her hands, guiding me down her body.

I ran my lips and tongue along the crease of her thigh as I trailed my fingers over her. By the time I'd reached the delicate skin between her legs, she was drenched and gasping. Running my tongue lightly over her, I savored it. Every touch, every sight, every taste was another reminder that I could've lost her. She clenched around me as I slid my finger inside her, curling it toward my mouth as I licked at the little bundle of nerves that was growing more swollen by the second. Lucy sobbed, leaning up on one elbow to watch as her hand smoothed down the back of my neck and alongside my jaw. She threw her head back as she came, her feet pressing against the bed as she pressed herself against my mouth.

Her eyes met mine as I rose, soft and adoring. I swallowed hard, knowing that I was looking at her in much the same way.

Reaching down, she curled her hand around my erection, her thumb gliding back and forth across the tip. I shuddered. I needed to be inside her. But when I paused, kneeling between her legs, the sight of the bandage on her thigh stopped me in my tracks. I ran my thumb along the edge of the tape, hesitating.

Lucy huffed impatiently and flipped over. Rising onto her hands and knees, she arched her back. The bandage disappeared, hidden between her thighs and protected from any friction.

The round globes of her ass brushed against me as she swayed from side to side.

"Gods," I muttered, running my hand down her spine. The tattoo on her back stared at me, a reminder that she had belonged to me long before either of us had known it.

I watched as I slid my fingers along the crack of her ass before pushing one and then two inside her. She was so wet that the sound of it played havoc on my self-control.

Lucy dropped down onto her elbows, giving me an even better view, and that self-control was gone. Rising onto my knees, I fisted my erection and fed it inside, watching her stretch around me as she mewled, her hands fisting the pillow beneath her head.

"Is that better, mate?" I asked softly, pulling out and sliding back in again.

"More," she ordered, moving in counterpoint.

Leaning over her back, I braced myself next to her shoulder. Our tattoos lined up so closely that they might as well have been kissing.

"You're so beautiful," I murmured into her ear, kissing anything I could reach.

How the hell had I gotten so lucky? Why had the Gods finally let me have her? Was it all just luck, or had I finally proven myself somehow? Whatever the reason, chance or fate, I was grateful.

Wrapping an arm around her waist, I found her clitoris with the tip of my middle finger and circled it, pressing a little harder with each pass until she was writhing against me, trying to both meet my thrusts and push herself harder against my finger. When she finally gave up control and arched into me, I pressed harder, and she came with a muffled scream, her body shaking beneath mine.

Smiling, I lifted my wrist to my mouth and nicked the skin. Carefully, I slid it beneath her and without a word, Lucy's mouth found it and began to suck. My mouth watered as I pressed my lips against her neck. I licked it softly before pressing my teeth against the pulse there.

The moment she came again, I pierced her flesh and let the taste of her roll through me. There wasn't anything else in the world like it. There would never be anything even remotely close.

I came with my body sheltering hers and her lifeblood flowing through me.

It was what I'd been made for, I realized as she delicately licked the blood from my arm. For that moment and all the ones that came after. I'd done a lot of things in my life that I was proud of and a lot of things that I wasn't. I'd probably killed more than I'd saved. I'd made wrong decisions and right decisions, I'd said terrible things and I'd said kind ones. I'd led an entire life before I'd ever met her.

But all of that had just been preparation for the real reason I was there.

I'd been put on the earth to love and protect Lucy Franklin.

CHAPTER 15
LUCY

I woke up in the middle of the night, wrapped in Ambrose's arms. I'd pushed in so close to him that his chest pressed fully against my back. I'd cocked one knee so that my stitches wouldn't touch anything, and his legs surrounded my other leg, his hips aligned with mine. My cheek rested on one of his biceps, and his other arm was wrapped around my waist, his hand pressed against my chest.

I was still freezing.

Curling my hands up by my chin, I lay there listening to his soft breaths.

When I'd realized that I was Ambrose's mate, I'd been so dubious of the entire thing. Even after I'd watched my brother fall in love with Zeke so quickly, I hadn't understood. I'd assumed Charlie had fallen so fast because that was just who he was. Romantic. Always seeing the best in people.

I wasn't like that. I hadn't been waiting for my Prince Charming to whisk me away. I'd had the life that I'd built, and I had Charlie, and that's all I'd needed. Did I like dating? Sure, sometimes. But I hadn't felt like I was missing anything when I was single. I hadn't been searching for someone to make a life with.

Then Ambrose showed up with his perfect face.

He was everything I'd never realized I needed.

He protected me. I'd proven how capable I was at protecting myself, but that didn't matter. He *wanted* to care for me, from washing me in the shower to making sure I ate, to letting Charlie lie in bed with us for hours watching stupid movies that no one but my brother liked.

It was something I'd never had before. Someone anticipating my needs and providing them before I'd even realized that they were missing.

He looked at me like I was the most beautiful woman in the universe. The smartest. The kindest. There hadn't been a moment since we met that I didn't feel the full weight of that. It was constant. Unwavering.

I really had won the lottery when I was least expecting it. I couldn't imagine ever going back to what I'd had before, carrying the weight of everything alone. Just the thought of it made my nose sting with tears.

"I love you," I whispered into the darkness, pulling his arm closer against my chest.

"I love you too, baby," he whispered in my ear, scaring the crap out of me.

"When the hell did you wake up?" I asked, turning my head to look at him.

"You've been moving around for the last fifteen minutes," he replied, his voice hoarse from sleep. "You okay? Does your leg hurt?"

"No. I'm freezing," I said with a huff, dropping my head back down.

So much for trying out the words before I said them for real.

265

"You shouldn't have thrown the comforter on the floor."

"It was a mess," he replied tiredly. "All those little crumbs would've driven me crazy if they fell in the sheets."

He moved to get up, but I clutched his arm to my chest as his words reminded me of the textured top of Zeke's quilt, running my finger over the embroidery.

"Get up," I ordered, flinging his arm away from me.

"What's wrong?" he asked in alarm as I crawled to the edge of the bed.

"Up!" I grabbed my shirt and pulled it over my head. "Get dressed."

"Lucy, what the hell is wrong?"

"Nothing's wrong," I assured him as I pulled on the lime sweatpants he'd been wearing earlier. "Hurry."

"You're worrying me," he said as he strode to the dresser. "Why am I getting dressed?"

"We need to go to Charlie's room."

"It's the middle of the night," he said flatly as he got dressed. "Can't this wait—"

"No," I said stubbornly, standing in the doorway. "Come on."

I had to give it to Ambrose. He was a good sport about it. He followed me across the house without a word as I rushed to my brother's room. I wanted to make sure that I was remembering right before I said what I was thinking. If I was wrong, then I'd look a little crazy, but he wouldn't be disappointed. If I was right, he'd be glad that I hadn't waited.

"Charles," I called as I entered his rooms. "I hope you're dressed."

"What the hell are you doing in here?" Charlie whined as I flicked on the overhead light. "Go away."

"No," I replied, reaching for the quilt that covered him. I yanked it off the bed.

"What are you doing?" Charlie grunted angrily as I threw the blanket out until it landed flat on the floor.

"Just a sec," I said as I kneeled down next to it.

Starting at one corner, I checked each scar of embroidery, one by one.

"Baby," Ambrose said gently from where he stood above me. "It's four in the morning."

I ignored him as Charlie sat up on the edge of the bed. "What are you looking for?" he asked blearily.

I'd almost given up when my finger caught on a little hard piece inside the blanket. My throat tightened. I was right.

There was something inside the quilt.

"Here," I said, keeping my pointer finger next to the red embroidery snaking across the quilt. "It's right here."

"What is?" Ambrose asked, kneeling down beside me. He reached out and set his finger next to mine, running it along the edge of the stitching.

"Feel it?" I asked, looking over at him.

"Holy Gods," he breathed.

"Charlie, get me scissors."

My brother stared at me blankly.

"Scissors," I snapped my fingers. "A knife, nail clippers, *something*."

Charlie grumbled as he shuffled to the bathroom.

"What do you think it is?" I asked, looking back at the quilt.

"A chip," Ambrose replied softly.

Charlie walked back in and dropped a pair of nail clippers on top of the quilt. "*You're* going to ask Mom to fix it if you put a hole in it," he said worriedly.

I handed the clippers to Ambrose and watched as he

carefully clipped the threads, pulling on them until they unraveled enough that he could slip his fingers inside. He pulled them back out, pinching a small black rectangle no bigger than my thumbnail.

"What is it?" Charlie demanded.

"It's a microSD," Ambrose said, holding it up to get a closer look as he sat back on his heels. He looked at me. "How the fuck did you know it was there?"

"I felt it," I replied, staring. It was so small.

"When?"

"Right before the sedation kicked in." I shrugged. "I fell asleep before I could tell you."

"What's on it?" Charlie asked, worry lacing his tone.

I frowned at my brother. "You know as much as we do," I reminded him acerbically. "Zeke didn't exactly label it."

Ambrose rose and walked to the wall, pressing the intercom on the wall. "Chance, is Danny home?"

It was silent for a few moments.

"How the hell would I know?" Chance griped angrily. "What the fuck?"

"Call him," Ambrose ordered.

"You call him," Chance shot back.

"Lucy found a microSD in Zeke's quilt," Ambrose said, looking at me like I'd invented the earth.

A few more moments of silence.

"I'll call him," Chance mumbled.

Ambrose pushed a different button. "Beau."

"This better be good," Beau replied.

"Come to Zeke's room."

"Okay."

We sat in silence until Chance barged in. He was wearing a pair of ratty sweatpants that were cut off at the knees and no shirt.

"My eyes," I hissed, covering my face.

"You're welcome," he replied. The sound of him slapping his belly was unmistakable.

When I opened my eyes again, Ambrose was staring at me in amusement.

"Where's the card?" Chance asked.

Ambrose handed it over.

"It was in the quilt?"

"He'd stitched it in," Ambrose confirmed.

"Tricky little fucker," Chance said, a small smile pulling at his cheeks. "And the idiots brought it right to us."

"He knew there was a good chance it would be shipped back to us," Ambrose said, reaching down to help me off the floor. "Shit, you're bleeding."

"No, I'm not," I argued, looking at my arms.

"Your thigh." A little circle of blood had started to seep through the sweats.

"Shit."

"Danny's on his way," Chance said as Beau and Reese walked quietly into the room. "Take her to Alice. We'll meet you in my rooms."

"I'm fine," I argued. "It doesn't even hurt."

"I'd like to get dressed," Charlie announced.

He was sitting there in his boxers, his cheeks red with embarrassment.

I wanted to argue more, but Ambrose was already pulling me across the room.

"It could've been worse," Reese said behind us. "What if you slept naked?"

I heard my brother laugh as the door closed behind us.

Alice was sleeping, her hand holding Sven's, when we got to the hospital room. Silently, Ambrose led me over to the bed and helped me take off my pants. Beneath them, the bandage was even bloodier.

Without a word, Ambrose gently took the bandage off. Most of the stitches were still intact. It was only one that had snapped and was sticking out at odd angles. I looked away as Ambrose used a pair of tweezers to pull the thread out of my skin. A few minutes later, he'd bandaged it again and was pulling my pants back over my hips.

Once we were making our way through the kitchen, he lifted my hand to his lips and kissed it. "It's healed enough that you didn't need a new stitch," he said quietly. "You need to be more careful until it's fully healed."

"I will," I assured him.

He stopped and picked me up at the bottom of the stairs.

"I think I can manage stairs," I said against his ear as he carried me up.

"Why chance it when I like having you in my arms?" he replied.

I wondered if he was filled with as much anxiety as I was. There was a chance that the only thing on that memory card was porn or bank statements or a million other things that Zeke could've wanted to hide. He could've hidden that memory card years ago and forgotten about it. We wouldn't know if it held anything until we opened it.

I wrapped my arms around Ambrose's neck and slid my hand through his hair as he reached the top of the stairs.

Pausing, he set me gently on my feet and grabbed my hand.

When we entered Chance's room, I was surprised to see that instead of a living room like the other brothers had, he'd turned his main room into a giant office. There was a huge L-shaped desk with four computer monitors set up, a thousand cords and wires, and other assorted tech stuff that was only familiar because I had no idea what any of it did. Everyone stood around waiting for us.

"How'd you get here so fast?" Ambrose asked Danny.

"I was already on my way home," he replied. His light-brown hair was a mess, and his beard was scragglier than I'd ever seen it. "You found a memory card?"

"Lucy did," Ambrose clarified. He looked at Chance. "You can read it?"

"We'll see," Chance said. For the first time since I'd met him, he seemed unsure of himself.

"You're offline?" Beau asked.

Chance nodded. "Closed system."

My brother had been leaning against the fireplace mantel, but he moved to my side as we grouped around behind Chance.

At first, nothing happened.

Then, all of a sudden, a little box showed up on the screen. Inside were smaller squares. There had to be hundreds of them.

Charlie's hand found mine.

"Files," Chance said grimly. "Should I just start at the top?"

I held my breath.

"Top left," Ambrose ordered, sliding an arm around my shoulder.

I didn't understand what we were looking at when the file opened, but by the sharp inhales around me, the Boucher brothers did. They didn't speak as Chance scrolled down, reading through whatever it was. After a moment, he opened the second file. Then the third.

I was too far away to read whatever was on the

computer, but I stood beside Ambrose for a long time as he read them over Chance's shoulder.

Eventually, I moved over toward the fireplace and sat down on the floor with my back against the wall. Reese and Charlie followed me. We watched as the Boucher brothers scoured their baby brother's files, discovering what he'd felt was so important that he'd hidden a memory card in the last place anyone would look.

"Is anyone else dying to know what they found?" Reese asked quietly.

I nearly laughed, knowing that they could hear everything she said and there was no reason for her to whisper.

"I'm cool waiting to get the CliffsNotes," I replied.

I knew how Zeke must have died. I didn't want to read any information that had anything to do with the people who'd killed him. Ambrose would tell me what they'd found when he was done, and I wouldn't have to risk seeing something I couldn't forget.

We sat there for hours. Beau and Danny sat down in kitchen chairs after a while, but Ambrose stayed on his feet, his hands on his hips and his eyes never leaving the monitor in the center of the cluster. Reese fell asleep, curled onto her side with her head resting on her arm.

Charlie and I just sat there quietly, pressed together from hip to shoulder, while we waited to hear what the brothers had uncovered. My thigh began to ache, but I ignored it.

And then they were done.

Chance pushed away from the desk with a curse. Both Danny and Beau turned to Ambrose.

"Baby brother was busy," he said after a moment. "Get some rest, and then this afternoon we'll split this up and go over it with a fine-tooth comb. Danny, you take the names. I want to know if someone had a cavity in one of their baby teeth. Chance, you and I will follow the money. Split it up however you think it makes sense, and then we'll compare notes and see where things intersect. Beau—"

"I'll start tracking down their families," he said quietly. "If we're looking for answers, there's a good chance that they are too."

"Before you get in touch with any Vampire's family, we need to talk it over and decide what we're willing to share and whose help we're willing to take. Just because they've lost someone doesn't mean we can trust them."

"Who's going to tell Mom and Dad?" Danny asked, locking his fingers together behind his head.

Ambrose glanced at the window where the sun had come up hours ago. "I will after I get Lucy to bed."

"I sound like a four-year-old," I complained to Charlie.

Ambrose shot me a look over his shoulder.

I tried to rise as Ambrose strode toward me, but my legs and ass were numb for sitting so long on the floor. Both he and Charlie had to help me to my feet.

"What was it?" Charlie asked as we walked across the landing to his rooms.

Ambrose didn't answer until we'd closed the door behind us. After a moment, I realized it was so his parents couldn't hear what we were talking about until he'd had a chance to tell them.

"Zeke must've been looking into things before you met, because there's no way he could've compiled so much information in so little time. There are notes on experiments." Ambrose grimaced and gripped the back of his neck. "Including Vampire and mate medical records. Financial statements. Names and phone numbers of collaborators. It's a mess of information, and we don't have a clear view of it yet, but we will."

Charlie nodded. He let out a sad, hiccuping laugh. "I'm glad," he said, smiling even as tears dripped down his cheeks. "I just—"

"There's a file in there with your initials on it," Ambrose said kindly, reaching out to give Charlie's shoulder a squeeze. "We didn't look at it. If you go back in there, I'm sure Chance is waiting."

Charlie's eyes widened, and he was nodding before Ambrose had even finished his sentence. Without a glance, he hurried back out of the room.

"I hope it's a letter," I said as the door swung halfway shut behind him.

"Me too," Ambrose said tiredly. "Come on. I'll walk you to our room."

"*Our* room?" I teased, leaning my head against his shoulder.

"For now," he replied. We walked across the house slowly, my leg still protesting the movement. "Beau and Reese are building a house on the property. We could do that if you wanted."

I nodded, but I could barely even think of the pros and cons, I was so worn out. We'd only gotten a couple of hours of sleep before I'd woken Ambrose up.

I climbed back into bed and let my mate tug the sweatpants down my legs as I groaned and closed my eyes. A few seconds later, I heard him snap the comforter in the air and then felt it settle over my body.

"Do you want me to come with you?" I asked, opening my eyes again. "I don't mind."

"Sleep, baby," he said, leaning over to kiss me. "I'm going to talk to my parents, and then I'll be back up."

"It's been a long night," I whispered, reaching up to smooth his beard.

"But we're one step closer," he whispered back.

Another kiss, and then he was gone.

I floated in that twilight space somewhere between wakefulness and sleep for a long time, thinking about the sacrifice Zeke had made. If he'd had solid information before he'd seen us at that café, he must've been terrified when he'd realized that he'd found his mate. Unable to walk away and pretend it hadn't happened, he also hadn't been willing to stop searching for answers. He'd been stuck between a rock and a hard place, both wanting to stay with Charlie and knowing that if he didn't leave, my brother might never be safe.

I just wished he'd reached out to his own brothers. They could've helped him the way they were following his clues now.

"You're an idiot, Zeke," I grumbled.

I could almost see him rolling his eyes as he flipped me off.

Sometime later, Ambrose came back into the room and crawled in next to me. He didn't say a word as he wrapped his body around mine, careful not to jostle my legs. I fell asleep almost instantly.

CHAPTER 16
AMBROSE

I'd been staring at financial records for two days, and I still hadn't figured out how they were connected to the conspiracy we were investigating. That's what it was. A fucking conspiracy. There were lists of names we recognized in Zeke's files, some with asterisks next to them and others with question marks. We weren't sure if he'd discovered that they were part of the group who were kidnapping Vampires and their mates or if he'd been checking them out and decided that there wasn't a connection.

It was as if my baby brother had left us a 3D puzzle with a million pieces, assuming that we'd figure it out.

The financial records belonged to both humans and Vampires. There didn't seem to be any organization or method to the information he'd compiled. I'd been cross referencing deposits in one account with withdrawals from the others. I'd found enough connections to know that I was moving in the right direction, but not enough to see any discernible pattern. It was infuriating.

I looked up from the table as Lucy threw her leg over

the arm of the couch. She was reading a novel she'd borrowed from my mother that didn't seem to be holding her attention. Every few minutes, she shifted like she couldn't get comfortable.

"You don't have to sit in here with me," I told her, setting the papers down. Chance had laughed his ass off when I'd asked him to print out the financials instead of looking at them on my laptop. There was something to be said about holding information in your hands while you studied it.

"What else would I do?" Lucy asked, popping up to smile at me over the back of the couch. "I'm good."

She disappeared again, but I couldn't make myself go back to studying the accounts.

Historically, the period after a Vampire met their mate was a time for the two to discover each other and enjoy themselves. It was the equivalent of what humans called a honeymoon period. We should've been in a hotel some-where, ordering room service and lounging naked in bed all day.

Instead, we'd been mourning my brother, escaping kidnappers, going under sedation in an attempt to avoid the mating heat, fighting off attackers, healing from gunshot wounds, and trying to unravel a plot that seemed to grow bigger with every piece of information we uncovered.

I fucking hated that she wasn't getting the experience that she should've had.

"Come on," I said, rising to my seat. "Let's go do something."

"Like what?" she asked, sitting up on the couch. "It's not like we can be out in public with these neon targets on our backs."

"We'll go for a walk on the property."

"I thought you needed to decipher those statements," she said, gesturing at the messy table. "I'm not trying to distract you. I can go read in the bedroom."

"Then I'd be more distracted," I confessed, pulling her to her feet. She was moving much easier now that the stitches had been removed from her leg.

"The heat hasn't been so bad," Lucy said, leaning into me.

"That makes sense," I replied, running my fingers down her spine. "In theory, mating heat should be inherently *good* for you. It's the way we recognize the person who is specifically made for us."

"It definitely takes the guesswork out," Lucy joked.

"So when you were hurt, it should've mellowed. Your body was already trying to heal itself. Adding severe mating symptoms to that would've been counterproductive."

"That makes sense," she replied. "Also, Severe Mating Symptoms would be a good band name."

"It also might be subsiding because we've already completed the bond."

"We're stuck now."

I smiled. "It won't ever go away completely, though."

"Oh, goody."

"It's nature's way of keeping us connected."

"Because we obviously couldn't have done it on our own."

"I don't know," I teased her. "You seem like a runner."

"I resent that." She smiled as I backed her toward the bedroom. "I'm a fighter, not a runner."

"I can't argue that."

"Your parents still can't go very long apart, can they?" she asked, walking backward.

I shook my head. "It's painful for my mother. I've

heard a lot of theories, but Alice believes that the heat symptoms are more severe in human mates longer because it keeps them near their physically stronger partner."

"So they're protected," Lucy said in understanding. "You gotta love evolution." She got a strange look on her face.

"What?"

"I wonder if that's why the symptoms were so bad when I was sedated," she said thoughtfully. "Because I knew somewhere in the back of my mind that something wasn't right, and the bond was like, *Danger, Will Robinson!* That could be why you didn't feel it as strongly. Because you thought you were doing the right thing."

"Could be."

"So you're *agreeing* that you need to listen to me from now on because my body has some kind of magical barometer for danger?" She nodded. "Cool."

"Or maybe you just missed me," I replied, leaning down to kiss her.

"Fair point," she whispered against my lips.

I pulled away slowly. "Come on. Let's get some fresh air."

The downstairs had been cleaned up the day after the humans tried to storm the house, but there were still things left to do to get the house back to its original condition. Cleaners had come in and scrubbed the walls and floors, but the couch was a loss, and so was the large area rug that had covered most of the hardwood. It was nearly impossible to get that much blood out. Windows still needed to be replaced in the front and back. The floors needed to be sanded and refinished. The front porch needed to be repainted.

It was a work in progress. We'd boarded up the

windows until the new ones came in, so Lucy hadn't seen the living room in full daylight yet. She paused at the bottom of the stairs in shock as my father and Beau lifted one of the replacement windows into place.

Beau cursed, and Reese laughed. She was curled up in a chair, watching them work.

The noise must've snapped Lucy out of it because she strode forward.

"Sorry," she said dryly. "I think that's the one I broke."

"Then you should be lifting it into place," my father replied, grunting as he positioned the window from the porch.

"I'm still healing," Lucy said with a grimace and a shrug.

"You look fine to me," Beau grumbled.

Lucy looked at me over her shoulder. "Aren't you going to offer to help?"

"We've got plans, remember?" I reached out, and she grabbed my hand.

The front porch was stained so badly that I took Lucy out the back so she wouldn't have to see it. When we got outside, she tipped her head back and took a deep breath.

"How did you know I needed some fresh air?" she asked happily. "God, it smells good out here."

"You haven't seen the sun in days," I said dryly, leading her further from the house.

"I know. I was turning into a Vampire," she said with a mock shudder.

I laughed and tried to tickle her, but she jumped just out of reach.

"Funny," I replied, nodding.

"Really? No issues with sunlight, huh?" She clicked her tongue.

"Humans have gotten it wrong for centuries," I said as

we wandered into the woods. "The only thing they got right was the blood."

"But we didn't even get that right," she said, turning toward me and walking backward. "We thought you went around biting people."

I smiled. "Only the ones we like," I joked.

"Look, you can't even see the house," she said, pointing over my shoulder. "That was fast."

"It's pretty thick out here."

"Should we go back?" she asked nervously.

"We have six Vampires on the perimeter," I assured her. "Motion sensors, trip wires, and Chance is monitoring cameras placed throughout the property. We're—" I stopped before I said it. I'd told her she was safe before, and I'd been wrong.

"So we should probably keep things PG then," she said, ignoring the mine I'd just avoided. She raised her voice and lifted both her middle fingers into the air. "Since *Chauncey* is watching."

I just shook my head. Their animosity had started out genuine, but I was beginning to see that it had changed into a running thing between them. I was glad. Reese had softened Beau a lot, and by the time Lucy met him, he'd started keeping most of his shitty comments to himself. But Chance didn't have anyone to soften his harsh edges. Beau had been a quiet jerk. Chance was an in-your-face one, which made him twice as obnoxious.

"Why are you frowning at the trees?" Lucy asked, moving closer to run a finger between my brows. "It's a beautiful day, and no one is currently trying to kidnap us."

The words were light, but they hit me like a slap in the face. When she started to pull away, I stopped her.

"I fucked up," I said quietly, cupping her face in my hands.

I'd had one job. I'd been waiting for it my whole life, had prepared for it, dreamed of it, and I'd failed. Protecting my mate was what I'd been put on the earth to do, and I'd failed. Watching her as the sunlight coming through the trees dappled her skin in light and shadow, it hit me. We could've missed this moment. I'd gone off on some harebrained plan, convincing myself that it was to rescue Finau's mate when the truth of it was that I was trying to avenge my brother's death...and I'd left her behind when we had wolves at the door.

"When?" she asked, searching my face.

"You told me not to do it—"

"I told you to leave Charlie behind," she reminded me. "I didn't tell you not to do it."

"I *knew* you didn't like it."

"I don't like a lot of things."

"I put you in danger."

"Ambrose, come on," she said, tilting her head to the side. "I was already in danger, remember? That's how we met."

I couldn't seem to draw air into my lungs.

She'd been trying to reassure me, but she'd done just the opposite.

Lucy was right. I'd known she was in danger before I'd even known she was my mate. In my hubris, I'd assumed that once she was on our property that she'd be safe from the danger that threatened her. I couldn't have been more wrong.

"What's going on?" she asked, wrapping her hands around my wrists. "Where is your head at?"

I'd been going through the motions since we found out that the perimeter had been breached at the house, and we'd been an hour away. Focusing on the next thing I had to do, then the next thing, then the next thing. It was the only way I'd been able to function without completely losing my mind. That had transformed into my obsession with making sure that Lucy was okay, that she was healing, that she had everything she needed. I'd sat beside her while she slept, changed and re-changed her bandages so I could check on her stitches, braided her hair back from her face.

Once she was awake, I'd been determined to give her whatever she needed to be okay emotionally. A punching bag? Of course. I'd deserved every bit of it. A shoulder to lean on. No question. A third wheel while she and her brother watched bad movies and talked about things I had no reference for? Any time.

Then we'd found Zeke's files, and I'd been distracted by those. They were a tangible thing that I could work on. Another step closer to keeping Lucy safe indefinitely. If we could find out for sure who was funding the operation, we could take it out at the knees.

Follow the money. Follow the money. Follow the money.

It wasn't until we'd stepped away from it all, and I'd watched her scampering through the woods, smiling and healthy, that the wave of guilt finally hit me.

It sat solid and unyielding in my chest. Too heavy to carry. Too big to ignore anymore.

"Oh Gods," I mumbled, staring at her beautiful face. The freckle on her cheek. The big brown eyes and straight nose that curved up a little at the end. The plump lips that had started to tremble as she stared back at me.

I could've lost her.

"Ambrose, *what*?" she whispered.

"I am so sorry," I choked out. "I'm so sorry, baby."

"For what?" she asked, trying to shake her head. "You're scaring me."

"I wasn't here to protect you," I ground out, my hands tightening on her face. "I abandoned you."

"No, you didn't."

"I did. I fucking left, and I was too far away to get back to you."

"Stop," she pleaded. "Just stop."

"We came as fast as we could," I continued. "I swear. Danny went twice the speed limit, but it didn't matter. I was trying to get back to you. Did you know I was coming?"

At some point, I'd started to cry, and I couldn't seem to stop. I blinked hard, trying to clear my eyes as her face grew blurry.

"Of course I knew," she said softly, reaching out to slide her hand around the back of my neck.

"I got back as fast as I could," I repeated. "I tried."

"I *knew* you were on your way."

"It took so fucking long to get home," I ground out. "And you were here waiting, and I didn't come."

"You *did*," she argued. "You got here."

"I was too late. You waited for me to come, and I was too late."

"Stop," she cried softly, pressing her hand on top of mine on her cheek. "Stop it. Where is this coming from?" She turned her head and kissed my palm. "Baby, you came for me. I know that. I always knew you were coming."

"It happened again," I rasped, staring into her eyes. "It happened again, and it was my fault this time."

"Ambrose, let's go inside," she said, her hand on my cheek, my neck, my shoulder. "I don't know what's going on. *What* happened again?"

"He waited," I explained, my words tumbling over each other. "I know he waited for us to come get him. He knew we'd come for him. He was sure of it. I know he was sure of it, and *we didn't*."

"Oh," Lucy breathed, her eyes filling with tears.

"I held him first," I continued, the words so fast that they were barely understandable. "My father caught him. He was so small. And he was covered in all this gross shit, and he went to hand him to my mom but she said *no*. She said, 'Give him to Ulf. Ulf should hold him first.' So I did. And he weighed less than my father's axe. He was so small and wiggly, and he was crying, and she said, 'Don't forget to protect his neck.'"

Pulling away from her, I turned and vomited onto the ground.

I braced my hands on my knees as I heaved over and over again.

Protect his neck, Ulf.

Moments later, Lucy's hand landed on my back, and she rubbed it in a slow circle.

It took a few minutes before I was able to stand up straight again. Using the bottom of my shirt, I cleaned off my face before turning to back toward her.

"Let's go inside," she said quietly, reaching for my hand.

The silence was deafening as I followed her back to the house. I couldn't get my head straight. The pressure was so intense, I felt like I was about to implode. I'd messed up too badly. I wasn't sure how she could ever trust me again.

I still had no idea how my parents had ever forgiven me.

When we reached the kitchen, Lucy pulled me to a stop.

I lifted my head to find my father leaning against the counter.

He opened his mouth to say something, then shut it again, dropping his head. When he raised it again to look at me, my throat tightened.

"It's not your fault," he finally said. "You're not all-seeing, Ulf."

I struggled for air.

"None of us knew until it was over. That was your brother's decision. He could've informed us at any point, and he chose not to." He cleared his throat. "You need to forgive yourself for that. It was never your fault to begin with."

Lucy's arm slid around my waist.

"I'm going to take him upstairs," she said.

I let her tow me to our rooms. Inside, it was cool and quiet. I stood inside the door, unsure.

"I want to talk to you," Lucy said, her voice low as she walked toward the bedroom.

I followed. When I stepped through the doorway, she was taking off her shirt.

"I think this discussion will work better without clothes," she said simply. She stripped completely bare and then came to me. I let her pull off my shirt and tug my pants and boxers down my legs. Kneeling, she peeled my socks off.

Without a word, she led me to the bed.

When I lay down beside her, she scooted in close, wrapping her leg around my waist. She tucked her arms between us and cupped my jaw in her hands. The comfort of her skin against mine was instantaneous.

"Are you with me?" she asked.

"Yes," I replied, my voice crackling and hoarse.

"You came for me, Ulf," she said firmly. "I knew you would. Every second was a countdown to when you'd get here. There was never any doubt in my mind. Not for a moment. Okay?"

I nodded.

"I knew I just had to do my best to get to that point." She leaned up and kissed my chin. "I had to outlast them long enough for you to get there."

My stomach lurched. "I understand."

"I don't think you do," she replied, her thumb coasting over my cheekbone softly. "So I need you to hear this next part, okay?"

I nodded again, bracing myself.

"I have never in my life been able to count on someone to save me," she said, her eyes sad. "I've always had to save myself. Always. Even as a child. I learned how to fight, and I learned how to shoot because I knew no one else would."

"Luce," I muttered, my chest aching.

"Until you." She smiled. "I *knew* you were coming. I railed at you about how you left me behind because I was angry. That was wrong, and I'm *so* sorry. *I* fucked up when I did that. From the very beginning, you've done everything you could to keep me safe."

"But I didn't."

"No, you didn't," she replied. "I did. But that's not the point. I knew you were coming, baby. Don't you see? *That's* the point. The fact that you didn't make it in time means nothing." She gave a quick jerk of her head. "I knew you were coming, and that means *everything*."

"I'll always come for you," I promised, sliding my hand into her hair.

"I know you will," she replied.

"I tried." My voice cracked.

"I know you did."

"I'm sorry I lost it outside."

"Hey," she said soothingly. "Everyone has their moments. I think you probably needed to get some of that out."

"I have nightmares sometimes," I confessed. "Zeke's sitting in the room where they held him, and he's waiting for us. Every time there's a noise outside, his head shoots up because he thinks it's us, but we never come."

"You saw where they held him?"

"It's how I found you," I replied. "The prisoners had a little hiding place in the wall where they left things. You know, little pieces of proof they'd been there. He put a photo of him and Charlie inside."

Lucy let out a little breath, her lips curling up in the corners. "Of course he did."

"We didn't even know he had a mate until we found that photo."

"Figures," she said, her hand sliding down to wrap around my chest. "Seems like he kept a lot of secrets."

"It kills me that I didn't know about any of it."

"I know."

"He couldn't keep a secret to save his life when he was little," I muttered. "Danny noticed everything, but we could generally count on him to keep his mouth shut. With Zeke, all you'd have to do is look at him and he'd start confessing to things he *thought* of doing."

Lucy laughed. "What a little narc."

"He was so cute, though," I mused. "It was hard to stay mad at the little bugger."

"It's okay to be angry at him now, you know," she said carefully. "He deserves it. I'm pissed."

I smiled at her and pressed a kiss to the end of her nose.

"He made bad choices, and he paid too much for

them. I'm devastated by that. Not angry. I wish he'd come to me."

She tucked her head under my chin, and we lay quietly for a long time. Eventually, I dozed off. When I woke back up, she'd pulled the comforter over us and was watching me silently.

"What time is it?" I asked.

"I was just about to wake you for dinner."

"Shit," I grumbled, reaching up to rub my eyes.

"Have you slept in the past few days?"

"Yes."

"I'm guessing not enough," she said wryly. She'd tucked her hands under her cheek, and her hair was fanned out over her bare shoulder. "From now on, I hope you'll come to me when things are too much."

"I can do that."

"I've been thinking—"

"Were you watching me sleep this whole time?" I asked.

She rolled her eyes and leaned up on her elbow. "You'll always come for me, and I'll always be your soft place to land, okay? That's what I wanted to say. I realize now that it sounds kind of stupid out loud."

"It doesn't sound stupid," I argued, pushing her onto her back so I could lean over her. "It sounds perfect."

"You just...you carry all of this *weight*, you know?" Her hands glided over my chest and around my back. "I can see it even when you try to hide it. But I'm here now. I'll help you carry it if you let me."

"My mate," I whispered, running my lips along the tendon in her neck.

"We're in this together now," she whispered back.

"No matter what happens," I promised. "No one will ever keep me from you."

"I'm counting on it."

Leaning back so I could look into her eyes, it felt like everything settled into place inside me. All the good and bad that I'd done, every decision I'd made, every order I'd followed, every lesson I'd learned and relearned. All of it had led me to her. If I hadn't been a soldier, I would've never known to go back to search the facility where Zeke had been held in case we'd missed something, and I would've never found that photo. If my parents hadn't instilled the importance of family loyalty into us from the cradle, I may never have searched for Zeke's mate. Every piece of my life had been preparing me to find her.

Lucille Franklin was every dream realized.

"You're my reward," I said, cupping her cheek. "The best gift I've ever been given."

"You're welcome?" she said hesitantly, a little smile playing on her lips.

"I'll love you long after I'm gone," I said.

When her eyes began to glisten, I knew she remembered where she'd heard the phrase before.

"I love you too," she said. "You're worth *every* sacrifice."

CHAPTER 17
LUCY

The sense of relief we'd felt when we'd found Zeke's memory card and realized that he'd done so much research dwindled as it took longer and longer for the Boucher brothers to make any sense of the information. It had been two weeks of studying the files and passing them around in the hopes that new eyes would see something the previous ones had missed, but it was no use. Without the information available in Vampire Command's computers, the Boucher brothers were stuck.

Rejoining their units was out of the question.

From what I'd gathered, it was pretty much unheard of for Vampires to separate from Vampire Command before they'd found their mates. It was a bit of a scandal. Vampires wanted to know why Ambrose, Chance, and Daniel had quit. They called Matilda and Erik throughout the day, both asking for answers and offering tentative congratulations in the hopes that either one of the parents would confirm that their sons had mated. Since they hadn't reported me or Daniel's mate to their government, Erik and Matilda had decided to just tell everyone that they'd made the decision to leave Vampire Command because of Zeke's death.

It wasn't a lie, but it wasn't exactly the truth, either.

All of us were becoming stir crazy. We were cooped up in the house with little to do and no idea when all of it would end. When you added in the stress the males were under, the house was pretty much a powder keg.

On the fourth day, Reese had walked outside and screamed at the top of her lungs in frustration. I didn't blame her, considering that she'd been there almost twice as long as I had. I would've applauded, but within less than a minute, a Vampire I didn't recognize had come running from the woods, his gun drawn. Reese started screaming for real, Beau had lost his ever-loving mind, and the Vampire had gone back to the perimeter with his tail tucked between his legs. He'd thought that something had happened and left his post, which was both admirable and stupid.

No one had let out their frustration that way again. Instead, we'd started jogging. I fell back into the swing of it pretty easily. I'd always enjoyed being in shape, but Reese and Matilda moaned and groaned like they were being tortured. They still came with us, though. Sometimes Beau ran with us, sometimes Erik. Occasionally, Ambrose came. I liked those days best.

After Charlie got Zeke's note from his files, he'd been pretty low. He spent most of his time in bed, wrapped in Zeke's quilt like a burrito. Matilda had kindly urged me not to push him for more than he could give. She spent hours in Charlie's room, just sitting with him in the quiet. One day, she re-stitched the scar that Zeke had left on the quilt, not even bothering to take it from Charlie. She'd found it down by his feet and neatly repaired it while he was wrapped in it.

Charlie's depression weighed heavily on me, but I tried to remember that he was surrounded by people who loved him and, eventually, he'd be interested in joining the land of the living again. We made sure he ate and showered and spoke to at least one of us a day, but beyond that, he felt out of reach. It left a hole that I struggled to fill, but I was learning to let go a little. It wasn't easy.

It helped that Ambrose and I were nearly always together. Even when he pored over Zeke's documents, he was never very far away. I sat with him while he worked, watching movies, reading books, and doodling on one of the multiple sketchbooks he'd ordered for me. Dinner was always a family affair, but afterward was just for us. We showered together, driving each other crazy until we either gave in and had sex against the wall or stumbled out to the bed or whatever other piece of furniture we bumped into. We'd had sex in every inch of the apartment, and we'd discovered every inch of each other's bodies. It was a small bright spot during those gloomy days when nothing felt like it was going right.

A pall had fallen over those of us in the house, no matter how we tried to avoid it. Every day seemed closer to some new confrontation, but we had no idea which direction it would come from. Frustration and worry built.

It didn't help that Sven still hadn't woken up, and Alice had become a shell of herself. Her mate lay quietly sleeping, but I wasn't sure if she'd slept more than a few hours since the house had been attacked. She repeated over and over again that he just needed time, but the rest of us had begun to wonder if Sven would be a casualty of Finau's deception.

Danny seemed to be the only one of us that hadn't fallen victim to the gloom. He was constantly moving, constantly talking, constantly disappearing. He didn't mention his mate—ever—but I knew he must've been seeing her somehow. I couldn't imagine how they managed to stay apart as much as they did. We didn't even know her name.

Something was strange about that whole situation, but I didn't feel like it was my place to ask about it. With someone out there kidnapping and torturing mates, I didn't blame him for being cautious. In the darkest parts of my mind, I was glad that he hadn't introduced us to her. It would be one less person for me to mourn if something bad happened...and it would be information that I wouldn't be able to give if I was ever taken.

Ambrose had taken me down to the home gym off the garage once I was fully healed. It had everything you could possibly want in terms of exercise machines and weights, but I'd been most glad to see the sparring mats and punching bag. My skills had gotten rusty. It had been pure luck, desperation, and a little muscle memory that enabled me to crawl out from under the man I'd killed, but I wasn't willing to bet on those things again.

Every morning, we sparred in the gym. Beau and Reese joined us. Reese clearly hadn't had any professional training, but she was scrappy as hell, and she fought dirty. Both of those things worked in her favor.

Sometimes Reese and I grappled, but not often. Based on what we'd seen so far, the humans we were fighting were male. She needed to know how to fight off an attacker who was larger and stronger than her. I taught her some moves that I thought were a good foundation, but she spent most of her time training with Beau.

Erik, Chance, and Danny joined us too, but because of the mating heat, I rarely sparred with any of them unless I fought a little dirty myself and ambushed them. Ambrose was adamant that I spare myself from the burn, but I figured that if I ended up needing the skills again, I'd need to know how to navigate fighting while I was on fire.

I couldn't count on the fact that the heat would be secondary to everything else, like it had been the night we'd been attacked. The chances were that they wouldn't try a full assault the next time, and I'd be caught unaware. Even a split second of hesitation could mean the difference between escape and torture.

Walking with casual nonchalance across the gym, I glanced over to where Ambrose was glaring at me, a bottle of water halfway to his lips.

He shook his head slowly.

That's when I pounced.

I'd found that grappling with Erik wasn't as bad as with Chance or Danny, so he was usually my target.

Wrapping my arms around his neck, I gripped him with my legs as he roared in surprise. It was always trickiest when I attacked without taking his legs out from under him first. I never won, but at least when he was already on the mat, I didn't have to try staying on his back while he attempted to throw me off.

"No mercy!" I yelled.

Erik paused to laugh, and I settled myself more securely on his back.

"You're a menace," he said, reaching backward.

I knew he was trying to grab my armpits. That was what he always did. So I squirmed and jostled around, avoiding the move, and stupidly lost my secure grip on his back.

The minute he felt me loosen my legs, he bent quickly at the waist, and, using my T-shirt, flipped me over his back.

I landed on the mat with a thud, the wind knocked completely out of me.

"Pathetic," Chance called from across the room.

"*You're* pathetic," I wheezed, staring at the ceiling.

"She can't best me," Erik said conversationally, looking down at me. "Yet, she keeps trying."

"I'll get you one of these days," I gasped. "Old man."

"Doubtful," he replied, crossing his massive tattooed arms across his chest.

"Can you breathe?" Ambrose asked as he pulled me to my feet.

I coughed and nodded. "Yep. Totally fine."

"Good."

Before I could even plant my feet, he'd swept them out from under me, and I landed on the mat again.

Then it was on.

I loved wrestling with Ambrose. Not only did I enjoy having his body pressed against mine, no matter the situation, but I also loved that he didn't go easy on me. After the first day, when I could tell he was testing my skill level, he'd never let me win. We were careful not to cause any lasting damage, but otherwise we fought dirty. Like the world was ending. Like it mattered. Because it did. Knowing the correct way to strike a blow or take down someone who was prepared for the move was all well and good, but I'd gotten that man's arms from around my hips by gouging his eyes out, not by doing some fancy maneuver.

By the time I tapped out, Ambrose's legs were wrapped around mine, and he'd pinned me flat, his hands holding my arms above my head.

The room around us was silent. Turning my head from side to side, I found that at some point, the rest of the occupants had left.

"I think your swearing scared them off," Ambrose joked, smiling down at me.

"My prowess, you mean," I countered, shoving my hips upward like I could throw him off.

"Oh, I'm sure it was that."

"Ugh." I dropped my head to the mat and sighed. "You wore me out."

"This morning?"

I looked at him in confusion for a moment before I realized what he was talking about.

He'd woken me up by playing with my nipples, and I'd paid him back by riding him into two orgasms. My thighs had burned for an hour afterward.

"That too." I smiled, tilting my head so he'd lean down and kiss me.

His tongue slid over my lips so softly that I groaned, but when I tried to press closer, he pulled back, just out of reach. He did it again and again, not putting enough pressure to satisfy me, but dragging me along the edge until I wanted to smack him.

"Kiss me," I ordered as I stared into his eyes. They crinkled at the corners as he smiled.

"Say please."

I loved the playful side of Ambrose that I'd seen more and more as the days passed and our connection deepened, but I had no patience for it in that moment.

Fire raced down my spine, and my back arched, pressing our lower bodies together even more.

"Oh, it's like that," he said, his eyes darkening.

He let me go in an instant and flipped me over before I could reach for him.

I felt the sting before I'd even realized what he'd done, but I was prepared for the second time he smacked my ass.

He paused, waiting for my reaction. When I tilted my

hips up in response, he groaned and smacked the first cheek again, making it throb.

"We can't do this here," I reminded him as both of his hands gripped my ass, kneading them with his fingers and prolonging the burn.

"Up," he whispered in my ear.

I scrambled to my feet and grabbed his hand as he strode toward the door to the garage. We hurried through the house like a couple of kids trying to get away with something, but we'd only made it to the second stair when Charlie surprised us by calling out my name.

I spun around in shock to see him making his way through the living area.

"Hey," I called, jumping back down the bottom two stairs. "What's up?"

"Do you still have that camera?" Charlie asked. "You know, the one you had in Europe?"

"Of course." It was still in my bag. I should probably unpack that thing and take over a couple of Ambrose's dresser drawers. I needed to buy some new clothes too. It was getting pretty old washing them every few days if I didn't want to live in Ambrose's pajama pants and T-shirts.

"Could I see it?" Charlie asked. "I was talking to Mom, and I thought she'd like to see those pictures you have. I know I said I didn't want to see them before but, um, I think I would now."

"Absolutely," I said softly, reaching out to grip his bicep.

God, he was so skinny. He'd been eating, but without even the exercise of walking around the house, he'd started wasting away.

"I'll go get it, okay? Are you going to stay down here?"

"I thought we could maybe use the projector?" he said tentatively. "So everyone could look at them?"

"That's a great idea. Should we set it up in here?" I glanced at the windows letting sun into the living room.

"Let's set it up in my parents' rooms," Ambrose said, still standing on the stairs. "They have the most space."

Charlie left to round everyone up, and I followed Ambrose upstairs to get the camera and the projector that had been sitting on the counter for the past couple of weeks.

When we reached our rooms and the door shut behind us, Ambrose locked it quickly and pushed me toward the couch.

"Camera," I reminded him, and he pressed firmly on my back, bending me over it.

"We'll be quick," he replied, yanking down my leggings.

Cool air brushed over my skin before he pressed his lips against the cheeks of my ass, soothing the remembered sting.

I arched and widened my legs as much as my leggings would allow, and seconds later, he thrust inside me.

The feel of him hadn't gotten old. I didn't think I'd ever get tired of it. I braced my hands on the seat of the couch and moved in counterpoint as waves of warmth flowed through my veins, amplifying everything. It was fantastic every time. When Ambrose slid his hand beneath me and circled my clit with a single finger, I came with a cry. Less than a minute later, he followed me into the abyss.

Closing my eyes, I let my head drop onto my forearms as he slowly pulled out.

"Camera," he said huskily. "Projector."

"I don't want to move," I grumbled.

Ambrose chuckled and gently pulled my leggings back into place. "Go clean up, love."

I stumbled to the bathroom, and when I came back out, Ambrose was standing by the door holding everything we needed.

"You didn't have to wait for me," I chided him, throwing open the door.

"I wasn't just going to leave you."

It was as simple as that for him.

Everyone had already gathered in Matilda and Erik's main room when we got there, and while Chance and Ambrose set up the projector, I surreptitiously looked around. The room was bigger than the ones their sons had, but not by much. There wasn't a kitchenette or dining area, and in the middle of the wide room, they'd placed a small sectional couch. The fabrics and carpets were all done in light neutrals, giving the space an airy feel that the other rooms lacked with their masculine furniture. I loved it, and I wondered if Matilda would let me see what she'd done with the bedroom and bathroom before we left.

Erik sat in the center of the couch with Matilda curled up next to him. He had his arm around her, and she'd pulled her knees up to her chest with her toes tucked halfway beneath his thigh. To their right, Beau sat with Reese in his lap. Then Danny, with his elbow on the arm of the couch, his chin resting on his hand.

Charles sat down next to Matilda, clasping his hands nervously between his knees. She reached out and rubbed his back.

I walked over and sat down on Charles's other side.

As soon as the lights had been dimmed and the projector turned on, Ambrose handed me the camera. I turned it on and scrolled to the first photo, the one with

Zeke standing behind Charlie, his arms wrapped around Charlie's chest.

My brother let out a shuddery breath beside me.

"This was the first picture I took," I explained as we all stared at Zeke's handsome face. "I think that was the day after we'd met Zeke. Right, Charlie?"

"Yeah, the day after," Charlie confirmed quietly. He nodded, and I knew I could move on to the next photo.

I moved through the pictures, explaining what was happening in them and trying to give as much detail as I could. Charlie added things sporadically, correcting me when I got something wrong, but for the most part, he just sat there silently, tears rolling down his cheeks.

Everyone else sat silently, absorbing the little piece of Zeke that they'd never seen.

A thousand memories bombarded me, but I thought I kept it together pretty well. I loved seeing Zeke and Charlie together in the photos. It reminded me briefly how well and how deeply my brother had been loved. Plus, I just missed my brother-in-law. For all his faults, he'd been genuinely good and kind and funny.

I knew I was reaching the end of the photos when a picture popped up on the big screen of Charlie and Zeke cuddling on the couch in the last hotel room we'd stayed in together.

"This was in Belgium," I explained. "A day or two before Zeke left. It was late, and we'd just finished way too much dessert from room service. I think Charlie was complaining that he'd eaten too much and Zeke was babying him, even though we'd both told him that he was going to make himself sick."

"It was so good," Charlie mumbled, making the family around us chuckle.

I stared at the photo. Zeke was sitting on the couch,

and Charlie was lying next to him, with his legs thrown over Zeke's thighs. One of his feet dangled off the edge of the couch, but the other was held in Zeke's right hand. He'd been rubbing Charlie's feet.

Zeke was in profile, his head tipped down toward Charlie's. My brother had one arm curled under his head to prop it up so he could see his mate. The other was lying loosely across his belly.

Completely wrapped up in each other.

I pressed the button to go to the next photo, but all that was there was a black screen.

"Oh, I must've taken a photo of my finger or something—" I started to explain.

I jumped in surprise when the screen suddenly changed, and Zeke's face was staring back at me.

Charlie rose to his feet with a sob.

"Hey, baby," Zeke said, his eyes bright. "I'm not sure when you're seeing this. Hopefully, you're not, and I was able to come home to you and delete it from Lucy's camera before she ever noticed it."

I put a trembling hand to my mouth.

He was there. He was looking right at us. No, he was looking at *Charlie*.

"I didn't want to make this video. I put it off as long as I could, but now it's almost time for me to go, and I didn't want to leave without making sure you had it." Zeke looked down and ran his hand through his hair. The gesture was so *Zeke* that I heard more than one person's breath catch.

"Maybe we should go," I whispered, gripping Ambrose's thigh.

"Stay," Charlie ordered, not looking away from the screen.

"All right, before I lose my nerve," Zeke said with a

choked laugh. "I want you to know how much I love you. You're everything I ever hoped for, Charlie. Everything I could ever imagine. My perfect counterpart in every way. Even if this is all the time we had—and I really hope it wasn't—you gave my life meaning that I didn't even know was possible. I—" Zeke stopped and cleared his throat with a self-deprecating smile. "I think you are impossibly wonderful, Charles Franklin. If I could disappear with you to a deserted island and live happily ever after, I'd do it in a heartbeat. We'd take Lucy, of course, because we both know she'd go crazy without you."

Clasping my hand over my mouth, I forced myself not to make a sound.

"Speaking of Lucy," Zeke said, pressing his lips together for a moment. "She needs you, Charlie. I know that if you're seeing this, I'm probably gone. But I need you to stay, baby, okay?" Zeke paused and swiped his hand under his nose. He didn't bother with the tears on his cheeks. "I know it'll be hard, and I can't even imagine the pain you must be in. I'm so sorry, love. Please know how much I love you. Please know that someday, far from now, I'll be waiting for you on the other side. Okay? But for now, I need you to stay—and this is important—I need you and Lucy to find my brothers. Find Ambrose. They'll keep you safe when I can't."

Ambrose's hand tightened on my hand as Zeke smiled mischievously.

His grin faltered, and he let out a sigh, glancing over his shoulder.

"I can't drag this out forever, can I?"

"Please," Charlie whispered.

"I love you so much, Charlie."

Zeke's hand reached up to cover his mouth as his body

jerked in a silent sob. He pressed his eyes tightly closed for a long moment.

When he opened them, he dropped his hand and clenched his jaw.

"When you see my brothers, tell them that the stars are clear and the questions are answered. Only the unadulterated are guilty. If they don't know what it means right away, hopefully they'll figure it out." His lips quirked. "And if they don't, it'll be a way for me to piss Chance off indefinitely."

He straightened his shoulders.

"I love you, baby. Forever."

The screen went dark, and my brother crumpled to the ground.

I scrambled toward him, wrapping my arms around his shoulders and head as he cried silently, his entire body spasming with sobs.

The light turned on, and I lifted my head.

Every single one of the Bouchers sat around me, stunned. Their faces held a range of emotions. Sorrow, anger, love.

Charlie stiffened in my arms. When he raised his head, his eyes blazed with anger.

"That asshole," he rasped. "I was in bed behind him. I was right there. He could've just *told* me."

"He was hoping you'd never see it," I reminded him quietly, brushing his hair back from his forehead. "And if he had, you wouldn't have it now."

Charlie fell back onto his heels and nodded.

"I'm sorry," Matilda said after a moment. "That was private. We should've let you watch it alone."

"I don't mind," Charlie replied. "There was nothing in that video that either of us would want to hide."

"It's true," I said, pushing to my feet. "They were disgustingly affectionate. Nauseating, really."

Erik chuckled.

"Only the unadulterated are guilty," Chance said, shooting to his feet. "The stars are clear and the questions are answered—*only the unadulterated are guilty.*"

"You know what it means?" Beau asked, helping Reese off his lap.

"The list of Vampires," Chance said as he strode purposefully for the door. "Question marks and asterisks."

"Holy shit," Danny muttered.

Chance turned in the doorway. "I'm still really fucking pissed at him," he said. "But not for this."

Beau, Danny, and Ambrose hurried after Chance, but the rest of us took longer to rise from our seats. I unplugged the camera and handed it to Charlie. There wasn't anything on it that I needed more than he did.

Erik and Matilda stayed on the couch with my brother while Reese and I headed for Chance's room. His computers held all the information, and we correctly assumed that's where the brothers had gone.

When we opened the door, Danny had just thrown a glass across the room, and it shattered against the wall on impact.

"What?" I asked, searching out my mate. "What did you find out?"

"Thomas Keihley, Roderick Morren, Edgar Adamson," Chance replied grimly.

"Should I know those names?" I asked as Ambrose crossed the room. "Who are they?"

"Vampires," Danny said with a scoff, his hands linked behind his head as he stared at the ceiling.

"Okay, we know that there were Vampires involved, right?" I asked as Ambrose reached me. "We knew that."

"They're not just Vampires, baby," Ambrose said as he pulled me into his arms. "Two are generals and one is a lieutenant general. They answer only to the commandant and the Prime Minister."

"Americans?" I asked slowly.

"Every single one."

The knowledge was like a heavy blanket thrown over us. Suffocating and dark.

"I think," Chance said, his fingers typing furiously on the laptop. "Holy fuck. Okay. Okay."

"What?" Danny asked impatiently. "You think what?"

"Give me a second," Chance replied, his fingers still typing faster than anyone I'd ever seen. His head was jerking as he looked from one screen to the next. Little boxes popped up and then were whisked away over and over.

Ambrose wrapped both arms around me, and I lay my head on his chest.

Whenever we'd discussed it, we'd theorized that the Vampires leaking the information to the humans were nobodies. We'd assumed that lack of families and status within the community had been what caused them to turn on their own kind. But, if top generals were part of the plot, that wasn't the case.

"Got it," Chance barked, throwing his hands into the air. "Zeke had fucking proof. It's all there. Every single transaction can be traced to Morren, Adamson, or Keihley directly."

"Fantastic," Danny spat. "But that doesn't mean shit. They're so far up Arthur's ass I doubt we'd even get a fucking meeting."

Chance spun toward us in his chair and looked at each of his brothers. "Wait, we're not planning on taking this to command, right?" He rose to his feet and grinned, stretching his arms above his head. "Because I plan on going *hunting*."

Ambrose ushered me out of the room as his brothers began to argue.

I didn't realize that my hands were shaking until we were safely closed in our own room.

"Does hunting mean what I think it means?" I asked Ambrose, stopping in the center of the room. "Because we've played that game before, remember? It didn't end well."

"I'm not sure what the next steps are," he replied, locking the door. "But I know there's no need for you to worry."

"Well, too late for that," I snapped. The day wasn't even half over, and I was already tired to the bone.

"Baby, we talked about this, remember?" he asked softly, framing my face in his hands.

"You won't ever leave me behind again," I replied, closing my eyes as he brushed his lips across my cheeks.

"And if we're separated, I'll always come for you."

I nodded. Taking a deep breath, I opened my eyes again. "You're worth every sacrifice."

"I promise you won't have to sacrifice anything," he whispered back.

"I love you."

We fell into bed with a desperation born of uncertainty, but when I lay there afterward, with Ambrose's arm wrapped tightly around my waist, I was surprisingly calm.

Whatever came, we could face it. We'd done it before and survived.

Next time, we'd have immortality on our side.

A LOOK AT BOOK THREE

He'd do anything to protect her. She just wants him to stay.

Daniel Boucher has waited over a century to find his fated mate. The moment he hears Rosemary Whitlock's voice, he knows—*she's it*. Smart, capable, and already entangled in vampire affairs, Rosemary is nothing like the fragile human he expected. But with mates being hunted and war brewing in the shadows, Daniel will do whatever it takes to protect her, even if that means keeping her at a distance.

What he doesn't see is how much that distance is tearing them apart.

Rosemary isn't new to this world. With mated vampire-human godparents and a lifetime of witnessing what real bonded partnerships look like, Daniel's sudden disappearances feel less like protection and more like rejection. She's not the type to sit back and wait to be rescued—and she won't let herself be left behind.

As the Bouchers close in on a deadly truth, love and loyalty are tested from every side. And if Daniel and Rosemary can't bridge the growing rift between them, their bond may not survive what's coming.

Is fate enough to hold them together when everything else is pulling them apart?

AVAILABLE NOVEMBER 2025

Acknowledgments

To my fella, my kids, my parents, and parents-in-law: Thanks for pitching in to help me finish this novel without completely losing it. This one was a whirlwind, and I couldn't have finished it without you. Love you guys.

To Michelle, Pam, and Bea: Thank you for everything you do.

To Donna: Thanks for blogging about my first book. I wouldn't be here without you.

To the readers who've come with me this far: Thank you for your support and love these past 12 years. I couldn't do what I do if you weren't doing what you do.

And to Ellie, who read the premise of the Bouchers series and said, *I want it*. Thank you a thousand times. Love you, dude.

Nicole Jacquelyn started writing before she started elementary school, however she didn't start publishing her stories until her senior year in college. Today, she's the author of the bestselling Aces series, the Fostering Love series, the Kellys series, and The Bouchers series. She loves to read, drinks too much coffee, and lives in Oregon with the coolest children in the entire world.